Praise for the Baby Boomer Mysteries

"Reading Susan Santangelo's books is like taking a masterclass in voice. Local politics, dogs, and the always funny Carol Andrews make the ninth book in the *Baby Boomer Mystery* series, **Politics Can Be Murder**, a clear winner."
—Sherry Harris, Agatha Award Nominated Author of the *Sarah Winston Garage Sale Mysteries* and the *Chloe Jackson Seaglass Saloon Mysteries*

"Susan Santangelo's always chatty (and sometimes catty) amateur sleuth Carol Andrews is back! In the ninth *Baby Boomer Mystery*, Carol gets herself, her posse of friends, her skeptical husband and her new-mom daughter entangled in a tale of local politics, a hit-and-run death, a sweet little dog, and a spoiled-rotten cat. Even Sister Rose, the iron-willed nun who has terrified Carol since high school, gets involved. And of course, there's a recipe—the 19th century classic Hartford Election Cake. Is **Politics Can Be Murder** a winner? I vote yes!"
—Carole Goldberg, National Book Reviewer

"Susan Santangelo's Carol Andrews is one retiree who is not content to bake cookies and babysit her grandchildren, and having solved nine *Baby Boomer Mysteries* with wit and homely wisdom, it would be a serious mistake to underestimate her sleuthing skills. I'm eagerly awaiting her next adventure, and I'm sure other mystery lovers are, too."
—Leslie Meier, Author of the *Lucy Stone Mysteries*

"When a friend becomes the victim of a hit and run driver, Baby Boomer Carol Andrews and her Fairport gal pals decide to help a successful local businesswoman run for Fairport Town Council, via a pedestrian safety-focused campaign. What could possibly go wrong?"
—Anne L. Holmes, APR, "Boomer in Chief," National Association of Baby Boomer Women

"In **Politics Can Be Murder**, Santangelo serves up a humorous story with a serious underpinning and an appealing main character—you have to love a woman who always tells you what she would have said but didn't."
—Leslie Wheeler, Author of the *Berkshire Hilltown Mystery* Series

Politics
Can Be Murder

Every Wife Has a Story

A Carol and Jim Andrews Baby Boomer
Mystery

Ninth in the Series

Susan Santangelo

SUSPENSE PUBLISHING

POLITICS CAN BE MURDER
by
Susan Santangelo

PAPERBACK EDITION
* * * * *
PUBLISHED BY:
Suspense Publishing

COPYRIGHT
2020 Susan Santangelo

PUBLISHING HISTORY:
Suspense Publishing, Paperback and Digital Copy, September 2020

ISBN: 978-0-578-70369-5

Cover and Book Design: Shannon Raab
Cover Artist: Elizabeth Moisan

Publisher's Note: The recipes in this book are to be followed exactly as written. The publisher and the author are not responsible for a reader's specific health or allergy needs which may require medical supervision. The publisher and the author are not responsible for any adverse reactions to the recipes contained in this book.

Acknowledgements

Thank you to my wonderful family—David, Mark, Sandy, Jacob and Rebecca. And especially to my husband Joe, who keeps me on my toes and inspires me every day.

A big thank you to my First Readers Club, especially Marti Baker, Beth and John Getker, and Ellen Evans for their helpful comments and suggestions.

Thanks to Elizabeth Moisan for once again providing terrific artwork for the front cover.

A big thank you to all my long-time friends from New England for their ongoing support, and to the new friends I've made in Clearwater, Florida, especially the members of the Clearwater Welcome Newcomers Club, St. Brendan's CCW, my pals at The Attic, and the staff of the Clearwater Library, Beach Branch. Words can't properly express my gratitude to the entire staff at Susan Cheek Needler Breast Center at Morton Plant Hospital. You guys rock!

To all my friends and cyber friends from Sisters in Crime, especially the New England, Northeast Florida, and Gulf Coast chapters, thanks for sharing your expertise with me. I always learn something new, and the support is fantastic.

Boomer and Lilly send special doggy love to Lynn Pray and Courtney Lynn Ross, Pineridge English Cockers, Rehoboth MA.

To Shannon and John Raab, and everyone at Suspense Publishing, who help me in so many ways, thank you for continuing to come with me on this incredible journey.

And to everyone who's enjoyed this series—the readers I've met at countless book events, those who have e-mailed me, and especially those who've posted online reviews for the books—thanks so much! Hope you enjoy this one, too. And keep those chapter headings coming!

To my awesome grandchildren, Jacob and Rebecca. You are the hope of the future.

A woman's place is in the House, the Senate, and the Oval
Office.
–Carol Andrews

All politics is local.
–Tip O'Neil

Politics
Can Be Murder

Every Wife Has a Story

A Carol and Jim Andrews Baby Boomer
Mystery

Ninth in the Series

Susan Santangelo

Fairport, Connecticut, Late Fall

The email was unsigned, succinct and confusing as heck. "The memorial service and reception for Mary Pat Ryan will be held at noon Saturday at Maria's Trattoria. Attached is a list of people, with emails and phone numbers, for you to contact concerning their attendance. The list must be completed by tomorrow night at the very latest."

I squinted at my computer screen and re-read the email again. Who was Mary Pat Ryan and why in the world did I get this email ordering me to help organize her memorial service?

"It's probably a mistake," I said to Lucy and Ethel, my two English cocker spaniels who were snoozing on the couch near me. "This should have been sent to another Carol Andrews."

I was about to delete the message when I glanced at the address of the sender: SR at Sallyscloset.org. The email was meant for me after all, and it was cc'd to my best friend, Nancy Green. It was from our long-ago high school English teacher and personal nemesis, Sister Rose.

Chapter 1

Why do today what you can easily postpone until tomorrow?

I'm embarrassed to admit it, but there are some people in life who can intimidate me without even trying. Even someone whose power over me ended the day I hung up my navy blue blazer, matching pleated skirt, and white blouse with a Peter Pan collar for the last time. The actual graduation ceremony wasn't nearly as important as my banishing the hated high school uniform (especially the navy and white saddle shoes that required a daily polishing) to a trunk in the attic and throwing away the key, figuratively speaking. If you think that's an extreme reaction, one of my friends actually threw her saddle shoes out the school bus window onto Fairport Turnpike to celebrate our last ride home from Mount Saint Francis Academy. Fortunately, her aim was bad so she didn't hit anybody.

I can sense that some of you are shaking your heads and wondering why the heck I'm telling you all this, so perhaps I should introduce myself. My name is Carol Andrews, and I live with my retired husband, Jim (he's retired from his public relations job in New York City, not from our marriage, to be clear), in Fairport, Connecticut, a shoreline town on Long Island Sound. We've been married almost forty years, and have two adult children. Our daughter, Jenny, is now married to Fairport Police Detective Mark Anderson and has just made me a grandmother for the very first time. Our son, Mike, owns a wildly popular bistro, Cosmo's, on Miami's South Beach. We don't see him as often as I'd like, but I remain hopeful that situation will change. And, yes, I went to Catholic school with my three best friends, Nancy, Claire and Mary Alice. Believe it or not, we're still best friends today.

Our two dogs, Lucy and Ethel, are my primary confidantes because they can keep a secret better than anyone else. And they never disagree with me, either, as long as I feed them on time. So it was perfectly natural (for me) to consult them about the email from Sister Rose.

"Let's take a few minutes and consider some options," I said to my two canine companions. "There's no reason why I have to get this done right away. Nancy got the same email. Maybe she's dealt with it and I don't have to do anything. No sense in our duplicating efforts."

I thought about the possibility of this happening and realized it was as likely as me fitting into a pair of size 2 jeans—impossible, even when I was 2 years old.

On the other hand, there really was no reason I had to drop everything and do the good sister's bidding immediately. "In fact," I said, warming to my idea of stalling as long as possible before even downloading the list she'd sent me, "Sister Rose didn't tell me to report back to her until tomorrow night." I didn't verbalize what Sister had actually written: "Tomorrow night at the very latest." Once I said that part out loud to the dogs, I knew both of them, especially Lucy, would give me dirty looks until I had completed my assigned task. Sometimes, in a wild flight of fancy, I imagine that Sister Rose and Lucy are a single entity which manifests itself in two different forms, because they both enjoy bossing me around so much. I know. Stupid.

To prove my point, Lucy chose that moment to make a flying leap from the sofa onto my lap. "Oof, Lucy," I scolded, trying to dislodge her. "What the heck did you do that for? I can't breathe with you sitting on me."

Ignoring me as usual, Lucy made a half circle and positioned herself directly in front of the computer screen. She turned her head, gave me a look, then turned back to the screen again.

"Oh, give me a break," I said. "If you want to download the list and contact everybody yourself, go right ahead. I'll even lend you my cell phone. In the meantime, get down." And I wiggled just enough to dislodge her. After all, who was running this house—her or me? Wait a minute. Don't answer that.

"As I was saying," I said, directing my attention to sweet Ethel and ignoring Lucy, "since I have oodles of time to do Sister Rose's bidding, there's no need for me to change my schedule for today." I paused, then said, "What is my schedule for today? It seems to me that I'm supposed to be somewhere this morning, but I can't remember where."

Does this ever happen to any of you? Do you go into a particular room to do something, and then forget why you're there? To tell the truth, the older I get, the more this happens. Since it's also common among my circle of friends, I chalk it up to the aging process.

"I'm sure it'll come to me if I think about something else," I said to the dogs. "So don't worry about it."

I re-read Sister Rose's email, and realized the memorial service for the mysterious Mary Pat Ryan would be held at Maria's Trattoria, one of my very favorite restaurants in the whole world. It was a sure bet that Maria would have some insider information about the event to share with me. She might even know why Sister Rose had commanded me to confirm the guest list.

Of course, a quick email, text, or phone call to Maria was the most logical way to find out what she knew. But where was the fun in that? No, this was definitely the Good Lord telling me that I had a moral obligation to take myself out to lunch today and, if I was lucky, enlist one or more of my posse of pals to come with me. If I was really lucky, one of my pals would know who Mary Pat Ryan was, and why I'd been roped into being part of her memorial service. Multi-tasking at its best!

I knew my phone was charging on the kitchen counter. It gets very cross when I interrupt the process and, like me, it takes longer and longer to get to 100 percent power. I figured I'd eventually have to give in and either replace the battery or the entire phone, but since that particular device and I have shared so many adventures over the years, I was reluctant to let it go.

I snapped my fingers and said, "Come on, girls. Snack time." In a flash, both canines were bounding into the kitchen before I changed my mind. "You two make me laugh," I said, tossing each of them a Milk Bone. "Now, go to your crates for a snooze. I have things to do."

Naturally, both dogs ignored me. Instead, they headed toward our bedroom and in a flash were muzzle to muzzle on top of our king-size bed. Oh, well.

I switched my computer reading glasses for my regular reading glasses so I could fire off some texts without squinting. My phone was at 58 percent capacity, so I figured that gave me plenty of power for a group text. But before I even had the chance to compose something witty, I realized I had a new text from Jim to deal with.

Jim: *Will be out most of the day. Remember to take your car to Fairport Garage at 10:00 to get tires rotated. Don't be late. And don't let anyone talk you into buying new ones. The coupon is only for a tire rotation, and it expires today. What time is dinner?*

And, just like that, my lovely lunch plans were probably ruined before I even had a chance to make them.

I allowed myself the brief luxury of a pity party while I was sprucing myself up for my forced trip to Fairport Garage. I don't normally share my secrets with anyone but the dogs, but I trust you to keep this confidential, so here goes.

First of all, I want to go on record as saying that I love my husband. I really, truly love him. Except...sometimes, he drives me nuts. And this has been happening with alarming frequency ever since Jim retired a few years ago. How I long for the good old days, when my time was my own to do with as I pleased, just as long as the kids were taken care of, the house was clean (thanks to our weekly cleaning service, now a victim of Jim's budget cuts), and dinner was on the table when Jim walked in the door from his daily commute to the Big Apple. I had plenty of time to tackle the freelance editing jobs that came from a variety of sources, and indulge in some retail therapy whenever I felt the urge. There was no one looking over my shoulder, asking me where I was going and when I'd be back and why did I feel I had to go out in the first place? Or checking the credit card balance online daily to see if I had indulged myself in a tiny purchase. Or two.

We also had clear job descriptions in those days. Jim handled the outdoor chores himself, except the major ones like painting the house or installing a new roof. I handled the inside ones. Jim was also responsible for car maintenance, and I was responsible for picking out the color of any new vehicle. All in all, a very satisfactory system, from my point of view.

And then Jim retired, and was home most of the time with not a lot to occupy him except me. My normal routine (see above) was completely disrupted, never to return to my version of "normal" ever again. I suspect I'm preaching to the choir here, as I'm not the only woman in the world this has happened to. Thank goodness Jim finally got that freelance job, writing the State of the Town column for our local newspaper. The assignments continued to come, making both of us happy for entirely different reasons. Jim appreciated the chance to give his opinion—in writing—on whatever was going on in Fairport. I was thrilled the job got him out of the house.

I looked at myself in the bathroom mirror, sans makeup, and was shocked. *This is the sight that greets Jim every single morning and he still finds you attractive after all these years. So give the guy a break and go get those tires rotated. It's for your personal safety, because he cares about you. He'd do it himself but he's working at the paper today. You can't have it both ways.*

I just hate it when I argue with myself. I never know which

side I'm really on. Oh, well. I guess it didn't matter. I just hoped that Jim, Lucy and Sister Rose didn't ever get together to hash over all my shortcomings.

Chapter 2

An old woman goes to a wizard to ask him if he can remove a curse she's been living with for the last 40 years. The wizard says, "Perhaps, but you will have to tell me the exact words that were used." The old woman says, without hesitation, "I now pronounce you man and wife."

When I walked into Fairport Garage, the smell of rubber was so overpowering that my first reaction was to hold my breath so I didn't gag. How in heaven's name did people work in such an unhealthy atmosphere without becoming sick? I certainly couldn't.

"You get used to the smell after a while."

I turned and saw a well-dressed woman sitting on one of the plastic chairs in a corner of the so-called waiting room. Frizzy hair framed an unlined face, so either she had remarkably good genes or a recent round of Botox injections. I tried to reply, but couldn't. I just wanted to keep holding my breath so I didn't have to inhale the noxious odor.

"Here, take this," she said, offering me a square piece of fabric she was holding in the palm of her hand. "I breathe into it every so often when the tire fumes are too much for me. I've been here for a while, so the odor doesn't bother me anymore."

I hesitated. I'm no germaphobe, but I wasn't sure if I wanted to breathe into the exact same item that a complete stranger had used. Instead, I coughed, smiled and said, "Thank you, but I'm getting used to the rubber smell already. It was just the initial shock of walking in the door and being assaulted by it. My car is only having the tires rotated, which should be pretty quick." I hope.

"Is there anyone here to help me?" I asked. "My husband made the appointment, but I'm not sure who he spoke to."

"Everyone's in the back right now," the woman said. "Doug's the owner, and he's the only one who really knows what he's doing. The man working on my car had a question and Doug went to help him. He should be back soon to take care of you. Meanwhile," she patted the seat next to her, "you might as well sit down."

"Thanks," I said, "but I'll stand by the door, so I can open it and breathe some fresh air."

The woman shrugged. "Suit yourself," she said. "I was just trying to be friendly."

Oh, boy. Now I'd offended a perfect stranger, and she was mad at me. If there's one thing I really have a hard time dealing with, it's knowing someone is mad at me. Even though I'd probably never see this person again, I felt compelled to apologize for my behavior. The woman was just trying to be friendly, and nobody can have too many friends, right? Of course, right.

"On second thought," I said, planting my posterior onto the chair next to her, "you're right. I should sit down. Who knows how long I'll have to wait, and I should be comfortable." I flashed her a friendly smile, which was not returned.

Sheesh. Some people are overly sensitive. Not that I'm criticizing, mind you. I would never do that.

Since I am a glutton for punishment, I tried again. "How long have you been waiting for your car?"

"Too long," the woman snapped back. "I'm a busy person and I have a business to run."

Hey, lady, don't take your frustrations out on me. I've got my own problems. I didn't really say that out loud, of course. She probably would have decked me.

The woman marched across the room and into the back of the garage, ignoring the sign on the door indicating that customers were not allowed beyond the waiting room. In a flash she was back, followed by a man whose customized shirt identified him as Doug. The man had enough to deal with at the moment, so I settled back in my chair, took small breaths so I wouldn't pass out, and waited my turn like a good girl. I was really curious as to how this drama would play out. Some people claim that mechanics and repairmen tend to take advantage of a woman alone, bumping up the price of their basic services or doing unnecessary things to pad the bill. The woman had calmed down a little, although it was obvious she was still angry at the long wait she'd had to endure.

"Now, Mrs. T," Doug said with a wink, "you wouldn't want me to hand your keys back if I didn't think the car was safe to drive, would you?" Without giving Mrs. T a chance to answer such an obvious question, he continued, "I thought you wouldn't." He held up his hand. "I know what a busy woman you are, and how many people depend on you. But I have a responsibility to my customers. When Tom discovered the problem with your wheel alignment, we had to fix it. It took a little longer than we expected."

"It took a *lot* longer than I expected," the woman said, not giving up without having the last word.

"You're right," Doug said, "and because you're such a special customer, the extra service is my gift to you. Your safety is very important to me. I hope you know that."

I practically fell off my chair. He was extending this cranky woman an offer that no one in her right mind could ever refuse. Jim would never believe it. No, wait a minute. I'd better not tell him, because he'd ask me why she got the free offer and I didn't.

"That's so nice of you," the woman said. "But you and I both know that in business, you never give anything away."

"What about those free cookies you give us every week?" Doug responded, a broad smile on his face. "Please don't tell me you'll stop doing that. The guys in the shop would be so disappointed.

And so would I."

The woman burst out laughing. And, in a minute, I did too. They both looked at me like I was crashing a private party, which embarrassed the heck out of me.

"All right, Doug," the woman said, "baked goods in exchange for taking such good care of me seems fair. I'll send someone over with a tray of assorted goodies sometime this afternoon."

"And don't forget the body work," Doug said. "That's worth at least two trays of cookies."

"Now you're pushing it," she said, laughing again. "And one of the delivery trucks needs servicing. Can you take care of it late Thursday?"

"Of course. Whatever you want."

Satisfied, the woman whipped out a credit card from what looked to my untrained eye like a genuine Prada bag. "Now, let's settle up for the other work and then I can get out of here. Your next customer," she said, indicating me, "has been very patient but I know she's just as busy as I am and needs your attention right away." She gave me a megawatt smile.

In the time that it took for the financial transaction to be completed, something clicked in my brain. I had seen that smile before, but for the life of me, I couldn't remember where. Before I had the chance to ask her if we'd met another time, she was gone.

"Isn't she something?" Doug asked, addressing me directly for the first time. "We play the same game every time she comes in here, especially if there's another customer in the shop. She always complains about being kept waiting too long, and I offer to comp her part of the service, and she says no, and then we do the barter thing. With all her money, she certainly could afford to pay me in full, but she thinks the barter thing is a lot of fun, so I go along with her." He winked. "But I always add the cost of any extra job we've done for her into the bill. I just don't break it out separately, so she never catches on." He patted his tummy. "But I gotta admit, those free goodies she drops off are creating havoc with my waistline. And there are always a few of her bakery trucks that need servicing. I could retire on what she pays me, alone."

Well, this friendly chat was all well and good, but I still hadn't given Doug my car keys so he could do the tire rotation I was here for. I also had places to go, people to see, and—rats—Sister Rose's list to deal with.

"You know who she is, don't you?" Doug asked me.

I was torn. Part of me (a very small part, since I shrink from any kind of confrontation) wanted to point out that I'd been waiting for service for a long time, too. But the other (larger) part, the very curious part, was dying to know who that customer was. Because...that smile. I knew I'd seen it before, and I also knew that it would drive me crazy until I figured out where. In the interest of preserving what little vestiges of sanity I had remaining, I said, "She looked very familiar, but I can't place her."

"That's Mrs. T," Doug said.

"Well, yes, I know that's what you called her. But who's Mrs. T? Should I know that name?"

Doug gave me an incredulous look. "Haven't you ever heard of Mrs. T's Tasty Treats? That was Donna Trumbull, the owner and brains behind the whole operation. She's become a multimillionaire since her husband died and she took over the business."

Oooh, this was getting good. Almost as good as those supermarket tabloids that are crammed into the newsstand near the supermarket checkout. Not that I've ever stooped so low as to pick one of those up and actually read it. My literary tastes are much more refined than that. But I have been known to allow my baby blues to scan the headlines on occasion. Just killing time until it was my turn to check out, understand.

I should be ashamed to admit this, but I leaned forward eagerly to hear more juicy tidbits about Mrs. T, a.k.a. Donna Trumbull. "Now I know why her smile was so familiar," I said. "I've seen her face on all the delivery trucks."

"That's an old photo," Doug said. "It was taken right after Mel Trumbull died. He started Mr. T's Tasty Treats years ago in a small storefront on Fairport Turnpike using a few recipes his wife had created. The products used all fresh ingredients, and were absolutely delicious. They caught on right away because Mrs. T used to sit in front of the bakery and offer free samples to anyone walking by." Doug frowned. "You probably couldn't get away with that today. People might be afraid there was something funny, even dangerous, about that kind of a giveaway. When Mel died, she took over the business and changed the name to Mrs. T's Tasty Treats. The rest, as the old saying goes, is history. She's a shrewd businesswoman, and I wouldn't want to cross her. She has a real killer instinct."

At my look of alarm, Doug added, "Figuratively speaking, of course."

"Of course," I said. "Well, this is all very interesting, but I'm here to have my car's tires rotated. My name's Carol..."

"Andrews," Doug finished. "I know who you are. Your car's all finished and ready to go."

I was confused. "I think you're mistaken," I dangled my car keys in front of Doug. "I still have my keys."

Doug laughed. "Your husband dropped off a set of keys yesterday when he made the appointment for you. He wanted to make it as easy as possible, because he told me you wouldn't want to stay here any longer than you had to."

Honestly, that Jim is full of surprises.

"That was very nice of him," I admitted. I fumbled in my purse for my wallet. "How much do I owe you?"

"Nothing," Doug said. At my shocked expression—how could the man stay in business if he kept on giving his services away?—he added, "Your husband also paid me in advance. He used a coupon he found in the local *Pennysaver*."

I smiled to myself. My husband loves his coupons. In fact, I tease him that he loves them more than he loves me.

Chapter 3

Always be sincere, even if you don't mean it.

I sat in my car, mulling over my options for the rest of the day, and realized two things: it was too late to plan a lunch date, and contacting perfect strangers about a memorial service for another perfect stranger was something I wanted to postpone for as long as possible. (Please don't remind me that it's my own fault Sister Rose can still intimidate me into doing whatever she wanted. I already know that.)

Then I remembered how Mrs. T had let Doug know, in no uncertain terms, that she was a busy woman and her time was valuable. He'd said something about her being a shrewd businesswoman, and that she had a killer instinct. Well, I may not be a shrewd businesswoman, but I was no shrinking violet, either. Maybe being in Mrs. T's presence for a short time and watching her in action rubbed off on me a little. I was mulling over that possibility and giving myself a pep talk when my phone bleeped.

Deanna: *Where r u? U're 20 min. late!*

Oops. Deanna was my hair stylist and one of my closest confidantes. And it looked like I had screwed up.

Me: *Do I have appointment 2day?*

Deanna: *Yes! And I worked you in as a favor!!!!!!*

Hell hath no fury like a scorned hair stylist.

Me: *Mea culpa. On my way.*

Look on the bright side, Carol. Deanna's mad at you now, but she'll get over it. And a hair appointment is a perfect excuse to put off taking care of Sister Rose's list.

My guardian angel must have dozed off, or decided to have a huge chuckle at my expense. Because when I breezed into Crimpers, the best hair salon in all of Fairfield County as far as I was concerned, thrilled with the prospect of a long, lovely, uninterrupted hair appointment and intimate chat with Deanna, who do you think was already there? Go ahead, guess. If you guessed the one person I'd been trying so hard to avoid, you'd be absolutely correct. Who knew that nuns ever went to beauty salons?

Fortunately for me, I spotted the good sister before she spotted me, so I had a chance to paste a big smile on my face before I greeted her. I hope I get points for that, because my first instinct was to turn around and run back to my car.

"I've been waiting for you, Carol," Sister Rose said, a trace of impatience in her tone. "When I heard Deanna calling to remind you about your appointment, I knew this would be an ideal time for you to catch me up on the progress you've made on the list I emailed you."

I shot Deanna a pleading look. *Help me. Please. I promise I'll never keep you waiting again.*

"I'm not really mad at you, sweetie," Deanna said, throwing her arms around me and giving me a hug. "What the heck's up with you two?" she whispered in my ear.

In a millisecond, I came up with the perfect diversionary tactic to get Sister Rose off my case.

"It's perfect that you're here, too, Sister," I said, doing my best to sound sincere. "I can share pictures of the world's most perfect grandchild with both of you at the same time." I whipped out my cell phone and handed it to Sister Rose. "Isn't CJ the most adorable baby you've ever seen? I'm so lucky that Jenny and Mark live close to Jim and me. Now that they've both gone back to work, I've been taking care of CJ every day. I'd forgotten how exhausting looking after an infant can be. The days just fly by. It's a good thing you texted me, Deanna. That's the best way to reach me these days. Assuming I have my phone on, of course. When CJ takes one of his frequent naps, I always turn it off so it doesn't disturb him. Sometimes I forget to turn it back on again."

I looked at Sister Rose. "Isn't he adorable?"

But Sister Rose was not to be diverted, no matter how cute my pictures were. She gave them a quick glance and handed the phone back to me. "Yes, he's very cute," she said. "I always think all newborns look like Winston Churchill, though."

Well! On behalf of my darling grandson, I was offended.

"Then CJ will grow up and become prime minister of Great Britain," Deanna said, sensing my reaction. She grabbed my phone and oohed and aahed over the baby pictures. "What a little doll. I hope you'll bring him into Crimpers sometime, Carol, so I can meet him in person."

I smiled. "I promise that you'll be the one to give him his first real haircut," I said. "If Jenny and Mark approve, of course. I'm only the grandmother."

Sister Rose coughed, then said, "Now, about the memorial service for Mary Pat Ryan, Carol. How many attendees have committed to coming?"

I thought fast and was able to come up with a whopper of a lie that I hoped Sister Rose would take at face value and not question. (Hey, years of practice with Jim has made me a real champ in that department.)

"I talked to two people," I said, "and they had no idea who Mary Pat Ryan was." The two people I was referring to were Lucy and Ethel, in case you didn't get that. Even though they're technically dogs, they're more like real people to me. "I didn't know what to tell them, because I wasn't sure how much you wanted me to share about her. I'm so glad I ran into you here today, so you can clarify things for me."

To my surprise, it wasn't Sister Rose who answered me. It was Deanna. "Isn't she the hit-and-run victim? I remember she was out walking her dog when some creep hit her and then drove off, leaving her there to die." She shook her head in total disgust. "I don't understand how anyone could do something like that. I hope the police catch him and lock him up. And the sooner, the better."

"Deanna's right, Carol," Sister Rose said. "I guess you were too preoccupied with being a new grandmother to be aware of the tragedy."

Not only did I remember about the recent accident, but at first I thought that my son-in-law's annoying mother, Margo, a.k.a. my Houseguest From Hell, was the driver of the car. (She wasn't, thank goodness, but mum's the word about my making her suspect number one, okay?) "I certainly know about the accident," I said. "But I didn't remember the victim's name. I've had a lot on my mind lately."

Sister Rose tsked. "You of all people, being a Mount Saint Francis girl, should definitely remember Mary Pat."

At my quizzical look, she continued, "Mary Pat was two years ahead of you in high school. She was in your Big Sister class and you were in the Glee Club together. As I recall, you were both altos, but I could be wrong about that."

I searched my memory bank but came up empty. No surprise. It had been a long time since I wore my navy blue blazer and saddle shoes, and I'm not going to tell how long that was so don't bother to ask. "Sorry, Sister Rose, I don't remember her at all."

"I pray that it was quick, and that she never realized what was happening," Sister Rose said, her eyes moist. "So you can see, Carol, now that you know Mary Pat's connection to Mount Saint Francis, why it's so important that we have a large showing for her memorial service."

Deanna checked the clock, then said, "I don't want to rush you both, but I have another client coming in about 45 minutes. Carol, if you want your highlights touched up, you need to put a smock on right away while I mix your color." She gave me a pointed look that told me to quit the chatter and do as I was told, then disappeared into the back of the shop.

"You go ahead, dear," Sister Rose said, settling herself into her chair. "I'll just sit here and wait for you and we can continue our conversation about the details for the service itself."

Oh, goody. I came to the hair salon as an oasis of calm, not to talk about planning a memorial service for someone I hardly knew.

Don't be so selfish, Carol. Sister Rose is asking for help, and you need to stop whining about it. And count your blessings instead.

But I couldn't help but wonder why Mary Pat's family wasn't making the arrangements. As I was slipping on the black smock that made me look like Darth Vader's older sister, it suddenly occurred to me that it was just like Sister Rose to take over an event like this without considering the family's wishes.

Maybe involving the family hasn't occurred to Sister Rose, and if you suggest that to her, you'd be able to bow out of the arrangements gracefully. Brilliant, Carol.

I plopped my keister back into a chair in the main portion of the salon and faced Sister Rose. "I'm not trying to weasel out of helping you," I said, although we both knew this was exactly what I was trying to do, "but what about Mary Pat's family? Don't they have the primary responsibility for the memorial?"

Sister Rose sighed. "Mary Pat had no living relatives," she said. "She was a science teacher at Fairport High School for years, and never married. Her whole life was centered around breeding and showing dogs."

My eyes widened. The mention of dogs brought back a sudden memory from my youth, as sharp and clear as if it had just happened. My mother never allowed me to have a dog of my own when I was growing up, and I wanted one more than anything. I remembered going to an older girl's house during my freshman year. She wasn't anyone I knew very well, but she'd seen me crying and telling my friends that, once again, I'd asked my mother for a dog and she had refused. The other girl felt sorry for me, and invited me to her house to meet her dogs. She lived way out in the country, and I had to get special permission to take another school bus to get there. It was quite an adventure.

Her dogs were so sweet and cuddly that I fell in love with them right away, especially after they covered my face with wet, sloppy kisses. I remember that their coats were long and incredibly soft. They were adorable.

"Her dogs were Coton de Tuléars," I said. "She was one of the first people around here to own one." Now it was my turn to cry. I knew who Mary Pat Ryan was. And I also knew that, because of her kindness to someone she barely knew, she gave me one of the best afternoons I've ever had. Thanks to her, dogs have become an integral part of my life.

"I'll do whatever I can to help you organize Mary Pat's memorial," I said. "I can't believe I didn't recognize her name. I owe her a tremendous debt, and organizing her memorial service is the only way I can pay her back for what she did for me."

At Sister Rose's questioning look, I added, "Let's just say that my life would probably be a whole lot different without her. And not as happy."

"Ready, Carol?" Deanna said, interrupting the conversation and turning my chair away from Sister Rose just as she was about to speak again. Boy, I had to admire Deanna. No way would I ever have that kind of nerve.

"Yep," I said, settling back in the chair and steeling myself for the sharp comment coming from Sister Rose at Deanna's moxie. But surprisingly, all she said was, "I'm glad we had a few minutes to talk about this, Carol. Please check in with me after you've completed the list. Since you have Nancy to help you, I'm sure you'll have it done quickly."

I nodded my head and Deanna said, "Stop moving, Carol, or I'll spill some of the solution on you."

Oops.

"It's my top priority," I said. "I'll try to get it completed by tomorrow morning."

"Excellent," said Sister Rose. "Thank you for your patience, Deanna. Carol, I'll wait to hear from you. Thank you." And she vanished out the door before I could reply.

I sighed and tried to clear my mind of sad thoughts. I was finally in one of my happy places, and I was going to relax and enjoy myself as much as possible.

"I appreciate you speeding things along with Sister Rose and me," I said as Deanna continued to apply the magic elixir to my locks. "She tends to be abrupt. Even bossy. Especially with me. But I know she has a good heart and she really cares about every single girl who ever graduated from Mount Saint Francis Academy, no matter how long ago that was."

Deanna laughed. "You don't have to explain Sister Rose to me. She's been coming here for the past few months because she wasn't satisfied with her old salon. The hair stylist there wanted to change her look and she had a fit and walked out."

"That sounds just like her," I said. "But you seem to get along with her very well. What's your secret?"

"I've been changing her hairstyle gradually, making it more up to date," Deanna said. "So far, she hasn't noticed the changes. I pretend I'm following the same lines as her old cut, and that's good enough for her."

"I guess when I make my next appointment with you, I'd better check first to be sure the coast is clear."

"So what about this memorial service?" Deanna asked, bringing me back to reality with a thud. "You knew the hit-and-run victim personally?"

"Yes," I said, "but I didn't remember her name until Sister Rose mentioned her dogs."

OMG. "I just had a terrible thought. Her dogs. Mary Pat was hit while she was walking a dog. Did the dog survive?" I started to sob. I just couldn't stop myself. The thought of her dog also being injured—or worse—by the car made the hit-and-run even more tragic.

"I need my phone," I said to Deanna. "If you hand me my purse, I know I can find it without moving my head. Please. I have to find out more about the accident."

Deanna knows me well. In fact, she probably knows me better

than some members of my own family. She knew I'd be a crying mess until I could get some answers, so without giving me an argument (like you-know-who would have done), she reached in the outer pocket of my purse, found my phone and my reading glasses, and put them both in my hand. "Here. Be quick. I'd like to have you finished and out the door as soon as possible." She must have realized how that sounded, so she added, "Please don't take that the wrong way. You know you're one of my very favorite clients."

"No problem," I said, busily scrolling Google and coming up empty.

"Rats," I said. "I can't find anything new about the accident. The latest information is two weeks old, and it doesn't mention anything about the dog."

"Try the Fairport Patch," Deanna suggested.

"You mean the Fairport Snitch?" I asked.

"You just call it that because they've mentioned your adventures a few times," Deanna said, which brought a smile to my face.

A quick search of the Patch revealed nothing. Frustrating. I knew I wouldn't be satisfied until I'd exhausted all possible search engines.

Then I realized I had my own personal search engine, who wasn't always willing to cooperate with me when I peppered him with questions, but still.... Now that he was a new father, perhaps my darling son-in-law, the Fairport police detective, would be more receptive to my request for information. Especially since he and Jenny depended on me (and Jim) for babysitting the adorable CJ. My route home from Crimpers could be altered just a tad to include a quick stop at his favorite donut shop, and then on to police headquarters.

Am I good or what?

Chapter 4

I didn't say it was your fault. I said I was blaming you.

Of course, the line of customers at Debbie's Donuts was extra-long, and the choice of baked goods at this time of day was limited. I was lucky to snare a dozen Fairport creams (the official donut of the Fairport police department) when I whispered that I was buying them for Detective Mark Anderson, who happened to be my son-in-law. Magically, a box filled with the tasty delights, still warm, appeared from the back room of the donut shop, and the clerk at the counter even added a glazed donut (my favorite) to the order, on the house. I hoped that my accepting the freebie didn't mean I'd accepted a bribe, but I was willing to risk it. And I'm not ashamed to admit that I scarfed the whole donut down on my drive to the police station. I'd deal with the sticky steering wheel when I got home.

I breezed into the station bearing my box of goodies and gave my name to the volunteer seated at the information desk, whose name tag identified her as Bobbie. She eyed the box suspiciously, and I assured her I was bringing in baked goods for Mark Anderson. I opened the box just enough to release the wonderful scent of freshly baked donuts in her direction.

"Yum," Bobbie said. "I hope I get to eat one." In no time at all, she buzzed me through the security door and I headed down the hall toward Mark's office.

I tapped on his door, then opened it and poked my head inside. Mark was seated at his desk, eyes closed, snoring quietly. My goodness. It was a good thing I was the one to interrupt his nap, not his boss.

I coughed, and Mark's eyes popped open. "I wasn't really sleeping," he said. "I was just resting my eyes for a second." He rubbed them for effect. "I've been working on the computer, trying to catch up on all this damn paperwork, and my eyes were feeling the strain."

I nodded in sympathy, not that I bought his story for a single second. I'd been a new parent, too, and I knew how sleep could be elusive with an infant in the house.

Mark eyed me suspiciously. "What are you doing here, Carol? Did Jenny send you over to check on me? Is everything okay at home?"

"Everything's fine, as far as I know. It's wonderful that she's only teaching one class this semester, so she has a lot of time to spend with CJ." I placed the box of donuts front and center on Mark's cluttered desk. "I come bearing gifts for the new father," I said. "I thought you might need a burst of sugar, or more, to keep you going, so here I am."

"You were right," Mark said, reaching for a donut with impressive speed. "Thank you. CJ's colic is pretty much gone now, but he still has his fussy moments, especially in the middle of the night. I haven't had a good night's sleep since he was born. Not that I'm complaining," he hastened to add. "Being a father is awesome." He nudged the box in my direction. "Want to share one with me?"

"I'm way ahead of you. I already had one on the way over here," and held up my sticky hands as proof.

Mark rooted in a desk drawer and came up with a small bottle of hand sanitizer. "Here. I always keep this handy, just in case."

"I don't want to keep you from your work," I said, spritzing my hands and wiping them on a napkin the donut shop had thoughtfully provided. "But since I'm already here, I was wondering about the hit-and-run accident that happened while you were on Daddy leave. Do you have any new information about it?"

"Atta girl, Carol," Mark said, grinning. He had a huge blob of donut filling on his chin, and I resisted the urge to wipe it off, the way I would have done when he was a kid.

"What do you mean?"

"I wondered how long we were going to discuss donuts. And when we'd get to the real reason why you stopped by. These..." he waved his hand over the box, "were merely a diversionary tactic to get me in a good mood before you sprung your trap. And don't try to deny it. I know you too well."

Busted, darn it.

"I'm not going to deny anything," I said, figuring I wouldn't get away with it anyway, so why bother? But I didn't want Mark to think that I'd become one of those nosy old women who live vicariously through the trials and tribulations of others. (Not that I consider myself old in any way, understand.)

"To set the record straight, though, my interest in this accident is very personal. The victim, Mary Pat Ryan, was a schoolmate of mine at Mount Saint Francis Academy. Sister Rose contacted me to ask for my help in arranging Mary Pat's memorial service, since she left no living relatives. Of course, I agreed. I'm in the process of contacting old classmates right now, and some questions have come up about the accident that I can't answer. That's why I came to you. Bearing donuts."

Mark looked a little embarrassed. "I didn't mean to imply that you're some kind of old busybody or ambulance chaser," he said. Left unsaid were the words, "Like my partner, Paul Wheeler does." I knew Paul thought I was both of those things, and a lot more. Personally, I think Paul's just jealous because I've been able to figure out several cases that have stumped the Fairport police. Jealousy is a terrible thing. I always step back and let the police take credit for solving the crime, though. Despite what you may have heard, I'm a very modest person. But Paul was the person who saved my best friend Nancy a few weeks ago, so he wasn't all bad.

My son-in-law nodded and helped himself to another donut, then put it back in the box. "Jenny says I should watch my snacks or I'll get fat and she'll leave me. I don't think she was really serious, but just to be sure I don't give in to more temptation, I'm going to put these in the break room for everybody else to enjoy. They'll be gone in minutes."

His expression turned serious. "So, you want to know more about that hit-and-run accident. All I can tell you is that we're nowhere closer to finding the driver than we were when it happened. There were no witnesses, and because there's never money allocated in the town budget to install cameras at intersections, we don't have a description of the vehicle that was involved. Be very careful when you cross a street in town. Pedestrian accidents are becoming much more common. This is the first fatality we've had in years, and I hope there won't be any others."

"I'm very careful, Mark," I assured him. "I only cross the street at a pedestrian crosswalk, and even then, I always check both ways first for oncoming traffic, to be sure there are no cars in sight. Not every driver honors those crosswalks, though."

"That's what happened to Mary Pat Ryan. Some car apparently came barreling around a corner and didn't stop. And then just sped away."

I leaned forward in my chair. "So, to get to the point of my visit...."

Mark raised his eyebrows. I could tell he was thinking, "Finally." But he didn't say it aloud.

"To get to the point of my visit," I repeated, "what about the dog Mary Pat was walking when she was hit. Is there anything about that in the accident report?"

"Hmm," Mark said, turning in his chair and scrolling through his computer. "I guess that's not top-secret information. I can share it with you, unlike some of the things you've asked me about before."

I didn't respond to the implied criticism. I knew that, despite his protestations to the contrary, Mark usually appreciated my interest in cases that were baffling the Fairport police.

"Here it is," Mark said. "The pedestrian died at the scene. But apparently, she'd let go of the leash and the dog ran to the sidewalk, so it wasn't hit. A local veterinarian checked it out. The dog was fine. That's all I can tell you." He closed the screen abruptly.

"I'm so glad to hear the dog survived," I said. "That's all I wanted to know. Thank you, sweetie." I leaned over and gave Mark a kiss on the top of his head.

"I'll let you get back to work now," I said. "Or back to resting your eyes. I'm on my way home to start contacting more classmates about the memorial service." And I made a hasty exit before Mark could say another word.

Chapter 5

We never really grow up—we only grow taller and learn how to behave properly in public.

I'm not embarrassed to admit that all I wanted to do when I got home that afternoon was spend an hour of quality time cuddling with Lucy and Ethel. I knew that Ethel would immediately snuggle up to me on the couch in the family room and fall asleep, and I was counting on the comfort of a sweet puppy to calm me down after what I'd discovered about Mary Pat Ryan and her tragic death. I knew that Lucy, being the suspicious type, would take a lot longer to settle down. She'd know that it was completely out of character for me to take time during the day to indulge in what was, in her opinion, a nighttime activity for me. I hoped she'd cut me some slack when I explained the situation to her.

So you can imagine that I was less than thrilled when I turned onto Old Fairport Turnpike and found Nancy's car parked in my driveway. Knowing that my best friend had a key to my house, I figured she'd already let herself inside and made herself comfortable. She probably wanted to complain about another demanding real estate client or a greedy homeowner with unrealistic expectations about how high to price a house for sale. Or maybe she wanted to share another outrageous story about her sort-of-married-to-but-not-living-with husband, Bob.

Don't be stupid, Carol. Nancy got an email about the memorial service from Sister Rose, too. That's why she's here.

"I hope she made a pot of tea," I muttered, walking slowly toward my kitchen door. "Or, better yet, started dinner." That last thought made me laugh, because Nancy hasn't cooked a real meal in her own kitchen for years. She's even worse than I am. That's why Claire, Mary Alice and I have given her the title, "Queen of Takeout." Her refrigerator is filled with so many white boxes of leftovers that she could subsist on them for at least a week, if not longer. (The food inside them, not the actual boxes, in case that wasn't clear to you.)

I was busy with my own musings, so when the driver's side of Nancy's car suddenly opened, I jumped.

"Hi, Carol. I was wondering when you'd show up."

"Nancy!" I said, surprised. "What are you doing sitting outside? Why didn't you wait for me in the house? Or text me and let me know you were coming over?"

Instead of answering my question, Nancy said, "Your hair looks nice."

"I had a Deanna fix today," I said, leading the way inside. "Sit down and I'll make some tea." I looked at her closely and saw the expression on her face. Something was definitely up, and it wasn't good. My always impeccably made-up, stylishly dressed best friend looked like, well... a four-letter word that made my mother send me to my room when she heard me using it.

"Tea sounds fine," Nancy said, sinking into a kitchen chair and snapping her fingers so Lucy and Ethel, who'd been taking a nap in their crates (where else?) would come to her. She bent down to give each of them a head scratch, then burrowed her face in Lucy's fur and burst into tears. "I'm such a mess. I haven't had a good night's sleep for weeks. I keep having horrible nightmares."

I was at her side in a flash and put my arms around her. "Oh, sweetie, I'm so sorry. What's going on? Is it Bob? Is he seeing some other woman?"

Nancy started to laugh. "If it were only that simple. I could handle another woman. It's being afraid all the time that I can't handle." She brushed the tears away from her eyes. "Is my mascara running all over my face? I bet I look a mess."

"Nancy, despite everything, you look as beautiful as always," I said, giving her a squeeze. "You're one of the fortunate ones who can cry and not end up looking all red and puffy, like I do." I plopped down in a chair and drew it close. "Now, please tell me what you're talking about. What are you so afraid of? What are these nightmares about?"

"If I tell you, I'm sure you'll think I'm stupid. Or nuts. Just like I'd probably think about you if the situation was reversed."

"No matter what you tell me, I promise I won't think you're stupid. Especially after all the things we've been through together over the years, when you had the chance to say that exact same thing to me and didn't. I'm going to get the tea now. You just sit here and think about what you want to say. Take your time. I'm not going anywhere."

I don't remember how long we sat at my kitchen table without saying a single word to each other. But if it was more than ten seconds, that would be a record. Finally, Nancy spoke. "I can't get beyond what happened a few weeks ago, when I found a real estate client's dead body at his house. Today I had an appointment to show a listing to a potential buyer, and when we got to the property and went up to the front door, I was afraid to go inside. The buyer thought I was nuts. And look what happened to me here. I was afraid to come into a place that's a second home to me. I'm going to lose my job if I can't get myself under control."

Nancy jumped up and started to pace around my kitchen. Then she whirled around and said, "Dealing with dead bodies all the time never seems to bother you. I think you actually enjoy it when you find one."

I came within a hair's breadth of lashing out at my very best friend and saying things I would regret for the rest of my life. But I didn't. I hope you're all proud of me, because it was one of the hardest things I've ever done.

"Just to be clear," I said, gritting my teeth, "I do not enjoy any association with dead bodies. In fact, if I could figure out how to avoid finding them, I would. It's not my fault that I've been unlucky since Jim retired and a few bodies have fallen into my lap. One of them quite literally, remember? You were there that time." I shivered, remembering when one of my fellow weight-loss pals had keeled over onto me during a meditation class. There have been several other incidents, but I won't bore you with them now.

What this situation needed was a little comic relief to break the tension. "It's probably Jim's fault," I said with a straight face. "After he retired and started hanging around the house more and driving me crazy, I had to find a new hobby. Unfortunately, as my very best friend, you're involved, too."

This was so patently outrageous that it made Nancy laugh. Thank goodness.

And then I heard a familiar voice say, "What's my fault? What did I do now?"

OMG. Jim was home and he'd overheard every word I said. I was in big trouble now. So I did what any other smart, slightly devious wife would do—I embellished the truth. Okay, I lied.

"I didn't mean you, Jim," I said. "Nancy and I have another friend who's married to a man named Jim. And he's only been retired for a short time. He's driving her crazy."

"That's not what you said, Carol," Jim replied. "Not driving *her* crazy. I heard you say, 'driving *me* crazy.' You were talking about you and me. Fess up."

Nancy knew better than to get in the middle of this husband-wife "discussion," so she grabbed her purse, gave me a quick smooch on the cheek, whispered "thanks" in my ear, and headed for the door, intent on making a speedy exit. The traitor.

I was trapped. And I was desperate. But I always believed that the best defense is a strong offense. I think I read that in a biography of George Patton. Or, maybe it was Douglas MacArthur. Both those guys were winners on the battlefield, right?

I grabbed Nancy's wrist, stopping her in mid-flight, and said, "Don't leave yet. I know how upset you are. I was just trying to make you feel better and make you laugh." I turned to Jim and said, "Do you see what you've done now? I hope you're sorry!

Nancy came to me, all upset, and I was trying to help her. And now, you've interrupted us and ruined everything. Why are you home so early, anyway? Did you feel you needed to check up on me, the way you always do? The tires have already been rotated, per your orders." I glared at my husband, then fired one more shot. "You misunderstood what I said. Your hearing loss is getting worse and you should do something about it. You just refuse to get hearing aids."

Of course, the poor man had absolutely no idea what I was talking about. Well, except for the part about having the tires rotated. That part, he got. The need for hearing aids was absolutely true, although there was a certain advantage for me when Jim didn't always hear/know what I was up to. I did feel bad, for about a millisecond, about my throwing him such a curveball the way I did. Even Nancy looked shocked.

"I'm sorry for this, Nancy, and I'm sure Jim is, too. Or he will be, once he thinks about it. And, to be fair," I said, throwing my husband a conciliatory lifeline, "you really had no idea you'd interrupted a heart-to-heart conversation, did you, dear? So, I forgive you." I gave him a peck on the cheek. "And I'm sure Nancy does, too. Maybe you and I should treat ourselves to an early dinner at Maria's Trattoria, Nancy, and continue our discussion in private."

"What about my dinner?" Jim asked, recovering his composure once the subject of food was raised. "I have to eat, too."

"I know you do, dear," I said. "I promise you won't starve. How about if I just have salad with Nancy and bring home some of Maria's lasagna for our dinner? You know how much you love it, and I never cook it for you anymore."

I thought I heard Jim mutter, "You never cook much of anything for me anymore," but I could be mistaken about that. And he stalked out of the kitchen.

"Works for me," Nancy said, freeing herself from my death grip and making her escape with impressive speed. "I'll go to Maria's now and save a table. See you there."

Now, Nancy may be my best female friend, but Jim was my life partner, for better or for worse, and I knew I'd made him angry and probably hurt his feelings too. I also knew I'd better make amends as soon as possible, before he changed the locks on the house so that when I came home from Maria's Trattoria my key would no longer work. (Only kidding, so don't worry.)

I found my long-suffering husband in his favorite spot, in front of his computer, banging on the keys with what I felt was excessive force. Obviously, Jim was still in a snit and taking it out on a poor, innocent electronic device. I leaned down and gave him a kiss on top of his head, noting that the hair on the crown of his head was still there, even if his front hairline was receding. "I'm sorry, Jim," I said. "I was backed into a corner and—"

"Do you really think your life is worse since I retired?" Jim asked me, looking like a hurt puppy whose owner had just dropped him off at the pound.

"No, Jim," I said. "But, it's different." I thought fast. "Mostly in a good way. But not good in all ways. Do you know what I mean?"

"It's more different for me than it is for you, Carol," Jim said, his face flushing. "I'm the one who had to get up before dawn every morning and commute to New York to put bread on this family's table, not you. And not once did I ever complain about it. So, what is your problem? I'd really like to know."

"When you put it that way, Jim," I said, "I guess I really don't have a problem. In fact, my life is very good, and I should quit complaining about it. And I know how you worry about me and my all-too-frequent forays into crime-solving."

"Since we're clearing the air a little," Jim said, "I have to admit, now that CJ is born and you're a grandmother, I hope you'll spend more time being his grandma and less time as Fairport's answer to Miss Marple. I do worry about you, and what you're up to when I'm not around." He frowned. "I never realized it before, but maybe I check in on you too much. And I expect you to stay around the house so you'll be here whenever I need you, when you want to go out and have some fun. I guess I've been very selfish."

"I'm the one who's been selfish," I said, guilt washing over me like a tsunami. "After all, who knows how many years we have left? I should be more aware of your needs, and not so consumed with my own. I know that retirement, and not going to a regular office all the time, has been a rough adjustment for you."

Of course, you do write for the local newspaper, so you have an office to go to anytime you want. I'd lose my mind if you were underfoot all the time. I didn't really say that, of course.

"I'm glad we had this talk, Carol," my hubby said. "I'll try to be more aware of your needs from now on. Nancy's waiting for you. You better go."

"I won't be too long," I said, giving Jim a smooch. "And I will bring us back dinner. See you later."

I knew this conversation wouldn't change a thing in the long run. So I got out of the house while, as the old saying goes, the gettin' was good.

Chapter 6

Money isn't everything. There's also Visa,
MasterCard, and American Express.

"Sorry if I kept you waiting, Nancy," I said, sliding into a booth way at the back of the restaurant. I took a good, long look at my lifelong best friend. She was shredding a paper napkin with impressive speed, a sure sign that she was still upset.

Nancy shoved the napkin aside and grabbed her water glass. "What took you so long? Are you and Jim still married? I was getting worried."

"Of course we're still married, silly," I said. "Till death do us part, remember? You were there, as my maid of honor, holding me up so I wouldn't faint."

"More like holding you back so you wouldn't run screaming up the aisle of the church and make your escape," Nancy said with just a trace of a grin. "You were a nervous wreck. You even cried at your bridal shower."

I started to protest, but then realized that she was right. I also realized that she'd given me a perfect opportunity to continue a difficult conversation.

"You've always been there for me," I said. "Even before Jim came into my life. And I'll always be here for you. So, let's figure out a way to get you over this crisis. I know that if we put our heads together, we can come up with a plan. We always have."

"I don't know if just the two of us can solve this one," Nancy said, looking sad again.

"I do," I said with more confidence than I really had. "Let's try." I grabbed a menu. "But, first things first. Let's order some salad, now, so we won't be interrupted."

That got a real smile from Nancy. "No matter what, food always comes first for you," she said. I would have argued that point, except that she was absolutely right.

"This may be a golden opportunity to do something we've always talked about but never done," I said as a truly brilliant idea popped into my conscious mind. I snapped the menu shut. "Let's forget about salad and just order dessert. And if we're still hungry when we've finished it, then we can order a salad or something. What do you say? Are you game?"

Nancy shook her head. "You're tempting me, but I can't. You know how careful I am about my weight, and I don't need any extra calories. I have to present a glamorous image to attract new clients. There are so many younger agents in my office now, and I have to compete with them."

"So, you're chicken?" I asked. "You won't do it, just this once? Come on, let's live a little. It won't be nearly as much fun if we don't do it together. I'm ordering tiramisu. What about you?"

"Oh, what the hell," Nancy said. "Just this once, let's live it up." She signaled for a server, and to my surprise, Maria Lesco appeared bearing a tray with three yummy desserts on it. "Just the people I wanted to see," she said, "and I come bearing gifts. This is a new recipe I'm testing before it goes on the menu. It's a combination of tiramisu and gelato, with a special secret ingredient." And she placed the three desserts on the table.

"Who's the third one for?" I asked. "Is someone else coming?"

"It's for me," Maria said. "I want to talk to you, and what better way to do it than over dessert?" She handed us each a spoon. "I didn't see what time you came in, though. Have you already ordered your main course? If not, tell me what you want and I'll take care of it right away. We can have this later."

"Not on your life," Nancy said, pulling her portion of the yummy concoction as close to her as possible so she didn't have to reach too far to gobble it down. "It looks delicious, and Carol just convinced me that this was the one time we should throw caution to the wind and eat dessert first. I consider this a sign from heaven that she's right."

"I do want to order some of your delicious lasagna to take home," I said. "That was the only way I could avoid cooking dinner tonight."

"I'd like a half portion of lasagna to take home, too," Nancy said.

"Knowing you, a half portion will last you at least three whole days," I said, laughing. "And put them all on the same check, Maria. My treat."

"No, this is entirely on me," Maria said, waving her hand at the hovering server and giving him the food order. He scurried away to tell the chef. When the boss lady talks, everybody moves extra fast.

"This is unusual for me," Maria said, pulling over a chair rather than sitting beside me in the booth. "I don't ever fraternize with the customers, but this is an unusual situation." She glanced around. "And, fortunately, things are quiet right now, so this is a good time for us to talk. But first, please try the dessert and tell me what you think."

It suddenly dawned on me that Maria joining us *was* a first, as far as I knew. I'd never seen her sit with any of her customers during a meal before.

I took one bite and savored it. Umm. Heavenly. Even though Nancy was only taking teeny bites, I could tell by her speed that she felt exactly the same way. In no time at all, the desserts were consumed. We all sighed with contentment, even Maria. There's nothing like a sugar rush to bring a smile to my face and joy to my heart. Well...almost nothing.

"I can see that you both enjoyed it," Maria said, pointing to our empty dishes.

"Actually," I said, blotting my lips with a napkin, "I may need an extra portion to eat at home, just to be sure."

"Good try, Carol," said Nancy.

"I won't do that, Carol," Maria said. "Until it's officially on the menu, I don't want any samples to leave the restaurant. I take these recipe pre-tests very seriously."

I could tell by Maria's tone that I was in big trouble. Her expression was as solemn as it used to be during all those parent-teacher conferences I endured when each of my kids had her as a grammar school teacher. She used to scare both Jenny and Mike to death. Me, too, truth to tell. I knew I had to apologize right away, even though, in my humble opinion, Maria was overreacting to what was my lame attempt to be funny.

"I'm sorry, Maria," I said. "What I should have said is that your new dessert is so delicious that I'd love to have a second helping. Or even a third." And I patted my tummy (was my waistband already tighter?) for emphasis.

"Well, why didn't you just say that, Carol?" Maria answered. "You and Nancy can have all the tiramisu gelato you want, as long as it's before the dinner rush starts and you eat it here in the restaurant. But the minute more customers start coming in, the tasting's over."

"Thanks, but no thanks," I said. "Sometimes too much of a good thing really is too much, at least for my waistline."

"Mine, too," Nancy put in. "Although mine is much smaller than Carol's to begin with."

I could have swatted her, but instead I burst out laughing, and in a millisecond, Maria joined in. What the heck. If my being the butt (no pun intended) of Nancy's joke would lighten her mood, I was willing. That's what best friends do for each other, right?

After a few minutes, the hilarity petered out. "I needed a good laugh," Maria said. "Especially right now."

"You said you wanted to talk to us," I reminded her.

Maria's expression turned solemn. "I do. It's about Mary Pat Ryan. I know Sister Rose has contacted you both about her memorial."

"What memorial? Who's Mary Pat Ryan?" Nancy asked,

looking confused.

"Don't you ever check your personal email, Nancy?" I asked.

"I've had a few things on my mind, Carol, as I told you a while ago," my BFF said. "I admit that I haven't been as attentive to my email messages lately as I should have been. Besides, you know the best way to reach me is by text. Email is so archaic. Will one of you please fill me in on what you're talking about instead of criticizing me?"

"Mary Pat Ryan is the woman who was killed in that hit-and-run accident last month," I clarified. "She was two years ahead of us at Mount Saint Francis, and Sister Rose sent me an email with a list of people to contact about attending her memorial service. She sent one to you, too." I looked at Maria. "The memorial and luncheon are going to be held here, which is why Maria is involved."

"That's not exactly true, Carol," Maria said.

Now it was my turn to be confused. "You mean, the plans have changed and you can't host the memorial here after all? Does Sister Rose know that? I'm glad I haven't starting contacting people on my list yet." Who says procrastination isn't a virtue? In this case, it had definitely paid off, because if the memorial venue was changed and I'd already done what I was supposed to do, I'd just have to do it all over again.

"That's not what I meant," Maria said. "Everything will still be here." Her eyes filled with tears. "Mary Pat was my friend. And it's my fault that she died."

Chapter 7

If jumping to conclusions was an Olympic sport,
I'd win the gold medal.

Wowser! What a bombshell. Did I hear Maria Lesco just confess to being the hit-and-run driver who killed Mary Pat Ryan? I couldn't believe it. I snuck a quick look at Nancy, who appeared to be as shell-shocked as I was. For once, I was at a loss for words. I fingered my cell phone, now having a nice little nap at the bottom of my purse. I hoped I didn't have to use it to call 911 and turn Maria in. But if I had to do it, I would.

Nancy finally spoke. "I'm sure you didn't mean to do it, Maria," she said.

"Nancy's right," I chimed in. "It was an accident, right?" *Please tell us that you hit her accidentally.*

"Oh, I meant it, all right," Maria said. "I made a choice. Though it kills me to admit it to you both."

Not as permanently as it killed Mary Pat. I didn't really say that out loud, of course.

"I need to tell someone what happened," Maria said, her voice shaking.

"Maybe we're not the ones you should be talking to," I said, pushing my dessert dish away. "I'd be glad to contact my son-in-law so you could talk to him instead."

Nancy nodded her head. "That's a good idea, Carol."

Maria looked confused. "But he's a police detective, if I'm remembering correctly. Why on earth would I want to talk to him?"

OMG. Maria Lesco, a woman I thought I knew very well, a respected teacher in Fairport for years, and now the owner of a successful restaurant, had just confessed to a hit-and-run and couldn't understand why I wanted to involve the local police. I realized she must be a sociopath, and I hadn't caught on until just now. I couldn't believe it.

"The Trattoria was very busy that night," Maria said. "When Mary Pat called and wanted me to stop by her house, I told her that if she wanted to talk to me, she'd have to come here. I suggested she come in the back way and go up the stairs to my office, because I knew she'd be bringing her dog with her. I reminded her that I abide by Board of Health rules, much as I hate the one that forbids dogs in the restaurants."

"I see," I said, although I really didn't. My mind was whirling with a billion questions, but I clamped my lips shut and waited for Maria to continue.

Did you really drive over to meet her instead? Did you know which route she'd take to walk to the Trattoria from her house? Did you deliberately set her up so you could nail her in the middle of the intersection and stop her from talking about...what? Did you let a customer bring a dog into the restaurant, and Mary Pat saw you do it? Did she threaten to report you to the Board of Health and have your license revoked? Was she blackmailing you?

OMG. That made perfect sense. Mary Pat Ryan was a blackmailer. Who knew? Poor Maria. She must have been desperate. I wish I knew the name of a good trial lawyer. Unfortunately, Larry McGee, my good friend Claire's husband, was retired.

If someone was blackmailing me—not that anyone ever would, because I lead a blameless life—I'd want to confront the blackmailer on my home turf. In fact, if I was really clever, I'd set up a trap to record our conversation and figure out a way to use it against her (or him). I didn't dare voice my support for the way Maria handled the situation because, of course, even if Mary Pat was a blackmailer, she didn't deserve to die that way. And I couldn't believe Maria, a woman I'd respected for years, would deliberately run over someone she called a friend with her car and just drive away.

I must have zoned out completely while I was concocting a reasonable defense that Maria's lawyer could use when I felt a sharp kick under the table. "Are you still with us, Carol?" Nancy asked.

"Sorry," I said. "I was thinking about CJ. Jenny said he was very fussy today. I hope he's all right." Isn't it impressive, the way I can come up with a quick untruth (lie is such a harsh word) without even trying?

Nancy gave me a skeptical look, then said, "Maria, maybe you'd better repeat what you were saying, because Carol was in her worried grandma mode and wasn't listening."

"Sorry, Maria," I repeated. "Would you mind going over it again? I really want to help you if I can."

Then I gave myself a mental slap. *For Pete's sake, Carol, why did you say you wanted to help her? She's just confessed to being a hit-and-run driver. You should turn her in, even if it means turning off your main source of Italian food forever.*

"I was explaining that Mary Pat and I met at a fall teachers' conference many years ago," Maria said. "I'd just been hired as the American History teacher at Fairport High School, and Mary Pat was the high school chemistry teacher." Maria paused in her narrative, and I didn't interrupt. But I wondered how long it was going to take to get to the point of our conversation—Mary Pat's foray into blackmail and then Maria orchestrating her death.

"We saw each other regularly at school, but never socially. Then I switched to teaching sixth graders instead of high schoolers. I used to see Mary Pat now and then around town in those days, and we were always cordial to each other. But we were never close friends, even when we were both teaching at the same school."

I have lots of those relationships, myself—people I say hello to on the street or in a store, just to be polite, but not anyone I consider a real friend.

"When I retired and opened the restaurant, Mary Pat started coming in for dinner at least once a week. She was always alone, so we chatted a bit. Then, about five years ago, she came in with a stack of travel brochures. She told me that she'd just had a big birthday and she realized that the time to check things off her bucket list was getting shorter and shorter, while the candles on her cake were getting more and more numerous. We had a good laugh about that. I could certainly identify with how she felt."

Maria paused again.

By this time, I wanted to shake her if that would speed things along. Nancy, always one to read my mind (unlike Jim, who never has a clue), gave me a warning look. So I kept my hands to myself.

"Anyway, one thing led to another and we started traveling together," Maria said. "We took at least one trip every year. We had some wonderful times. She was always ready to try a new place, or take off on a new adventure. This time, it was my turn to pick the destination, and I suggested a trip to Italy. I'd been there before but always wanted to go back. Mary Pat did some internet research and found a terrific deal. The trip included a stay in an Italian castle in Umbria, and on-site cooking classes. Even though Mary Pat never cooked a meal if she could avoid it, she knew I'd love it. That night she called to tell me all about it, and stressed that we had to book it right away or we'd lose out. I told her I couldn't take the time to make a decision until the dinner rush was over. She said she'd come right over and wait until I had a quick break to talk. That's why she was out that night. She was walking over to see me. And then some horrible person hit her and just left her there to die."

Go ahead and give me and my overactive imagination a slap, figuratively speaking. But at least give me points for keeping my big mouth shut.

"Her death is my fault. I should have taken some time to listen to her when she called me about the trip. If I'd just taken five or ten minutes, Mary Pat would still be alive. I'll live with this guilt for the rest of my life."

"Maria," Nancy said gently, "please don't blame yourself. It wasn't your fault. It's just an unfortunate coincidence that she was coming to see you when she was hit."

"Nancy's right," I said. "I'm betting that Mary Pat walked her dog around Fairport all the time, day or night. I know there's nothing that Lucy and Ethel love more than a good walk around the neighborhood. And, I have to confess, I don't walk them nearly long enough. I need to get them out more." Myself, too.

"I just wish the police could find the person who was driving the car," Nancy said. "I'd lock him up and throw away the key."

"How do you know it was a man?" I asked. "The police still have no clue who was responsible."

"I don't know, for sure," Nancy admitted. "But everyone knows that women are far more compassionate than men. A female driver would have stopped to help, not left the victim there, dying."

There was some truth to that. But every rule has exceptions. Some women I know, even some I've known since before we both got our driver's licenses, are really terrible drivers. Not mentioning anyone by name, understand. And some women tend to panic under stress, which could override any compassionate feelings. Again, not mentioning anyone by name, but if one should happen to pop into your head that fits this profile, well...that's not my fault.

"It's a miracle her dog wasn't killed, too," I said. "I heard from Mark that it was taken to a vet to be checked out after the accident, and it was fine."

"I wanted to adopt the dog myself," Maria said. "Her name is Harriet, and she's a real sweetie. I guess I figured we could mourn the loss of our friend together. But I delayed calling about her, and by the time I did, it was too late. Someone else had taken her. I hope she went to a good home where her new family will love her as much as Mary Pat did."

"I'm sure Harriet went to a loving home," I said. I couldn't imagine anyone else taking care of Lucy and Ethel and loving them as much as I did. But I didn't voice that to Maria. She was dealing with enough emotional baggage already.

The restaurant was starting to fill up with a line of prospective diners, intent on eating one of the Trattoria's yummy meals. Under normal circumstances, Maria would already be on her feet, racing to welcome the customers and apologizing for keeping them waiting for a table. But not this time. Instead, she signaled for one of her servers and indicated that he was to take over the hosting duties in her place. "And please offer them my apologies and five percent off their total check for keeping them waiting." The server nodded and scurried off.

In all the time I'd been coming to the Trattoria, I'd never known Maria to offer any bargains before. First, she was comping Nancy's and my meals, and now she was offering a dining discount. This was not the hard-headed businesswoman I'd come to know.

"You look surprised, Carol," she said. "It's just good customer relations. I don't want anyone telling their friends that they were kept waiting for a table here. I depend a lot on word-of-mouth to keep the patrons coming."

"That makes sense," Nancy agreed. "It's the same in the real estate business. I offer my clients the best service I can, so they'll refer others to me."

I rolled my eyes, anticipating another of Nancy's real estate lectures. I'd been subjected to them far too often over the years. Then I realized, if Nancy was going off on one of her boring (to me) Real Estate 101 lecture tangents, she must be feeling better. And that was good news to me.

"Customer service is certainly important in any business," I said, interrupting Nancy. But I had a sudden insight that wasn't the real reason for Maria's new policy. "I hate to play sidewalk psychiatrist," I said slowly, "because I'm certainly not qualified. But I wonder if you're suffering from survivor guilt, Maria."

"What?" she said, looking startled at my suggestion. "I have no idea what you mean."

"You admitted to us that you blame yourself..." I held up my hand as Maria started to interrupt... "wrongly, for Mary Pat's death. You can't do anything about what happened to her. But now, you have an overpowering need to do what you perceive to be the right thing for everyone else, as much as you can. Which also explains why you wanted to adopt her dog. You wanted to make it up to Harriet, too."

I sat back in the booth, waiting for both Maria and Nancy to shoot it down and tell me I was being ridiculous.

"You know," Maria said, looking thoughtful, "you may be right."

Say what? Really?

"I can't compare my situation to anyone who's been through a traumatic event like the death of a family member," Maria said. "But there may be an element of good sense in what you've said."

"That's a first," Nancy said, grinning to take the sting out of her words and show she really didn't mean them.

"When Sister Rose called me about having Mary Pat's memorial here, I jumped at the chance," Maria admitted. "I already had a fundraiser for Frank Bologna's re-election campaign booked for that same time, but I was able to move it to the following week." She frowned. "He gave me a really hard time about that, even though he hadn't even started to invite people to come. The irony is that he loves to tell everyone that he'll do anything in Fairport to help his constituents. What a joke. All he wants is to be re-elected so he can continue to do absolutely nothing for the town and the people who live here."

"He should be named Frank Baloney, because that's what he's full of," Nancy said. "I swear, that man never stops campaigning."

We were getting off track here—something I excel at, by the way, so I knew what I was talking about. It's a diversionary tactic I often use when I know I'm in hot water with Jim about some trivial matter (like maxing out the family credit card, for example) and need to change the subject to a more pleasant one, pronto.

"Nobody enjoys talking about local politics more than I do," I said, which was such a blatant lie that I couldn't even look at Nancy. "But right now, I have to get home and start contacting Mount Saint Francis alumni about Mary Pat's service. I hope my order is ready. I've been neglecting my culinary obligations on the home front lately and I'm counting on your fabulous lasagna to win me a few points with Jim." With everything Maria had shared with Nancy and me, I needed to get out of the restaurant and have some time to process it.

"Not so fast, Carol," Maria said, putting a restraining hold on my arm. "Before I check on your order, when can you give me a head count for the memorial service? I have to let my suppliers know as soon as possible."

"We were meeting here to talk about that very thing," Nancy said. I flashed her a grateful look, then realized she'd admitted less than twenty minutes ago that she hadn't even read Sister Rose's email. But since she'd given me a lifeline, I took it. And prayed that Maria had been so caught up in her guilt about Mary Pat's death that she'd forgotten what Nancy said earlier.

"Sister Rose wants the list completed by tomorrow, so we can give you a preliminary head count then," I said.

"We'll get on it right away," Nancy assured Maria.

"The memorial isn't until Saturday," I said. "Today's Tuesday. When do you need the final 'drop dead' numbers for your suppliers?"

Nancy gave me a shocked look and I realized what I'd just said. "I don't know what in the world made me use that expression, Maria. I am so sorry."

"Apology accepted," Maria said. But the hurt expression on her face told a different story. "I'll get your takeout order now." And she vanished into the kitchen.

"What the heck is wrong with you?" Nancy asked.

"Nothing's wrong with me. It's just that my mouth operates separately from my brain sometimes."

"All the time, if you ask me," Nancy shot back.

"I said I was sorry. And when, pray tell, do you plan on reading Sister Rose's email for the first time?" Yes, I was being snarky, in case you didn't get that. Sometimes my usual sunny disposition deserts me.

Nancy waved her phone. "I already did, while you were busy putting your foot in your mouth and then apologizing to Maria. I have a list of sixty names, all of them with either emails or phone numbers. I just hope the numbers are for cell phones. Texting is so much quicker."

"Who's the first name on the list?" I asked, scrambling for my glasses in my purse so I could read my own copy.

"Denise Albano Smith," Nancy read aloud. "And the last one is Jean Williamson O'Mara. I guess Sister Rose put the names in alphabetical order according to maiden name."

"Makes sense," I said. "All we have to do is split up the list between us and get the invitations out tonight. That's thirty people for each of us to contact."

"Why don't we make it extra easy and just forward the email Sister Rose sent to us?" Nancy suggested. "If we have the responses go directly to her, we'll get ourselves out of the middle."

"I just love it when you're brilliant," I said. "That's a perfect idea. But I think we should add one sentence explaining that Mary Pat was an alumna of Mount Saint Francis, in case some people don't recognize her name."

"That's why we're besties," Nancy said. "We can take one person's idea and combine it with the other's suggestions and make it even better." She gave my hand a squeeze. "In case I don't tell you this often enough, I'm so grateful for our friendship. I feel a lot better about my own problem now, after talking about it out loud with you. I refuse to let my mind dwell on negative thoughts any longer."

"I like that attitude," said Maria, who'd arrived back at our table with our orders just in time to overhear the tail end of our conversation. "I'm going to do the same thing." She leaned over and said in a low voice, "I'd appreciate it if neither of you would share what I told you about Mary Pat with anybody else."

"Of course we won't, Maria," I said, surprised that she thought either of us would break her confidence. "And just so you know, we're asking that all the responses for the memorial service go directly to Sister Rose, not us. It'll be quicker that way. No Mount Saint Francis girl will be slow to respond to Sister Rose. She wouldn't dare!"

"That's a good idea, Carol. That way I only have to deal with one person instead of three. Easier for me. But you better c.c. her when you send out all the emails and texts, so she knows that in advance."

"You mean, when I re-send them, don't you, Maria?"

"Oh, Carol, don't kid me. You haven't done anything about this yet, right?"

I looked down at my hands. "No, not yet."

"But tonight's the night. Promise," Nancy said, jumping up and grabbing the smaller takeout bag. "Text me later and tell me how you're doing, Carol." She blew me an air kiss and threaded her way through the crowded restaurant with ease.

I was impressed. Nobody can make a speedier, more graceful exit than Nancy. She even had a handsome stranger hold the door for her. I would have tripped over something and dropped the bag of food all over the floor.

"I really insist on paying you for this order, Maria," I said, whipping out my credit card. "It's only fair."

"I won't take money from you for this," Maria said. "Consider your dinner as payment for letting me spill all my troubles to you." She pushed the remaining bag over to me. "You better get home before this gets cold."

"Well, if you're sure," I said, grabbing the bag before she changed her mind. "Thank you very much. I know Jim will appreciate your delicious food even more than he usually does when I tell him it was free."

Chapter 8

Rule Number One: The woman is always right.
There is no Rule Number Two.

Would you be surprised if I told you that Jim was sitting outside on the steps, waiting for me when I rolled into our driveway? Well, don't be. And don't get any crazy ideas like, he missed me so much that he couldn't wait for me to get home again so he could tell me so. Ha! Ever since my darling husband retired a few years ago (although it certainly seems like longer), one of the few joys in his life is dinner served no later than 6:00 every night. As for the rest of them, well... I'm not telling.

"It took you long enough," Jim said, snatching the food order from my hands like a desperate man grabbing for the last life preserver on the *Titanic*.

"Maria prepared this meal especially for you," I said, knowing from years of having the same conversation over and over again that this was my husband's stomach talking, not his brain. I followed Jim into the kitchen and stopped short. My darling husband had not only set the table with my best china and wine glasses, he'd also picked the last of the roses from our garden and arranged them in a real vase, not the cheap water glass he usually favors for such impromptu floral displays. An open bottle of wine was chilling nearby, and there were candles on the table, too. Hmmm.

I gave Jim a big smooch. "This looks wonderful. What are we celebrating? Our anniversary isn't for a few months. And it's not my birthday." A terrible thought hit me. "Oh, Jim. It's your birthday and I forgot it! I'm so sorry. And you didn't say a single word about it when I sailed out the door with Nancy, after those terrible things I said about you bugging me all the time since you retired." Tears sprang to my eyes. "And here you are, being so sweet to me instead of me being sweet to you on your big day. How could I be so thoughtless?"

"As much as I'm enjoying the fact that you're filled with guilt, as opposed to the other way around, I have to confess that it's not my birthday. We celebrated that when Mike was home for CJ's birth, remember?"

I sank into a chair. "Phew. You really had me going there." Then I eyed my husband suspiciously. "So, what's up? Why go to all this trouble? It's just a regular weeknight supper for the Andrews family."

Rather than reply, Jim spread the takeout containers on the kitchen table, placing a serving spoon in each one. Now, that was really a first. He usually prefers to use his own fork to fill his plate directly from whatever pot I've cooked supper in, which drives me nuts. Especially when he dips the fork back into the pot after he's already used it to feed himself. I know we're married, but, sheesh. I guess familiarity can breed bad table manners.

"This really smells delicious," Jim said. "Want me to serve you some? Or do you want some wine first?" I noted that he'd uncorked a chardonnay, which he knows is my favorite wine, rather than a red wine like a cabernet or merlot, which would have been a more appropriate choice to serve with our meal. And which Jim prefers over white wine any day of the week. By now, my suspicion-o'-meter had revved up to warp speed. My husband was definitely up to something.

"I'll have just a little wine," I said. "I have a feeling I need to keep my wits about me right now." I took a tiny sip, then looked at Jim over my wine glass. "Okay, what's going on? This is totally unlike you."

Then I realized what was going on. "I bet Nancy called to tell you that Maria comped our dinner tonight, and this is your way of thanking me for making that happen. But it's Maria you really should be thanking, not me. And she did it because she needs help with Mary Pat Ryan's memorial lunch. That reminds me." I grabbed my phone and made a note, reminding me to edit Sister Rose's email and get it out to her list ASAP. Just as soon as I finished dinner, of course. The tiramisu gelato had become a distant, although pleasant, memory.

Jim now looked completely confused. He shook his head, then said, "No matter how many years we're married, I'll never be able to keep up with you and how your mind works. I didn't realize our dinner, which is probably getting cold now, was a gift from Maria, and who the heck is Mary Pat Ryan? Should I know that name, because I don't."

Keep your explanation short and simple. You know how sharing too much information makes Jim nuts.

"Mary Pat Ryan is the name of the hit-and-run victim," I said. "It turns out that she also went to Mount Saint Francis Academy, which is why Sister Rose asked Nancy and me to contact some schoolmates about attending her memorial service Saturday at the Trattoria. Maria needs help organizing it, which led directly to your free dinner." I decided to spare him the details about Maria's friendship with Mary Pat, and her feeling of guilt over Mary Pat's untimely death. And no way would I mention the tiramisu gelato tasting. Jim would be annoyed that I hadn't managed to sneak a teensy portion of mine to share with him.

"Now I remember the name," Jim said. "What a tragedy. And she was just out walking her dog when she was hit. You know, we both need to be extra careful when we're walking Lucy and Ethel. It could happen to either of us, too."

"That's a scary thought. But you're right. I've seen cars blow right through a stop sign at an intersection without looking first to see if either another car or a pedestrian was there. In fact, some people around town seem to gun the motor and go even faster, like it's a game or something. And the same thing happens when a traffic light turns yellow. Instead of slowing down, so many drivers take that as an invitation to speed up."

"They're not always kids, either," Jim said, warming to his subject even more. "I've seen some drivers our age, who are certainly old enough to know better, do exactly the same thing. Although perhaps they did check quickly, didn't see anyone, and then raced through."

I realized that I'd done the same thing myself on a few occasions, and then been startled when I saw there was another car in the same intersection at the same time. So far, I'd been lucky. But, still. If it could happen to me (and I consider myself a very good, safe driver most of the time), it could happen to anyone. Note to self: Be more cautious when approaching crosswalks and intersections.

"Maybe we should both sign up for the special course AARP offers for older drivers," I suggested. "It's free, and we could learn a lot."

"I don't need to do that," Jim said. "I'm an excellent driver. But go ahead and do it if you want to, Carol. In fact, I think you should."

I tried not to bristle at the implied criticism. Who did Jim think he was? I've seen him race across an intersection when the traffic light had already turned red. And I knew for a fact that he wasn't color-blind, either.

Let it go, Carol. And move on.

I took my own good advice. "I hope you don't mind cleaning up tonight," I said. "I have work I have to do, and I'm on a tight deadline."

"Well, why didn't you say so?" Jim said, a big smile on his face. "I didn't know you got a freelance editing job. I'm proud of you."

"No, Jim, that's not what I meant," I said, tamping down the surge of guilt that had reared up when my husband reminded me that I hadn't pursued any jobs that could contribute to the family's financial bottom line in...well, who knows how long? I certainly don't, and I'm sure none of you do, either. "I'm talking about the invitations to the memorial service."

"Oh," Jim said, clearly disappointed, which made me feel defensive.

"I'd think you'd be more proud of me for doing a good deed," I said. Not that I had any choice in the matter. "From my point of view, good works are more important than any freelance editing job."

"You're right, they are," Jim said. "And I am proud of all the times I've seen you jump in to help someone who needs you. You're a very selfless person. But...."

I tensed. I just knew there'd be a "but" coming, because I knew my husband so well.

"I worry about you a lot. There've been too many times that you've jumped into a situation without thinking, and gotten yourself into trouble as a result. I wish you were more up front with me about what you're doing. Maybe I could even help you. But you always turn to one of your girlfriends instead of me. I wanted our dinner tonight to be special because you mean a lot to me, and I don't show it often enough. You can always count on me. You just have to ask."

Wow. This was a revelation. Maybe I didn't know my husband as well as I thought I did. I thought carefully about my response. I certainly didn't want to hurt Jim's feelings, but he approaches a problem in a much different way than I do. He's so logical, and "logical" is one adjective that no one would ever use to describe me. I'm ruled by my emotions, like a lot of other women I know. Our different approaches often cause friction between us, because we're both so pigheaded and stubborn and convinced that the other one is wrong.

It suddenly occurred to me that Nancy and I had decided to split up the list, but we never figured out who would do which part. Plus, some of the names on Sister Rose's list had email addresses, others had cell phone numbers, and some had both. The list had to be organized before any invitations could be sent, and I was certain Nancy would never think of doing that. Not to speak ill of my best friend, but I figured that she hadn't given any thought to sending out the invites since we left the Trattoria.

Organizing the list was a perfect job for Jim. "Right now, I do need your help," I said with a smile. "In fact, you're the only one that I know I can count on to get the job done right. I'd like to forward you Sister Rose's list, and have you put the names into an Excel spreadsheet. I'm sure you'll be able to divide it the right way. And the names need to be in alphabetical order according to maiden name. You know what that means, right?"

Jim nodded, looking a little miffed. "Of course I know what a maiden name is, Carol. Give me a little credit."

Satisfied, I continued my instructions. "And then, if you could reword Sister Rose's explanation about Mary Pat and why we're all involved and should attend the memorial, that would be great. And please be clear that all responses are to go to Sister Rose, not Nancy or me. The first half of the list should go to Nancy, and I'll take care of the other half."

"Sounds pretty easy," Jim said. "I'll get right on it."

"I'll text Nancy and tell her what you're doing, so she doesn't duplicate your effort. And I'll clean up the kitchen, too."

"Give me half an hour," Jim said. "No interruptions."

"You got it," I said, giving him a smooch and pushing him out of the kitchen. "And thank you."

I fired off a quick text to Nancy telling her not to start contacting people until she heard back from me. In a skinny second, she replied that, as I'd suspected, she hadn't even started yet. What was it that was making both of us drag our feet over doing such a simple thing? I bet a shrink would have a field day trying to figure out our deep-seated lack of motivation.

Oh, well. On to more immediate tasks.

"Alone at last," I muttered as I started carrying our dirty plates and cutlery to the kitchen sink to rinse them. I wasn't really alone. Lucy and Ethel had both parked themselves under the table in the hopes of catching some stray morsels of food. Italian is one of their favorites, but we never feed them "people food," no matter how much they beg. "I know what you both want," I said. "But rules are rules. You'll just have to be content with sniffing the leftover lasagna, because you're not getting any of it to eat." This earned a reproachful look from both dogs.

"Forget it," I said as I turned on the water. "No dice."

"I swear, I think you talk more to Lucy and Ethel than you do to me," Jim called from the next room.

"That's because they always hear me the first time," I muttered. "Unlike you, who rarely hears a word I say unless I've repeated it at least twice."

"I heard that, too," Jim called.

Yikes. I better watch my step. Or my mouth. I'd already gotten myself in trouble with Jim earlier today, and I wasn't about to do it again.

But I couldn't resist asking, "How is it that you can hear what I'm saying when we're not even in the same room, but you don't when I'm sitting right next to you?"

"What?"

"I give up," I said, and turned the hot water on full blast to give the dishes the benefit of my frustration by scrubbing them so hard I took part of the pattern off one of the plates. (Not a lot, and nobody in the family will notice, so no criticisms, okay?)

I couldn't decide whether to load the dishwasher or not bother and leave everything piled up in the sink. Knowing Jim, he'd only rearrange everything anyway in the interest of optimum cleaning efficiency (his opinion, not mine).

"This is an interesting list," Jim called from the other room.

"What?"

"I said, this is an interesting list," Jim said, carrying his laptop into the kitchen and plunking it down in the middle of the kitchen table, which horrified me. "Stop. Lift up your computer so I can clean the table," I ordered. "Otherwise, you're risking getting something on it or in it, and you'll blame me. Or you'll ruin it and have to buy another one."

For once, he didn't argue. I was sure the threat of a potential major retail purchase was the reason.

"For the third time," Jim said, carefully positioning his laptop on a placemat, "I said that this is an interesting list. Some of the names on it sound familiar."

"Familiar because you dated some of these women while you were in high school?" I asked, tamping down the irrational jealousy that had stabbed my heart. Yes, I know. I was being ridiculous. But unlike so many other times, I actually *knew* I was being ridiculous. That's progress, right?

"As a matter of fact, I did," Jim answered. "Why? Do you have some sort of problem with that? It was way before I met you. We didn't even know each other in high school. We didn't meet until college, in case you've forgotten."

Jim waited for me to respond, and when I didn't (not wanting to admit that he had interpreted my reaction correctly), he sighed, then continued. "I've finished the spreadsheet and edited the cover message. Check it and let me know if you need any changes made." He waited a beat, then added, "I did it *exactly* the way you told me to."

I can read Jim-speak pretty well after all these years of marriage. There was a subtext to his last sentence that I found curious, but I didn't question him.

"I don't understand why I had to divide the list so you and Nancy could each send out half," Jim continued. "It'd be so much simpler if just one of you did it. I even thought of doing it for you, but I figured you'd want to check the wording first."

"Thank goodness you didn't send it out yourself," I said.

"Why? Are there some mistakes in it?"

"I'm sure there aren't," I said. "But I'd never hear the end of it from Sister Rose if the memorial invitations didn't go out from Nancy and me, the way she wanted. She'd probably accuse us of delegating all the work because we couldn't be bothered to do it ourselves."

My husband looked completely lost, and I knew I could never make him understand, so I gave up trying. Instead, I kissed him on the cheek and said, "You're the best. Thank you."

Jim waggled his eyebrows in a gesture I knew well. "You can thank me later," he said. "Right now, I'm going to walk off that delicious lasagna." He patted his midsection. "Gotta keep myself trim."

"Take the dogs with you," I suggested. "They both could use a walk, too."

As the threesome headed outside, I suddenly realized that it was dusk. The visibility for pedestrians and motorists would be limited, just like it had been for Mary Pat Ryan on that terrible night. I ran to the door and tried to stop them, but I was too late. "Be careful," I yelled. "Don't cross any streets. Just walk around the block and come right home."

Rats. I knew he didn't hear me. And if Lucy and Ethel did, they chose to ignore me. They both hate it when I hover. Oh, well.

"Check out Jim's spreadsheet carefully, forward Nancy her part, and get the invitations out right now," I ordered myself. "If you keep procrastinating, you'll be handing out printed copies at the door of the restaurant to complete strangers." Then I realized Jim was right about one thing. There was absolutely no reason why the invitations had to come from two separate computers. All I had to do was add Nancy's email and name to the signature line along with mine. Duh, Carol!

I figured Jim wouldn't mind if I continued to use his laptop, since it was already powered up and sitting on the kitchen table. We respect the sanctity of individual computers, and never use each other's, just like we never use each other's toothbrushes. Some things just aren't meant to be shared.

I resisted the temptation to check out Jim's recent email messages (see above—sanctity of individual computers) and went right to my own email and his Excel spreadsheet attachment. It was so...I searched for the right word and came up with... organized. I never could have done it as well. Even his cover memo was perfect, except he forgot to add that Mary Pat Ryan was a graduate of Mount Saint Francis Academy, and give Sister Rose's contact information for the responses. Well, nobody's perfect.

I made sure to copy Sister Rose on the invitation, and prayed she wouldn't give me grief about receiving the RSVPs directly. A few keystrokes later, the email invitations sailed off into cyberspace. I saw that Jim had emailed me the cell phone numbers, so I was able to do a cut and paste of the message and send out a group text invitation as well. Then I texted Nancy and told her she was off the hook. The invitations were out to the entire list. I knew some people would get both an email and a text, but that was no big deal.

In about a millisecond, I heard the ping of an incoming text. Of course, it was from Sister Rose. I figured she'd responded so quickly for one of two possible reasons, neither of which I wanted to deal with tonight. In fact, truth be told, I didn't want to deal with them EVER. She was either angry that I'd given her name and contact information to receive the responses, or—horrors—she had additional jobs for me to do for the memorial service. So I ignored it. And when Jim and the dogs came home from their walk, I surprised him by suggesting we go to bed extra early for a change. No more details will be forthcoming about that episode, so don't bother asking me.

Chapter 9

Old friends are the best friends. And I'm getting older all the time.

The house phone rang at the crack of dawn (at least, it was for me) the following morning, annoying the heck out of me. "Those darn telemarketers have a lot of nerve, calling so early," I muttered, grabbing the phone, ready to unleash my caffeine-deprived wrath on the person at the opposite end of the call.

Too bad I didn't check the caller ID first. I was stopped in mid-rant by a familiar voice, chilly enough to make hell freeze over. "I don't know who you think this is, Carol. But since you didn't answer my text last night, I assumed there was something wrong with your cell phone. That's why I'm calling on the home number. Is everything all right?"

I was tempted to hide under the covers and not come out until next year.

You can run, but you can't hide, Carol. Sister Rose will track you down and find you, no matter where you are. At least she's not at your front door. Or, even worse, sitting at your kitchen table. Was she?

"Everything is fine here, but I haven't read your text yet, Sister," I said, which was absolutely true. "I had my cell phone turned off last night." I peered at the bedside clock. "It's a little early for a phone conversation. I just woke up. Can I call you back after I've had my first cup of coffee?"

I could hear the tsk, loud and clear, implying that I was a lazy woman who was spending much too long getting herself up and ready to accomplish important things. Which would be whatever Sister Rose wanted.

"I wanted to thank you for your efficiency," the good sister said, ignoring my attempt to put her off.

"Jim was the one who did the spreadsheet," I said, giving credit where credit was due. "But Nancy insisted on checking everything before the invitations went out. Remember, you did ask us to work together on this. She was busy with real estate clients for most of the day, which delayed things even more." I knew I was a terrible person to blame my best friend when I was just as guilty of procrastinating as she was. I apologized to her silently and promised never to do that again.

This time, the tsk was unmistakable. "I was surprised to see myself listed as the contact person for the responses, rather than you and Nancy. But I understand from Maria Lesco that you and she felt that was more efficient."

I steeled myself for what I was certain would be coming next—a remark about how we had made this decision without checking with her first. But Sister Rose surprised me. "When I thought about it, I realized that the idea made perfect sense. Maria also wants to be involved in planning the entire memorial, not just the lunch, since she and Mary Pat were friends. So you don't need to worry about that, either. My text made it clear that you've been relieved of any responsibility now, except for one." *So you should have read it last night right when I sent it, and responded.* She didn't really say that, of course. But the implication was crystal clear.

I sat up in bed. Here it comes. And I haven't even washed my face or brushed my teeth yet.

"Maria asked that you find out who adopted Mary Pat's dog. And, if possible, to invite that person to bring the dog to the memorial. She feels strongly that Mary Pat would have wanted the dog included." Another tsk. "Not that I understand why. I'm not an animal lover, myself. Except for yours, of course."

"Of course," I said, my head spinning. How the heck was I going to accomplish this?

"Maria and I have decided that a printed program to hand out to mourners would be a nice touch. She has a lovely photo of Mary Pat with her dog and we'll use that for the cover." Before I could reply, she had clicked off.

"This is sounding more like an over-the-top Hollywood extravaganza than a service honoring someone who's died." My comment earned a reproachful look from Lucy. Or maybe it was the fact that my movement in bed had disturbed Her Majesty's slumber. (Ethel, of course, refrained from comment.)

"Everyone grieves in their own way," I reminded myself. "It's not your place to criticize. All you have to do is track down a dog. How hard could that be?" Especially after coffee and a hot shower to stimulate my little gray cells.

By the time I finally made it into the kitchen, Jim was already gone. Lucky for him, because he was spared a rant from me about Sister Rose's latest orders, to which he would have responded (assuming he heard me), "I don't know why you let her bother you so much after all these years. You're not in high school anymore." And then I'd respond by being defensive about my reaction, even though I knew in the small adult part of my brain that he was absolutely right.

At least Jim left a sticky note on the kitchen counter detailing his schedule for the day. I scanned it briefly while enjoying my first hit of caffeine and smiled. My husband had a breakfast meeting scheduled with the head of our local chamber of commerce. There were few things that Jim enjoyed more than a chance to get an inside scoop on what was going on in our town to use in the State of the Town column he writes for our local newspaper. I knew from personal experience that Jim would be gone for hours, because after the meeting, he'd go into the newspaper office to write up his notes, plus have a conversation—which would inevitably continue over a long lunch—with his editor. I was off the hook in the food department for most of the day. Now all I had to do was find Mary Pat's dog. And I knew just where to start my search.

Chapter 10

I'm a lifetime member of the Witless Protection Program.

Our area of Connecticut is lucky to have a 24-hour emergency veterinary office. We haven't needed to use it for our dogs, thank God, but I figured that's where Mary Pat's dog would have been taken after the accident. For some reason, a voice inside my head suggested I might get more information from the vet office if I told a little white lie about why I was calling. I whipped up what I thought was a plausible story and punched in the number.

"24-Hour Vets," a young female voice answered after only two rings. "What is the nature of your animal emergency? Do you need a house call, or can you bring the animal here?"

Wow. I wasn't prepared to answer any of these questions.

"Um, I really don't have an emergency at the moment," I said.

"Then why are you calling here?" the voice said, clearly annoyed that I was taking up precious phone time when another animal could need help. "This office is for emergency calls only. If you're looking for a local veterinary practice, please consult the Internet for a complete list."

This wasn't going at all as I expected. I had to think fast, or the woman would hang up. And I couldn't blame her, under the circumstances.

"My name is Carol Kerr," I said, giving the name I was born with and hadn't used in years. "I'm not calling to request help for any of my animals. I'm a freelance writer, and I'm doing a story for 'Canine Capers' on emergency veterinary services across the country. I'm sure you've heard of our publication." Which would be a miracle, since I'd just made the name up.

"I can't say that I have," the girl said, sounding less annoyed than she had before.

"May I ask you a few questions about what services you offer? I promise not to take up too much of your time. And I'll completely understand if you have to put me on hold to take an emergency call or take care of a client. I'm a very patient person." Which was another lie. I am the most impatient person in the world.

"Well, I guess it would be all right," the girl said.

"Let's start by your giving me your name," I suggested. "As I said before, I'm Carol. And you are...?"

"Marilyn," the girl answered. "Marilyn Woods, but my friends call me Merry."

"Of which you have many, I'm sure," I replied. Smooth, right? "And for background, how long have you been with 24-Hour Vets?"

"Five years full-time, ever since I graduated from high school," Merry answered proudly. "But I worked here part-time when I was in school, too. I just love animals. I'm saving up my money so I can go to college and become a veterinarian myself."

"Good for you," I said. And I meant it. I'm always in favor of women furthering their education. We all need goals in life, right?

"One of the questions my editor really wants me to include in this article is how emergency practices like this one handle a true emergency," I said, segueing casually into the real reason why I'd made the call in the first place.

"They're all true emergencies to us," Merry corrected me, sounding a little defensive. "Every client is treated exactly the same way, with expertise and compassion. We're known all over Fairfield County for our excellent care."

"That's what I've been told. But I need specifics for my

article." I paused for a few seconds. "For the sake of discussion, let's say I have a dog—I have two, by the way—and I bring her in to be checked because she's been vomiting constantly. How long would I have to wait to see a vet?"

"Why wouldn't you take her to your own vet?" Merry asked.

Thinking fast, I added, "I would, but the vomiting began in the middle of the night, and our regular vet's office was closed."

"Under those circumstances, we'd try to have someone look at her within ten minutes of your arrival," Merry answered. "Of course, the timing would depend on what other emergencies we were dealing with at the moment." I could hear the sound of a phone ringing in the background. "Can you hold a sec? I have to take another call."

I hummed along with Patti Page singing "(How Much Is That) Doggie in the Window?" for a few seconds, then Merry was back. "Sorry about that. Today's been pretty quiet up until now because the regular local practices are still open and seeing clients. We really start to get busy after they close at six o'clock. Sundays are the worst here. We have extra staff on duty to handle the volume."

"No need to apologize," I said. "I really appreciate your taking so much time with me. But you've raised an interesting point, something I'm sure my readers would want to know. Now, to continue with my example, let's say that I've brought my dog, Lucy, in to be checked because of constant vomiting. In the middle of the examination, another person brings in an animal who's been hit by a car. How does your office handle that?"

"That's a really tough situation," Merry admitted. "We generally don't pull a vet away from an animal they're already treating, but if the other animal is really hurt, and we're short-staffed at the time, then I guess we'd have to. I'd hope the original client would understand why."

"I certainly would," I said. "But here's another scenario my editor heard about, and wanted me to include in the story. There was a hit-and-run accident a few weeks ago in Fairport involving a woman walking her dog. The woman died at the scene, and the police took charge of the dog because there was no longer an owner. What would happen in a case like that?"

"Um...."

"My editor feels strongly that adding some personal anecdotes would really strengthen my story," I said, plowing ahead despite Merry's obvious hesitation. "Maybe you remember the accident I'm talking about. I'm wondering if you were working that night. Can you tell me if that dog was brought to 24-Hour Vets to be checked out? And if so, what happened to the dog afterwards?"

"I wasn't working that night, so I don't have any information for you about it," Merry snapped. "And even if I did, I wouldn't be authorized to tell you. If you need any more information about our services, I suggest you check our official website and email us."

"But...." The next thing I heard was the dial tone.

"Well, that was weird," I said to Lucy and Ethel. "Maybe one of you should make the next call. I think I'm losing my touch."

Sweet Ethel, sensing that I needed a shot of unconditional love, gave my hand a sloppy kiss. (Or maybe she was just checking to see if I had any food in my hand.) Lucy ignored me, which I knew was a criticism of my performance. And for using her name as part of the conversation without permission. She had a valid point, as always. And who knew that tracking down a dog would be so difficult?

"Okay," I said, "next time, I'll be more truthful about why I'm calling." I sat back and thought about exactly who I was going to call next. I didn't want to spend my whole morning on this.

I thought about the whopper I'd told Merry from 24-Hour Vets and decided it didn't sound convincing at all. No wonder she'd hung up on me. Of course, I was a perfect stranger, too. "Maybe she would have been more helpful if she knew me," I said aloud. And then I realized what I'd just said.

"Of course. I am so stupid. I'm going to call our own vet. With any luck at all, Karen or Meghan will answer the phone. We've been at that office so many times over the years that we should have a reserved parking space. And while I'm on the phone, I'll make appointments for you both to have your rabies shots. Perfect." I love it when I can multitask.

Lucy gave me a dirty look. She hates getting shots, and even more than that, she hates getting on the scale to be weighed every time we're there. I can sympathize.

"Don't worry," I told her, punching in the number on my cell, "we can always postpone the appointment. This is just a reason to start the conversation."

"Fairport Veterinary Hospital, this is Meghan. How can I help you?"

"Just the person I wanted," I said. "It's Carol Andrews. I'm calling about scheduling rabies shots for the dogs. I think they're due soon."

"Hi, Mrs. Andrews. Give me a second to check our records." I could hear the computer keys clicking at a rapid pace. "How are the two most beautiful English cocker spaniels today? And you too, of course."

I laughed. "I know what your priorities are," I said. "And I'm not the least bit insulted. Animals first, then humans." But she'd given me an opening of sorts to begin the real reason why I'd called. "I learned that lesson when I was in high school from a very good friend of mine. Mary Pat Ryan."

"Oh, wasn't that a terrible thing?" Meghan said. "The way that poor woman died when all she was doing was taking her dog for a walk."

"Very sad," I said. "Did you know Mary Pat, too?"

"She's been a client here for years," Meghan replied. "Well, of course, her dogs were the actual clients. I didn't put that exactly right, did I?"

"No worries," I said. "I knew what you meant." I waited a beat, then added, "Several of Mary Pat's high school friends are planning a memorial service for her Saturday at Maria's Trattoria. I'm one of the organizers. Maybe you'll be able to help me with it."

"Oh, Mrs. Andrews, I'd do anything to help if I could. A memorial service for Mary Pat is a wonderful idea. I really liked her a lot. But I work here full-time, and with my family responsibilities and all, I just don't have any extra time. My husband would probably divorce me if I took on anything else."

"I'm sure he wouldn't do that," I reassured her. "I completely understand how busy your life is. Actually, I'm trying to track down Mary Pat's dog. We thought it would be lovely if the dog could be brought to the memorial, since dogs were such an important part of Mary Pat's life. But I have no idea how to find her."

"Harriet is such a beautiful bitch," Meghan answered, which threw me for a minute until I remembered "bitch" is the official name for a female dog. "Mary Pat had planned to breed her to another champion, and we were all hoping for a litter. I know the puppies would have been gorgeous. But we haven't heard anything about the dog since the accident. Have you called 24-Hour Vets? Maybe they can help you."

"Been there, done that, got nowhere," I admitted.

"Well, I wish I could be more help, but that's all I know," Meghan said. "And things are starting to get nuts here. Do you want to make the rabies appointments now?"

"Tell you what," I said, "I'll call you back about that. I just realized I left my calendar in the car."

"No problem," Meghan said. "Good luck."

"Thanks," I said. "I'm going to need it."

I terminated the call and allowed my frustration level to reach its maximum potential. And, believe me, it doesn't happen very often, but when it does, you don't want to be anywhere near me. Just ask Jim.

"I bet this is why Sister Rose gave me this assignment," I said to the dogs. "She knew it was going to be next to impossible to find Harriet. Maybe she's even paying me back for all the times I was scheduled to volunteer at Sally's Closet and then cancelled at the last minute."

Oh, for heaven's sake, Carol. This is a nun you're talking about. A woman who's devoted her life to helping others. She doesn't have a vindictive bone in her entire body. Don't be such a baby. She's not going to flunk you if you can't find Mary Pat's dog. Have faith in yourself and don't give up so easily.

I suddenly realized I was also under a time crunch. I was due at Jenny's to watch CJ at noon so she could teach a class. I wasn't going to allow anything to distract me from enjoying every single precious second I had alone with my precious grandson.

"What I really need is some divine intervention."

I thought about what I'd just said, and realized asking for some heavenly help was a terrific idea. I considered asking Saint Jude for help. He's the patron saint of desperate cases and lost causes, in case you didn't have the benefit of a Catholic education like I did. Hmm. I decided to put him on the back burner because I wasn't that desperate. Yet.

Saint Anthony was supposed to be the go-to guy for finding lost things. I wondered how he felt about finding missing dogs. I hoped he wasn't allergic to them or, even worse, favored cats over dogs. There was only one way to find out. I Googled "Patron Saint of Lost Dogs" and up popped the name of someone I'd never heard of, Saint Felix of Nola, Italy. Fascinated, I read that a local peasant prayed at the tomb of Saint Felix because his oxen had been stolen. He asked Saint Felix to bring them back. When the peasant returned home, he found all his oxen safe in their stalls. Since then, Saint Felix is venerated as the patron saint who finds and returns lost animals. His feast day is January 14. I squeezed my eyes shut and was just starting to send up a prayer to Saint Felix when my phone buzzed with an incoming text.

Meghan: *I had another idea about finding Mary Pat Ryan's dog. Try contacting Furry Friends.*

Me: *What's that?*

Meghan: *New local animal rescue. 555-woof.*

Me: *I'll try them. Thanks!*

I sent up a quick thank you to Saint Felix, commending him for his speed and promising to spread the word about his good works. I figured even saints can use some marketing sometimes, and distraught pet owners should go straight to him and not bother Saint Anthony first, who was probably overloaded with requests already.

"This is my last shot for the morning," I informed the dogs. "So it has to work." I tossed each of them a Milk Bone. I don't usually encourage them to eat between meals, but I wanted to be sure I had their attention in case they had any suggestions for me.

"I've made two calls and used two different approaches. One was a blatant lie and the other was the truth. And each time, I got exactly nowhere." I thought for a minute, and then decided that perhaps a mixture of the two approaches might work. A "creative" mixture, if you get my meaning.

I thought about how having Lucy and Ethel had brought such joy to Jim and me. I was wallowing in the "empty nest" syndrome after Mike moved to Florida; when Jim retired, it got even worse. I don't know what I would have done if the dogs weren't in my life, needing care and feeding on a regular basis. Not as substitute children—I'm not one of those people who dresses up their dogs in different clothes and costumes. (Not that I'm criticizing, understand. To each her own, I always say.) And Jim, the old softie, loves having them cuddle on our bed, especially on a cold winter's night.

I know many people who are hesitant to add a dog to their household. They see it as a responsibility they don't want to deal with, as well as a hindrance to any travel opportunities that may come their way. I feel sorry for folks like that, because they're missing out on the joys of unconditional love. But that's just my opinion.

To be fair, Jim and I were lucky that my close friend, Mary Alice Costello, was more than willing to take care of the dogs any time. Widowed at a young age, with her children now grown up and gone, she confided to me once how she'd never gotten used to going home to an empty condo. Having Lucy and Ethel with her, even though it's just temporary, makes her feel so much better.

I suddenly remembered that Mary Alice had mentioned she might like to have her own dog instead of borrowing mine. It was probably a casual remark that she may not even remember saying, but that wasn't the point. I could call Furry Friends and ask about adopting a dog for her. Three guesses what dog breed I had in mind.

" 'Woof' translates to 9663," I informed Lucy and Ethel as

my fingers punched in the phone number of Furry Friends. "In case you were wondering."

Neither dog seemed the least bit interested in that piece of information. Although Ethel did raise her head and make quick eye contact with me. She's always the polite one.

After seven rings, I was about to give up and try another time. Then I heard a woman's voice say, "Jerome, you put that down right now. You know you're not supposed to touch anything that's on your father's desk." This was immediately followed by the wail of a baby crying. From the pitch, it sounded like a newborn. Clearly, I had misdialed.

"Hello, are you still there? I'm so sorry to keep you waiting."

"I'm the one who's sorry," I said, channeling my late mother, who had raised me to be polite under any circumstances. "I'm trying to reach Furry Friends, and I must have called this number by mistake."

"I'm so sorry for the confusion," the woman said. "This is Furry Friends. I'm the volunteer taking calls until 2 this afternoon, when my other children come home from school and someone else takes over. I apologize for being distracted when the phone rang. How can I help you? Are you interested in fostering one of our animals? Or, perhaps even adopting one?"

"I'm not calling for myself," I said, thrilled that I had the right number after all. "I have a good friend who might be, and she asked me to find out more about your organization. I understand from my own dogs' vet that you're new in town."

"Yes, we just formed about four months ago," the woman said. "Too many animals are being abandoned by their owners these days. It's very sad. We don't want to see any animal euthanized, no matter what. And did you say you have dogs of your own?"

"Yes," I said. "Two beautiful English cocker spaniels named Lucy and Ethel. It's not a very common breed. You've probably never heard of it."

The woman started to laugh. "Is this Carol Andrews?"

Startled, I stammered, "Yes. Why? Who is this?"

The woman laughed again. "It's Stacey O'Keefe."

"Oh, for heaven's sake," I said, laughing myself. "I didn't recognize your voice. I haven't seen you jogging around the neighborhood lately with the other mommies. Is everything okay?"

Stacey and her family are among the influx of younger families that now live on Old Fairport Turnpike. I love seeing young moms like her walking their kids to the school bus stop, or jogging behind a baby stroller. It takes me back to the long-ago days when I was a young mother. Not that I ever jogged behind a baby stroller, understand. Exercise and I have barely a nodding acquaintance. And I may have lots of clothes in my walk-in closet (too many, according to you-know-who), but I assure you that a pair of yoga pants is not among them. Even the ones made by my favorite designer, Lilly Pulitzer.

"Except for being exhausted taking care of a newborn, things are great here." She punctuated her answer with a yawn. "Oops. My bad. But I just can't seem to stop myself."

"Congratulations on the new baby," I said, embarrassed that I didn't even realize Stacey was pregnant again. "I had no idea. I guess our neighborhood grapevine isn't working these days. Is it a boy or a girl?"

"It's a little girl," Stacey said. "After three boys, I finally had a girl. We're just thrilled. We've named her Bridget Maeve, after the two grandmothers."

"What a beautiful name," I said, jotting myself a quick note on a napkin reminding myself to send her a baby gift. "I can't wait to meet her."

"And how's Jenny doing with CJ?" Stacey asked. "We haven't connected with each other for a while."

"All's well there," I said, glancing at the kitchen clock and realizing time was getting away from me. I needed to get this conversation back on track pronto or I'd be late for my very important date.

"I'll try to stop by and meet the new baby sometime soon," I said. "I promise to text you first. I know that new moms have to grab some shut-eye whenever they can. But as much as I love hearing about Bridget Maeve, what can you tell me about Furry

Friends? How did you get involved? You must have your hands full already, just taking care of your family."

"That's easy to answer," Stacey said. "The boys weren't too thrilled when we told them they were getting a little sister. They tried to guilt Mike and me into getting them a dog. So we had a family meeting and came up with a compromise solution. We'd all volunteer for Furry Friends, and see how the kids related to dogs without actually bringing one home to live. The two older boys help feed and walk dogs who are in foster homes, after school and on weekends. Calls like yours, from the information line, are forwarded to my number three afternoons a week. I answer any questions I can, and take messages when I have to for another volunteer if the questions are too complicated for me. So far, so good. We haven't gotten a lot of calls yet, because we're so new."

"I admire you teaching your kids about responsible pet ownership," I said. "How does someone adopt a dog through Furry Friends? I have a particular breed in mind, which may make it a little more difficult."

"Don't tell me you and Jim are adding to your canine family?" Stacey said, sounding surprised. "I'd think that taking care of Lucy and Ethel would be enough for you." *At your advanced years.*

Stacey didn't really say the last part, of course. But I could tell that was what she meant.

"Oh, it's not for us," I explained. "It's for my friend Mary Alice Costello. You may even know her. She retired from nursing at Fairport Hospital, although she still does some private duty there. She's a widow, and would love to have a dog for company. She doesn't want a puppy; she'd prefer an adult dog."

At least, I was sure she would, if I ever posed the question to her.

"I know of a few adult dogs in foster homes right now who may be suitable. Before we can start the process, we'd need to speak to Mary Alice herself. I'm sure you understand."

"Of course I do. And Mary Alice has allergies, which may make the search more difficult to find her the right dog. Although..." I paused, then continued, "I did read about one particular dog, a Coton de Tuléar, that would be just perfect for her. Harriet belonged to Mary Pat Ryan, a dear friend who was killed in that hit-and-run accident. I'm not sure what happened to the dog. I know it's a long shot, but is Harriet available for adoption through your organization?"

For a few seconds, I didn't hear anything from the other end of the phone. I figured that Stacey was keeping an ear out for any cries from the nursery and didn't hear me, so I said, "Are you there, Stacey? If you have to take care of the baby, I can call back in fifteen minutes or so."

"No, that's not it," Stacey said. "I checked on Bridget and she's sleeping like a little angel. I'm just trying to figure out how to answer your question."

"I don't understand. Isn't there a simple answer—yes or no?"

"I've been told not to answer any questions from callers about that dog," Stacey said. "But I know you, and I know I can trust you to keep this to yourself."

That proves you don't know me at all. I didn't really say that, of course.

"We've been told to keep track of any calls asking about that dog, and immediately contact the police whenever we get one."

"You mean she's in the Canine Protection Program?" I asked, which made us both giggle.

"I don't know about that, but it is odd," Stacey said.

At that moment, I heard a newborn's wail. "I guess Bridget's awake," I said. "You better go." I glanced at the clock again. Yikes. I had just enough time to exercise the dogs in the yard and get over to Jenny and Mark's.

"I'll stop by soon," I said. But Stacey had terminated the call.

Chapter 11

I finally realized I'll never be old enough to know better.

"I was afraid you'd forgotten to come," said Jenny, looking harassed and just a teeny bit annoyed at me. "It's not like you to be late for a date with your grandson. You should have texted me if you were running late."

"Something came up unexpectedly," I said. "I'm sorry." My eyes filled with tears. I can't stand having anyone mad at me, especially if it's someone in my own family.

"I'm sorry for snapping at you. Blame sleep deprivation for my bad mood. CJ has yet to sleep through the night, and Mark works such random shifts these days that I don't ask him to help out unless I'm really desperate." Jenny gave me a hug to show that all was forgiven.

"Next time, if I'm going to be late, I promise to text you. And if you want to blame anyone for my tardiness, it's Sister Rose. If she hadn't given me another job for Saturday's memorial service, I would have been early."

Jenny raised one eyebrow, a family trait she inherited from Jim. "Whose memorial service? A classmate?"

I made a shooing motion with my hands. "It's a long, complicated story and you don't want to be late yourself. I'll tell you another time."

"To tell you the truth, Mom, I'd built in some extra time today to have a quick coffee with one of my friends before I headed to class, like an actual grown-up. I really had an hour to spare."

"You rascal," I said. "Why didn't you tell me that right away? I thought I'd let you down."

"I should have," Jenny admitted. "My bad. I already texted my friend that I was running late and we decided to postpone getting together. It's really no big deal. CJ's sleeping like an angel right now, and I have time for coffee with you, if you trust me to make it. You know I don't do as good a job as Dad, but it's hard to make a mistake when I use the Keurig. Even Mark thinks I make great coffee since we got one. You really should get with the modern age and buy one, too."

"You must be kidding," I said, following my daughter into her kitchen. I was secretly glad for a chance at some mother-daughter bonding, even if it would only be for a short time. "Your father wouldn't ever spring for one. He thinks they're overpriced and totally unnecessary."

"Maybe CVS will carry them," Jenny said with a wicked grin. "Then you know he'd go for it."

"True," I said. "But I won't hold my breath until that happens."

"So," Jenny said, placing a cup of steaming coffee in front of me in less time than I'd ever thought possible, "I repeat, whose memorial service?"

"Mary Pat Ryan's," I said, taking a sip of the steaming brew. "I have to admit, this is pretty good coffee. Not as strong as your father's, but I like it."

"Mary Pat Ryan," Jenny said. "Isn't that the hit-and-run victim's name? I didn't realize you knew her."

"Mary Pat was two years ahead of me at Mount Saint Francis. She had no family left when she died, and Sister Rose decided that, because she was a Mountie, it's up to us to give her a proper send-off. Two days ago, she put Nancy and me in charge of inviting people to come to a memorial service this Saturday. If it hadn't been for your father's help putting a database together, the invitations never would have gone out. This morning, she contacted me again with another assignment. You won't believe what she's ordered me to do now."

"Knowing Sister Rose like I do, not much will surprise me."

"She wants me to find out who has the dog Mary Pat was walking when she was hit and bring the dog to the memorial. It sounded like an easy task, but I've run up against a stone wall everywhere. I ended up calling a new animal rescue program in town: Furry Friends. Guess who answered the phone? Stacey O'Keefe. Did you know she just had a baby girl?"

"I haven't seen her for a while," Jenny said. "I'll have to text her congratulations. Maybe we can get together one of these days. But what's this about Furry Friends?"

"Stacey and her boys are volunteering at Furry Friends. She figured it was a way to teach them about responsible pet ownership. The kids are walking dogs after school and she's taking phone calls for the program. I called to see if Furry Friends had Mary Pat's dog, but she said they didn't. I'm still looking for the dog, and Sister Rose is really on my case. I'm pretty desperate at this point. Got any ideas?"

Jenny flushed, and I felt bad. I realized, too late, that I'd put her on the spot. I try (I really do!) not to take advantage of the fact that my darling daughter might have access to insider information because she's married to a Fairport police detective.

In true Andrews fashion, instead of answering my question, she lobbed back one of her own. "Why would Sister Rose want you to bring that dog to the memorial? I didn't know churches allowed dogs."

"The memorial's going to be held at Maria's Trattoria, not in a church," I explained. "I'm not even sure any clergy will be involved. Maria and Mary Pat were both retired teachers and good friends. Maria's the one who wants the dog to be present. In fact, she tried to adopt the dog after the accident, but wasn't able to. It means the world to her to have the dog there, and I'm doing my best to find it. But so far, no dice. I hate to disappoint her."

I looked Jenny squarely in her baby blues, so like my own. I could tell by the look on her face that she was hiding something. I couldn't press her anymore.

"I may be able to help you, Mom."

I hugged Jenny and said, "That would be wonderful, sweetie. Thank you so much."

"But no promises," Jenny warned as the unmistakable cry of an infant sounded from the bedroom. "I'll try. And now, I have to get to class. Give CJ a minute or two and he may go back to sleep on his own. If not, there's a bottle already prepared for him in the fridge. You just have to warm it up. And I'm sure he'll need changing. I'll be back by 4. Thank you. You're the best!" She gave me a quick kiss and was gone.

I trusted my daughter. She knew how important it was for me to produce Mary Pat's dog at her late owner's memorial, even if she thought the whole idea was nutty. Even though I still didn't know where Mary Pat's dog was, I was hopeful that, thanks to Jenny, I'd be able to find the dog by Saturday.

I fired off a text to both Sister Rose and Maria.

Working on getting Mary Pat's dog to memorial service but no promises. Full-time grandma duties until then.

I hope Sister Rose, in particular, got the message—I've done all I can, so don't bug me anymore.

I smiled and headed toward the sound of my grandson, expressing his displeasure in higher and louder decibels. I picked him up and took a moment (well, more than one moment) to inhale his sweet baby smell. Even though, to be honest, CJ was not smelling his sweetest at that very minute.

"Hello, handsome," I cooed to the world's most perfect grandbaby ever born. "It's me, your favorite grandmother. I'm going to make you comfortable again. You can always count on me." As I busied myself performing necessary tasks, I thought about what Jenny had said. And, even more important, the way she'd said it. Or not said it. She always was the more cautious of my two children. While Mike was more inclined to rush headfirst into any project that attracted him without giving a moment's thought to any potential negative consequences, Jenny was inclined to deliberate so long before she made a decision that it sometimes made me nuts.

As I started to prepare CJ's bottle, it occurred to me that I'd sent a tentative RSVP to the memorial invitation on behalf of a dog. Thank goodness Lucy and Ethel didn't know that. I'd never hear the end of it.

Chapter 12

I may be wrong, but I doubt it.

"I don't recognize any of these people," Nancy whispered to me. "Did they all go to school with us?"

"No idea. I don't know any of them, either," I said.

The private dining space at Maria's Trattoria was jam packed, mostly with clusters of women of a "certain age" chattering non-stop, like they were at a high school reunion. Which, come to think of it, this was, in a weird sort of way.

I scanned the room for a familiar face and found an unexpected one. Good grief. I elbowed Nancy. "There's your knight-in-shining armor, Paul Wheeler. Why don't you go over and have a nice chat with him? And while you're at it, find out what he's doing here. I don't remember his name on Sister Rose's list."

Nancy tossed her head in a familiar gesture that always drives me nuts. "Paul was one of Mary Pat's students at Fairport High," she said. "I'm sure you knew that. You just forgot."

"How would I know who Paul's high school teachers were? I'm not buddy-buddy with him like you are," I said, annoyed at Nancy's implication that my memory was faulty, even if she was right. I gave her a little shove. "Go on over and say hello. He's one of the few men in the room and he looks very uncomfortable."

"No way," Nancy said. "There must be other people here who

were Mary Pat's students. He'll find someone to talk to. Let's pretend we didn't see him and walk the other way. I don't want him to get the wrong idea and think I'm romantically attracted to him, just because he saved my life."

"Honestly, Nancy, you can be so ridiculous sometimes."

I noticed several photos of Mary Pat in prominent spots around the space. Sadly, nobody seemed to be paying any attention to them. "Come on," I said, grabbing Nancy's hand, "we need to set a good example and look at the photograph displays. Nobody else is. It's disgraceful. We're here to honor a woman's life and mourn her tragic death and everybody's acting like we're at a big party instead."

We took some time to circle the room and stare at each of the photos, which were displayed in sequential order. The earlier ones showed a girl in her Mount Saint Francis uniform, and my eyes filled up to see her at the age when she'd had such a positive impact on my life. Many of the later photos showed Mary Pat at dog shows, winning ribbons for her prized dogs. The most recent photo showed her with a dog identified as Harriet. Mary Pat was wearing a neon green windbreaker and had a huge smile on her face.

"I'm glad there's one photo of Mary Pat with Harriet," I said to Nancy.

"I thought the dog was coming to the memorial," Nancy said.

"I tried to make that happen," I said. "But I'm still not sure it will." I turned toward the photos again, hoping she'd get the hint that I was changing the subject.

The sound of all those female voices in the small space was starting to get on my nerves. I noticed that some of the women were wearing black in deference to the occasion, but most were dressed in various shades of navy blue, an homage, no doubt, to the uniforms we wore when we were students at Mount Saint Francis a million years ago.

"Mary Pat must have been very well liked to have so many people show up at her memorial service," Nancy said. "I don't remember her from high school at all, but don't tell anyone I said that." She gestured around the room. "I think there are more people here than were on the invitation list from Sister Rose. How in the world could that have happened?"

"Maybe some women brought a guest," I said. "And there could have been a separate invitation sent to Mary Pat's teacher friends."

Or maybe a chance to chow down on some free food from Maria's Trattoria was the attraction. I didn't really say that out loud, of course.

I gestured toward a long table, which offered coffee, tea, and a variety of breakfast pastries. The pastries were going fast, and an efficient server was replenishing the trays as quickly as she could. I was impressed with her speed, and the way she arranged the baked goods so artfully.

"I think I've met that woman before," I said. "She looks familiar."

"You always say that," Nancy reminded me. "I can't count the number of times I've been with you when you see someone you think you know, and when you say hello, she says she's never seen you before in her life. Do you want to risk embarrassing yourself again?"

Nancy was right, but don't tell her that. I decided the woman looked familiar because she worked at the Trattoria and I was being stupid. "If you want a little snack, you'd better get one fast. These women are chowing down like they haven't seen food in a year."

"You must be kidding," she answered, speed-walking toward a row of chairs as far away from the buffet table as possible without sitting outside in the parking lot. "You know I never eat that kind of food."

"I know," I said, "but I was hoping we could get something and split it."

Nancy ignored me and chose a chair at the end of the row. "I may get a business text that I have to take," she said. "I don't want to interrupt the service. I can just slip outside if I need to." She shifted in her seat. "And I thought I had dressed appropriately, considering I didn't even know Mary Pat. But this burgundy suit makes me stand out, and not in a good way. I wish I had time to run home and change."

I put a restraining hand on my BFF. "You look fine. And don't kid me. You're just itching to get out of here, and using your choice of clothing or getting a text as excuses to bolt. I don't know any of these women, either. They were probably in Mary Pat's class, and she was two years ahead of us in school."

I released my hand, hoping Nancy wouldn't disgrace us and make a break for the door. "You certainly know Maria and Sister Rose. Mary Alice and Claire promised to come, too." I craned my neck. "Where the heck are they?"

"They're probably both still home, figuring out what to wear."

I gave Nancy a quick glance to see if she was kidding. Mary Alice has spent much of her life in hospital scrubs and couldn't care less about clothes. And Claire...well, let's just say her taste in attire leaves a lot to be desired. Of course, to be fair (and I *always* am), she's quite tall and big-boned, so it's hard for her to find clothes that fit her well.

Before I could think of a snappy comeback, I was conscious of two eyes boring into the back of my head. I didn't need to turn around to check who they belonged to. I'd been the object of that laser stare more times than I care to remember. Or intend to share with you.

"Don't turn around," I whispered to Nancy, scooching down in my chair and trying to look invisible. "Sister Rose just walked in." Which, of course, was all Nancy needed to hear. She turned and gave Sister Rose a wave. Then, to my horror, I heard her say in a loud voice, "There's plenty of room in our row, Sister. Do you want to sit with us?"

I gave Nancy a sharp kick. Good heavens, what was she thinking? I took a chance and looked over my shoulder. Sister Rose was shaking her head and pointing to the first line of chairs. OMG. She wanted us to sit in the front row.

Now, I don't know about the rest of you, but I never sit in the front anywhere. No exaggeration. I consider myself lucky that, before I married Jim and my last name changed to Andrews, I was Carol Kerr. The letter K has the perfect spot in the alphabet, right in the middle. When the nuns used to seat us in alphabetical order according to last name, I was always in an inconspicuous spot.

Sister Rose was not about to let us off the hook. Knowing her, she'd made a seating plan in her head, and Nancy and I were at the top of her list. She was beside us in a flash, and for a split second I thought she was going to grab my arm and pull me to my feet. Instead, she stopped beside my chair and gave me The Look, then threaded her way through the crowd, saying hello to several women on her march to the front row. Nancy and I meekly trailed behind her, just as she knew we would.

The aisle seat in the front row was already occupied. Which was nervy, considering that Maria had placed a large "Reserved" at the end of the row, indicating that only specific people were to sit there.

Nancy elbowed me. "Do you believe this?" she asked. "It's Frank Bologna. What the heck is he doing here? I thought Maria had postponed his campaign event to next week."

"He probably figured this was a golden opportunity to pitch himself as a close friend of Mary Pat's and win some votes," I said.

"That's disgusting," Nancy said.

"I agree. But you know how politicians are. He'll probably go to every Fairport funeral between now and election day and pretend that he's one of the mourners."

"I hope he doesn't expect to speak," Nancy said. "Sister Rose will never allow it. Maybe she'll even ask him to leave."

I had to admit that it was nice to see someone else besides me in the crosshairs of Sister Rose's wrath. Wasting no time, she tapped the politician on the shoulder.

Frank jumped to his feet, a solemn look pasted on his face. "Hello, dear lady. On behalf of all the citizens of Fairport, please allow me to express our condolences on the sad loss of your sister." He waved his hand around the crowded room. "This is a clear indication of the contribution to the community Margaret made. I am so sorry for the loss to your family. I'd like the opportunity to express my personal sympathies publicly, if that's allowed. She was too young to pass from a heart attack." He bowed his head. "Much too young."

It takes a lot to stop Sister Rose, but this guy had hit a home run in that department. Not only did he get the name of the deceased wrong, but he also misidentified Sister Rose as Mary Pat's blood sister. He didn't even get the cause of death right, which was ridiculous. The hit-and-run accident had been in the news for weeks because the police were still trying to find the driver. I couldn't wait to see what happened next.

I shot a quick glance at Sister Rose. I had to hand it to her. The only sign that she was completely flabbergasted was the way she narrowed her eyes and stared the man down. "For your information, Mr. Bologna," she said in a very low tone of voice, "we're here today to honor the memory of Mary Pat Ryan, not someone named Margaret. At the very least, you should know her correct name. She was not my sister, but a former student of mine at Mount Saint Francis Academy, where I taught English for many years. I am a nun, in case you didn't know that, either."

Bologna, clearly embarrassed at his colossal faux pas, started to answer, but Sister Rose didn't give him a chance. "Furthermore," she continued, her voice rising, "Mary Pat did not pass from a heart attack. She was the victim of a hit-and-run driver, who has yet to be apprehended, while she was out for an early evening stroll with her dog. She was at a clearly marked pedestrian crosswalk, and when she stepped out onto the road when she thought it was safe to cross, she was struck and killed. As an elected official of the town of Fairport who clearly wants to be elected again, what exactly do you propose to do to make Fairport safe so this kind of tragedy will never happen again?"

"I'm sorry," Bologna mumbled. "I guess I shouldn't have come."

"For once, you got something absolutely right," Sister Rose said. "And now, I think you should leave." I was worried the confrontation would continue, but Bologna was smart enough to make a hasty exit without making eye contact with anyone.

I patted Sister Rose on the shoulder in a rare gesture of solidarity. "Let's all sit down," I suggested. In a low voice, "You need a little time to collect yourself before the memorial service starts. You handled the situation perfectly."

"You were great," Nancy chimed in. "You made it pretty clear that Frank Bologna can't count on your vote."

"I need a little time to pray and ask the Lord for forgiveness," Sister Rose said. "I shouldn't have allowed myself to get so angry. I don't think I've ever been so angry at another human being in my life."

"Even me?" I asked with a grin, trying to lighten her mood. I was rewarded with a quick smile from Sister Rose and a loud laugh from Nancy.

All of a sudden, I realized it was very quiet in the banquet room. Then, one person started to clap. Another joined in. Pretty soon, everyone in the room was applauding Sister Rose's exchange with Frank Bologna.

OMG. It hadn't occurred to me that the argument had been overheard by every single person there. Nor had it occurred to Sister Rose, judging by her obvious embarrassment at the unexpected attention. Even the server who'd been so busy replenishing the pastry tray came up and shook Sister's hand. "I want to congratulate you on voicing things that all of us in town have thought for years but never quite had the nerve to say. Why don't you think about running for office, yourself? It's way past time that man is voted out. I bet you'd beat him in a heartbeat. I know I'd vote for you. I'm sure everyone in this room would, too."

From the look on Sister Rose's face, the woman's suggestion had knocked her for a loop. But once I thought about it, I realized it wasn't such a crazy idea, and I could tell that Nancy agreed with me. With all those alumni of Mount Saint Francis Academy who'd been taught by Sister Rose and who still lived in town, she'd win in a heartbeat. Heck, I'd even campaign for her myself.

"Thank you, but I could never do that," Sister Rose said. "My vows as a nun wouldn't permit it. Maybe you're the person who should run."

"If you do, let me know," I said to the woman. "Maybe I can help you."

The woman laughed. "I just might." She turned around and noticed a few more people around the pastry station. "I better go and replenish the baked goods again. This is a hungry crowd. I hope I brought enough."

I thought that was an odd remark for one of Maria's employees to make. I knew that Maria prided herself on only serving food that was made in her own restaurant kitchen.

My phone chirped, announcing an incoming text. I squinted at the screen. It was from Claire.

Claire: *Flat tire. Waiting for the auto club to put on the spare. Not sure if we'll make it. Mary Alice is with me.*

Me: *Come even if you're very late. Lots going on here and you'll be sorry if you miss it.*

Claire: *Will try.*

The room quieted again as Maria Lesco, who thus far hadn't been visible, made her way to the round table that would serve as a podium. Her face was strained, and I knew she was fighting not to lose control in front of the assembled guests. I was glad that she hadn't been around to hear the Sister Rose-Frank Bologna conversation.

"I want to thank you all for coming today to honor the memory of a fine woman whom I was proud to call a friend, Mary Pat Ryan," she began. "I'm sure all of you have personal memories of your own relationship with Mary Pat as well." Her voice quavered for a minute but, to her credit, she soldiered on. "I assure you that the staff at Maria's Trattoria has made an extraordinary effort to provide a menu that has something to please every palate as a tribute to Mary Pat, who loved nothing more than sharing a good meal with good friends. And I'd like to think that, in some way, she's sharing this one with us today."

Maria paused and looked down at the notes she had in front of her. "Many people were involved in putting this memorial together, but especially Sister Rose, whom I'm sure many of you remember fondly from your days at Mount Saint Francis

Academy." I knew from first-hand experience that Sister Rose kept a close eye on the life experiences of her "girls," as she referred to Mount graduates. Sometimes, too close, But that's just my opinion.

There was more applause from the assembled guests. I snuck a quick look at Sister Rose. Her cheeks were pink with embarrassment at being singled out by Maria.

"I'd also like to thank Donna Trumbull, owner of Mrs. T's Tasty Treats, for donating all the delicious pastries you've been enjoying during the coffee hour, and will continue to enjoy for our dessert course a little later."

The woman at the pastry table smiled and waved. "My pleasure," she said.

Now I knew why she looked familiar. We'd met at Fairport Garage when I'd had the tires on my car rotated. I couldn't wait to tell Nancy that this time, I was right.

My phone pinged with another text.

Claire: *We're here. Standing in the back.*

I sent back a smiley emoji and silenced my phone. With my luck, I'd get a call or text from you-know-who, asking how long I'd be gone and what did we have for lunch.

"Many of you have asked me for a chance to share personal reminiscences about Mary Pat," Maria continued. "I'm sure you all agree with me that she was a fine woman who always put other people's needs above her own." She looked around the room and asked, "Who would like to go first?"

That's when all hell broke loose.

Chapter 13

I never speak ill of the dead. I'm afraid one of them will come back to haunt me.

A woman in a navy blue pantsuit with salt and pepper hair was the first speaker. She introduced herself as Louise Baker, a classmate of Mary Pat's at Mount Saint Francis. She took a moment to compose herself and dabbed her eyes with a tissue. "Sorry," she said, "I'm a little nervous. I'm not used to speaking in public."

"That's all right, Louise," Sister Rose said. "Just take your time."

Louise took a deep breath. "I just want to say that I've never known a kinder, more selfless person in my whole life than Mary Pat Ryan," she said, her voice shaking.

"That's complete bullshit!" yelled a male voice from somewhere in the room.

I swiveled around in my seat, straining to see who'd spoken. It wasn't difficult to identify the person. Except for Paul Wheeler, he was the only male in the room. He had a woman standing next to him, possibly his wife, who was pulling on his arm, obviously trying to get him to be quiet. But without any success.

"You want to know what Mary Pat Ryan was really like?" he yelled, his face getting redder and redder. "I'll tell you. Elaine and

I had the great misfortune to purchase the house right next door to hers seven months ago, and we haven't gotten a good night's sleep ever since. She let that damn dog outside at all hours of the night, and when it would howl and bark, she'd ignore it. I called the police but they never did anything about it. They said it was something I had to work out with her."

"Marty, please stop," the woman pleaded. "You're embarrassing me."

"Too bad," the man said, glaring at his wife. "It's about time somebody told the truth about that woman. I'm not sorry she's gone, I'll tell you that."

"How dare you talk like that about Mary Pat," Maria said, marching toward the man, furious. "I want you to leave right now, or I'm calling the police."

"Oh, yeah," the man said. "Why don't you make me? Go ahead. Just try."

By this time, Maria and the man were eyeball to eyeball. The rest of the room was deathly quiet. I was on my feet, trying to see better, and that's when I noticed Claire and Mary Alice, a few feet away from the two combatants, huddling against the back wall to distance themselves from the argument.

Nancy nudged me and, just for a split second, I turned my head to see what she wanted. So I missed seeing Maria sock Marty in the face. He fell onto the nearby food table and plopped, head-first, into a full tray of Mrs. T's Tasty Treats.

The next thing I knew, Marty's wife started screaming at Maria. "How dare you hit my husband! You ought to be arrested!" And she grabbed Maria, spun her around, and pushed her face down onto the table beside her husband.

Sister Rose ran up the aisle, trying to save the memorial she'd worked so hard to organize from turning into a complete disaster. She helped Maria to her feet and said, "Pull yourself together. You're making everything worse."

Paul Wheeler pushed his way through the crowd and flashed his detective badge. "Sir, it's time for you to go. If you don't, I'll have to arrest you for causing a public disturbance. Now, why don't you and your wife leave quietly?"

Sister Rose grabbed Marty and handed him a wad of napkins from the table. "Use these to clean yourself up. You ought to be ashamed of yourself for the way you've behaved." She then turned her laser gaze on his wife who, by this time, was sobbing uncontrollably and saying, "I'm sorry. I'm so sorry."

"You ought to be," Sister Rose said.

"Let's go," Paul said, herding the couple toward the exit. "I'd hate to have to put handcuffs on you, but I will if I have to."

"We're going," Marty said. "But believe me, you haven't heard the end of this." And he and his still crying wife made their exit, Paul close behind. I figured he wasn't taking any chances on them trying to sneak back inside.

Sister Rose directed her next comments to Maria, who was attempting to clean up herself and what was left of the delicious pastries with the help of Donna Trumbull. "You might want to let Donna take care of that, dear," she said. "I believe your place is at the front of the room. And..." she looked around and located Louise Baker, "I believe you were starting to give a personal story about Mary Pat, Louise. Go right ahead. I'm sure we all want to hear what you have to say."

I had to hand it to Sister Rose. Despite all the upheaval in this memorial service, which would probably go down as the most memorable one in Fairport history once word got around town, she was determined that the show, so to speak, would go on.

But it was no use. Poor Louise mumbled a few platitudes that nobody listened to, and then sat down, looking as uncomfortable as all the other guests. Everyone was whispering to their friends about what they'd just witnessed and not paying a bit of attention to Maria or Sister Rose as they both tried to restore a sense of dignity to the proceedings.

OMG. It suddenly dawned on me that Jenny could show up now with Mary Pat's dog and add to the chaos even more. I fired off a quick text.

Me: *Don't bring Harriet to the memorial! Will explain later.*

Jenny: *Wasn't going to. Couldn't work it out. Sorry.*

Me: *No worries. Talk soon.*

Thank goodness something went right. With everything else going on, I hoped Sister Rose and Maria didn't realize that the dog wasn't here. (Or even remember that she was supposed to be.)

"I wish Sister Rose would figure out that this event is a complete fiasco and let us all leave," Nancy whispered in my ear.

"Me, too. But, knowing her, she won't give up. I feel terrible for poor Maria. She looks crushed at the way things have turned out."

"I hope she doesn't lose any customers because of her behavior," Nancy said, not bothering to whisper anymore. "She really socked that guy hard."

"He certainly asked for it," I said. "He's lucky it was Maria who hit him, not Sister Rose." We both started to giggle, which earned us a reproving look from the good sister.

"She and Maria need to end this," I said again. "But I don't think either of them knows how to do it."

The answer came from Donna Trumbull, who had corralled several of Maria's wait staff to pack to-go boxes of the food we were supposed to have after the tributes were over. She threaded her way to the front of the room carrying two of the boxes, and set them down in front of a surprised Sister Rose and Maria. "I hope you both won't think I'm interfering," Donna said with an apologetic look at the pair. "I thought it might be a good idea for us to reconvene at a later date to continue the program as planned. In the meantime, if it's all right with you, we've prepared carryout boxes for everyone to take their lunches home."

"Wonderful idea," said Sister Rose, a relieved look on her face.

Maria immediately jumped to her feet, held up one of the takeaway boxes, and made the announcement. "I want to thank you all for coming," she said. "Although the memorial didn't turn out exactly the way we'd planned, it was good to be together and celebrate the life of a remarkable woman who, thank goodness, also had a good sense of humor. I'm sure that if she's looking down on us right now, she's laughing. Please help yourselves to one of these luncheon boxes as you leave today. I hope you'll all come back to the Trattoria for a meal in the near future. I promise it won't be as exciting as today's was." And she laughed.

"What a great way to end this debacle on a high note," I whispered to Nancy as we made a break for the door to catch up with Mary Alice and Claire. "Let's get the heck out of here."

"That sure was something," Claire said, licking the spoon she'd dipped into a bowl of cherry vanilla ice cream I'd found stashed in the dark recesses of my freezer.

"It was a good idea to come back to your house after the memorial so we could talk privately," Mary Alice said, pushing away her bowl before I could offer seconds. "That was delicious, but sweets are best eaten in moderation, especially at our age."

"I don't agree," I said. "Look what happened to poor Mary Pat. Here today, gone tomorrow, whether she watched her sweet tooth or not. In the long run, what difference does it make?"

"Well..."

"Carol's right," Claire said, coming to my defense in a rare show of solidarity. She grabbed a clean spoon and helped herself to a little more ice cream.

"I feel terrible for the way the memorial imploded," Nancy chimed in. "It was horrible. Like watching a car wreck. Not that I've ever done that, of course."

"All our nerves are pretty frayed," I said, pushing away my half-eaten bowl of ice cream. "I can't even finish this, and you all know that no matter how upset I am, I can always eat."

"It was nice of Donna Trumbull to give us our lunches to take home," Mary Alice said. "I've never met her before. She seems very nice."

"All right," I said, "we've danced around the elephant in the middle of the kitchen table long enough."

"That is the most mixed up mixed metaphor I've ever heard," Claire said.

"Maybe it is, but I'm sure you get the point. Nancy and I were way in the front of the room, but you and Mary Alice were right there when the fight started. So...share. Tell us what you saw."

"Well," Mary Alice began, "you know we got there late, so we had to stand in the back."

"We know. We know," Nancy and I chorused. "But what did you see?"

"We snuck in and stayed by the door," Claire said, shooting me a look, daring me to interrupt again. "There was a young couple standing near the other door, the one that leads to the fire escape. I noticed them because everyone else in the room was our age."

"Old," Mary Alice clarified, in case Nancy and I were dense.

"There were a few seats available at the end of a row on their side of the room," Claire continued. "We couldn't get to those seats without causing a disturbance, but the young couple easily could have. I thought it was weird that they didn't sit down. The way they were standing, it was almost like they were positioning themselves for a quick getaway."

"And you think *I* have an active imagination," I said. "Even I wouldn't come up with such an outlandish scenario. You've been watching too many true crime shows on television." (I don't mean to criticize one of my dearest friends, understand. But Claire often accuses me of embellishing a story I'm telling, for effect. And here she was, doing exactly the same thing. I felt I should point that out in the interest of complete disclosure.)

Before Claire had a chance to defend herself, my cell phone rang out. I squinted at the screen. It read "Unknown Caller." I know, everybody gets calls like that and, if they're smart, ignores them. After all, it could be from a telemarketer, or even worse. But some of you may remember my recent adventure with a series of calls from an "Unknown Caller," which I did ignore. And that turned out to be a big mistake which almost cost a woman her life.

I took a chance and answered it.

"Hello, is this Carol Andrews?" a woman's voice asked. "This is Donna Trumbull calling. I hope you've recovered from the memorial service earlier today. What a shame things turned out that way."

I put my hand over the phone and mouthed, "It's Donna Trumbull," to my friends.

"Ask her what she wants," Nancy said, always one to get to the point.

"Even better, ask her if she has more leftovers to share," Claire quipped. "If she does, tell her to come on over." Mary Alice and Nancy started to laugh, and I shushed them. Jeez.

"Yes, this is Carol Andrews," I said.

Nancy mouthed, "Put her on speaker so we can all hear why she's calling." I ignored her.

"I'm sure you're surprised to hear from me so soon," Donna continued. "Or, quite frankly, at all. But I can't stop thinking about what happened today. I've decided to go for it, so I wanted to talk to you right away, before I changed my mind. Or lost my nerve."

"I'm sorry, but I'm at a complete loss here," I admitted.

"Isn't this Carol Andrews, Sister Rose's friend? We saw each other at the memorial today."

"I know Sister Rose," I said, thinking that calling her my "friend" was a stretch. "And of course I remember meeting you today."

"Well, thanks to your encouragement, Carol, I've decided to do it," Donna said. "I'm going to run for Fairport Town Council. And to honor Mary Pat Ryan's memory I want to make pedestrian safety the cornerstone of my campaign. You promised to help me. We have no time to waste. When can we get together and organize my campaign strategy?"

Congratulations, Carol. You and your big mouth have done it again.

Chapter 14

The only sure way to get a woman to do something is to tell her not to do it.

"How was your day?" Jim asked, coming into the kitchen freshly showered and smelling of my favorite aftershave. He gave me a quick kiss. "What's for dinner?" He waggled his eyebrows. "I hope I get what I want for dessert."

Honestly, that Jim.

The dogs danced around his feet, begging for a share of his attention. Like me, they appreciate good smells, especially those they find outside in the yard.

"How long have you been home?" I countered. "If you've been here a while and heard Mary Alice, Claire, Nancy and me talking about the memorial, you'd already know the answer."

"When I heard you all come in," Jim said, looking a little guilty, "I headed for the bedroom. All that girl talk gives me a headache. Besides, there was a football game on that I wanted to watch. I used the earphones you gave me for my birthday so I wouldn't disturb your coffee klatch." He yawned. "Fairport High School lost."

Note to self: Be very careful what you talk about with your pals, in case you-know-who is around. Some things are best kept from prying ears, even those with selective hearing. In my opinion, that's one of the secrets to a long marriage. That and separate bathrooms.

"I like the element of surprise," Jim said, a mischievous glint in his eye. "I thought you did, too."

"Only sometimes," I said. "Not all the time. You ought to know that after all these years." I handed him a bottle of Merlot and a corkscrew. "Talking to you about what happened today is sure to give *me* a headache, and I don't mean the football game," I said. "But this may help me relax. And we're having leftover beef stew for dinner. Thank goodness I made an extra-large portion last week. I'm not in the mood to start a meal from scratch today."

I thought I heard Jim mutter, "You rarely are these days." But then again, I could have been mistaken.

I put two bowls of steaming hot beef stew on the table and plopped onto a chair.

"Yum," Jim said, not wasting any more time talking. His priorities are always predictable.

I took a small sip of wine, then another, and immediately felt myself start to relax. "So, now do you want to hear about my day?"

Jim nodded without looking up from his bowl.

"It was pretty stressful," I said. "In fact, it was more than that. It was horrible."

"Memorials for a deceased person aren't ever fun and games," Jim pointed out, taking a long pull from his wine glass and returning his attention to his dinner. "What did you expect?"

"That's not what I mean. The whole memorial was a disaster. An insult to the memory of a fine woman. It all started when Frank Bologna crashed the memorial and sat down in the front row with Sister Rose. I couldn't believe the gall of the man, using the death of an innocent woman who was only out walking her dog to promote his own political campaign. He didn't even know the name of the deceased person, or her connection to Sister Rose. It was disgusting. But Sister Rose sure put him in his place, and insisted he leave immediately. In fact, she practically threw him out the door. She was terrific," I said, smiling at the memory. "Everyone in the room cheered and clapped. Some even shouted that she should run for town council, because she was sure to beat him. She said that because she's a nun, she couldn't. Which is really too bad."

"So Mr. Fairport is running for town council again," Jim said, entirely missing the point of Frank Bologna's inappropriate behavior and its aftermath. "He didn't mention it when I saw him earlier this week, but I'm not surprised. He has nothing else in his life and he's done a lot of good for the town over the years."

"Oh, really?" I asked, waving my fork in the air and preparing to challenge that assessment. "Like what? Name one thing Mr. Fairport has accomplished for the town in all the years he's been in office." I stopped for a millisecond and processed what I thought I'd heard Jim say. "Do you really believe a political hack like Frank Bologna should be re-elected just because he has nothing else going on in his life? You can't be serious."

"That's not exactly what I said, Carol. You're paraphrasing and missing my point."

"*I'm* missing the point?" I repeated. "You must be kidding. If there's anyone at this dinner table who's missing the point, it's you, Jim. I'm telling you that Frank Bologna showed up today to offer his condolences to Sister Rose on the death of her *biological* sister. Do you get that? Her biological sister. What an idiot. Plus, he didn't get Mary Pat Ryan's name correct, or know how she died. He was totally clueless. He was just looking for a way to promote himself to a gathering of potential voters. But instead of getting votes for himself, I'm sure there's not a single person who was there who'll vote for him now."

"I'm sure you're exaggerating how bad the situation was," Jim said. Left unspoken, but clearly implied was, "The way you always do."

"Every time I've interviewed Frank for my column, he's been right on top of the latest issues in Fairport," Jim continued. "And doing his best to solve problems about which you know absolutely nothing."

"Those are fighting words, buster," I said. "You're completely wrong about me. For your information, I follow local, state and national politics very closely. I'm just not obsessed with it, the way you are. Some people actually value my opinion. In fact..." I laid down my fork and stood up, for once taller than my husband. "In fact, just this afternoon I was invited to manage the campaign for someone who's going to run for town council against your friend Frank. I wasn't sure if I was going to do it, but now I definitely am. How do you like that?" Without waiting for an answer, I turned in the direction of the family room. "You can clean up the kitchen for a change." And I flounced out of the room.

I know what you're all thinking. Once again, I was behaving like a child. But before you start to criticize me, consider this: Who was the person in this marriage who majored in political science in college? I'll give you a hint—Jim majored in math. That's probably why he doesn't appreciate my creative financial methods as much as he should. (Although how he ended up with such a successful career in public relations after majoring in math is a complete mystery to me.)

As I sat on the couch in the family room, fuming and arguing with myself (silently, not that Jim would hear me anyway), I got a text from my daughter.

Jenny: *Sorry about Harriet.*

Me: *It's okay. Thanks for trying.*

Jenny: *Are you busy now? Got time for an in-person chat?*

Hmmm. This was odd. My maternal instincts went into overdrive. Something was definitely up.

Me: *Sure. I'll be there in 10.*

Jenny: *No! I'll come to you.*

Me: *Not a good idea. Somewhere else.*

Jenny: *Fairport Diner?*

Me: *Okay. On my way.*

Jenny: *K.*

I stuck my head into the kitchen, brandishing my car keys. Jim was busy loading the dishwasher, which should have made me happy. Except I couldn't help but notice that he wasn't scraping or rinsing the dishes first, which meant they wouldn't come completely clean. Arrgh. I'd probably have to run them through all over again.

"I have to run a quick errand," I said, ignoring the dirty dishwasher debacle my husband was creating. "I don't think I'll be gone too long."

"Don't go to the store and buy things we don't need," Jim cautioned. "Whenever you say you're running a quick errand, you come back with a car full of groceries."

Totally untrue. He was the one who always stocked up on paper towels, soap, salad dressing, etc., just because they were on sale. But we'd already had one "domestic" tonight, and I wasn't anxious to have another one.

"I promise you that I won't this time," I said, ignoring the barb he'd tossed my way. Instead, I gave him a quick kiss (I can behave like an adult when necessary) and was on my way out the door before he could respond again.

Chapter 15

I didn't say you were wrong. I merely pointed out that I was right.

"This is nice, honey," I said, sliding into a booth at the Fairport Diner and trying to ignore the stickiness on the table between Jenny and me. "I always love a chance for the two of us to get together for some special mother-daughter bonding." I took a good look at my daughter. It was obvious by her red-rimmed eyes that she was either very tired or very upset.

I reached over and grabbed her hand. "Or, maybe this isn't so nice. What's going on, sweetie?"

Jenny was silent for a minute, then said, "Why don't you talk first, Mom? Tell me how the memorial service was."

I know when someone's stalling for time. But I also knew that my daughter had a very good reason to suggest we get together tonight, and she'd tell me what it was when she was ready. So I launched into a summary of the memorial, including Frank Bologna's outrageous attempt to crash it, and the uproar involving Mary Pat's two terrible neighbors.

The latter made Jenny smile. "Did Maria really sock one of them? That must have been something to see. Did she throw them out?"

"Thank goodness Paul Wheeler was there. He made sure they

left," I said. Jenny looked surprised. She's never heard me praise Paul Wheeler for anything before.

"Paul was certainly helpful, but the person who really saved the day was Donna Trumbull."

"Who's that?"

"The owner of Mrs. T's Tasty Treats. She donated all the baked goods for the memorial. After the excitement had died down, everyone was really uncomfortable and just wanted to go home. Neither Maria or Sister Rose seemed to know how to handle the situation, so Donna Trumbull stepped in and organized takeout boxes for all the guests. There was practically a stampede for the door."

"You're exaggerating now, aren't you, Mom?"

"Only slightly," I said. I eyed Jenny, who seemed a little more together. "And now, young lady, that's enough chatter from me. What's going on? Is everything okay at home?" A sudden thought stabbed my heart. "Is it the baby? Is CJ sick?"

"No, Mom, CJ is perfect, as always. And Mark's home, so I was able to get away for a little while." Her face darkened. "And no, things aren't okay. I'm beginning to figure out that I married a big fat jerk and I'm stuck with him for life."

Oh, boy. Be careful what you say, Carol. You know that Jenny and Mark are crazy in love. They were meant to be together ever since grammar school. Don't take sides in this. Just listen. For once.

"We'll each have a cup of herbal tea," I told the server who had appeared magically at the worst possible moment. I decided not to mention the sticky table. After all, I'm not the world's greatest housekeeper, either. And the server looked like she was old enough to have been collecting Social Security for even more years than I have. (Oops, I didn't mean to let that slip. Forget I said that.)

"We had a fight," Jenny said. "It was all about Harriet, Mary Pat's dog. I told Mark that you wanted the dog to come to the memorial service, and that I said I'd try to help you.

"Mark said that anything he'd told me about the dog was in strictest confidence. He accused me of telling you that Paul Wheeler was taking care of her. I never did that. I volunteered to call you so you could tell him exactly what I said, yourself, but that just made him madder. So I left."

Oh, boy. This was all my fault. I already knew the police were still holding Harriet, and I'd taken advantage of my own daughter to do Sister Rose's bidding. Shame on me. The part about Paul Wheeler was a big surprise, though.

I didn't want to make things worse between her and Mark, so I didn't react right away. But my mind was whirling. Why would a Fairport detective (although usually an inept one) have Harriet in his personal custody? I'd joked with Stacey O'Keefe about the dog being in the Canine Protection Program, and what Jenny just told me made my fertile imagination go into overdrive. Sometimes I think I should write fiction, myself.

Don't be ridiculous, Carol. Maybe Paul Wheeler just likes dogs. Or just liked this dog because she'd belonged to one of his favorite teachers, and that's why he's taking care of her for a while.

That didn't answer why Harriet's whereabouts seemed to be such a deep, dark secret, though.

"Mom, you're a million miles away. Do you have any advice for me about Mark? I don't know what to do."

"Sorry, sweetie, I was thinking about the best way for me to answer you," I fibbed. I grabbed her hand. "First of all, this is the first time I heard that Paul Wheeler is keeping Harriet, and I won't tell anyone, even Lucy and Ethel. I promise. This whole thing is really my fault. You were just trying to help me, and I shouldn't have involved you. I'm sorry. I promise not to do it again. I'd be glad to straighten things out with Mark myself, just to clear the air, but it might be best to just let it go. If your husband is anything like mine, I'm betting that by the time you get home, Mark will feel terrible about the fight and all will be forgiven. He's probably just tired, and that's why he snapped at you. He didn't mean it. It's all part of the ups and downs of married life. Believe me, I know what I'm talking about."

Try taking your own advice for a change, Carol. You were ridiculous to get so angry at Jim the way you did. Go home and apologize to your own husband.

"Mark and Paul have been working double shifts this week," Jenny admitted. "They're trying to...."

I realized that we could be veering off into forbidden territory again by discussing one of Mark's cases. "Don't tell me anything else. It's time for both of us to go home to our spouses. Let's forget the tea. I didn't really want it, anyway." I turned, waved over the server, and pressed a $10 bill into her hand. "For your trouble."

I hugged Jenny. "Come on, let's go home."

Chapter 16

Beware of the dog. She is very sarcastic.

In case you were wondering, Jim and I did make up when I got home from the Fairport Diner. When I woke up the next morning I had a smile on my face, in spite of the fact that I had to face another day filled with situations I had no idea how to deal with. Tops on my To-Do-If-I-Could-Figure-Out-How list was figuring out the reason behind the current co-habitation of Paul Wheeler and Mary Pat's dog without letting my son-in-law figure out Jenny had tipped me off about it. For some reason, this was a big deal to Mark, and I didn't know why. But I was smart enough to realize that if I showed up at the police station the day after my mother-daughter coffee date, Mark was bound to be suspicious, no matter how many donuts I brought with me.

Then there was the issue of my suddenly becoming a political consultant for a woman I barely knew without my husband figuring out what I was doing. The lecture/tongue-lashing/ criticism I'd gotten from him last night about my possible foray into Fairport politics wasn't anything I'd care to repeat. Ever. So that definitely called for major diversionary tactics that I had yet to come up with, even with my fertile imagination and years of practice.

"Why is life so complicated all of a sudden?" I asked the

old woman looking back at me in the bathroom mirror. "Who the heck are you, and what have you done with the old Carol Andrews?" I suddenly realized what I was saying. This was the Old Carol Andrews. The Very Old Carol Andrews.

"Every day is a gift," I reminded myself, washing my face and applying a gallon of Oil of Olay to "regenerate youthful skin cells," as the advertisement had promised. The smart advertisers hadn't said how long it would take for the skin cells to regenerate to their former youthful selves, however. In my case, I figured it would take a decade or two, so I resigned myself to getting dressed and getting on with the main business of the day—plotting, planning, and scheming. There are only so many hours in the day and, as the treacherous bathroom mirror had reminded me, I wasn't getting any younger.

My musings continued over a cup of Jim's delicious coffee, one of the fringe benefits of his retirement. He always makes the coffee even when he doesn't stick around to share it with me—like this morning, for example. I seemed to recall in the fuzzy recesses of my brain that he'd mumbled something about a quick trip to CVS. Today, being Sunday, was the day the new coupons went into effect, and my dear husband always likes to be one of the first people in the store so he has his pick of the sale merchandise.

I checked the time on my cell phone, and laughed at myself. Confidentially, there was a time, not so very long ago, when I hated the darn thing. I never carried it, and it used to drive Jim nuts, because he never knew where I was or what I was doing. (That part hasn't changed much.) But now I've become so dependent on my phone that I don't make a move without it. I don't even wear clothes unless they have pockets.

I was just trying to figure out if it was too late to catch Nancy before she left for her first appointment of the day when my phone announced an incoming call. I checked the number, realized that it was Donna Trumbull, and panicked. I didn't want to talk to her. I didn't want to get involved in town politics. And, most of all, I didn't want Jim to yell at me.

What are you, some kind of 1950s television show mommie, letting your husband call the shots? Pick up the damn phone!

"Good morning, Donna," I heard a voice that sounded like mine say. "You're certainly up early today."

"Good morning, Carol," Donna said, sounding a little miffed. "I run a business, as you know. I'm always up early and it's certainly not early now. It's past 9:00. I've been up for hours, plotting our campaign strategy."

"Our?"

Donna's voice changed. "Of course, *our*, Carol. I may be the official candidate, but you, as my campaign manager, are an equal partner. Now, I want to call a meeting this afternoon at my home at 4:00 sharp to go over assignments. The first thing is to collect enough signatures to be sure my name gets on the ballot in time, so we have to get going. Who can you get to come?"

"Me?"

"Really, Carol, if the only thing you're going to do is repeat everything I say, we'll never get anywhere. So get a hold of some of your friends and tell them to come to a 4:00 meeting today at my home. And don't be late. I abhor tardy people." She rattled off an address on Jefferson Street and terminated the call.

"How do I get myself into these things?" I moaned to Lucy and Ethel. I had just wasted an hour texting everyone I knew in Fairport (only a slight exaggeration), starting with my three formerly best friends, and come up empty. Zilch. Not one person. I wondered if they'd talked ahead of time and planned excuses they could use when I leaned on them to attend a political campaign planning meeting for Donna.

Didn't anyone care about what was going on in Fairport anymore? What happened to all the cheering women at the memorial who were urging Sister Rose to become a candidate for town council and run against Frank Bologna? Were all of them just caught up in the heat of the moment after Sister Rose basically threw Frank Bologna out of the memorial service? Or would they only get involved if the candidate was someone they knew and were either terrified of or respected—the person who had already ruled herself out as a candidate.

Lucy, of course, gave me a cynical look which told me, loud and clear, that finding myself in situations like this all the time was my own fault. Sweet Ethel nuzzled my hand in sympathy, but I could tell from her eyes that she agreed with Lucy. She was just too polite to say it.

I raised my eyes heavenward (well, toward the kitchen ceiling, which was the closest I could get to heaven from where I was currently sitting) and said, "Dear Lord, please send me a sign. Should I try to get out of this right now, while I still can? Should I tell Donna Trumbull I'm much too busy to take on such an important and time-consuming commitment? If that's what You think I should do, I'm happy to go along with You. But I need Your help, because I don't know how to do it." I closed my eyes and hoped that the Good Lord wasn't too busy right now to listen to me and my stupid, petty problems.

When I opened them again, the answer to my prayer walked into the kitchen, proving that God does, indeed, have a sense of humor.

Chapter 17

Politics is the second oldest profession, and often resembles the first.

Jim gave me a kiss on the top of my head, and asked, "Got anything for lunch? I'm starving."

"There's a fresh supply of cold cuts in the meat drawer," I said. "Turkey, ham, and cheese."

"What kind of cheese?" Jim said, his head stuck in the refrigerator. "I don't see any."

I sighed. *Honestly, why can't men find things that are staring them right in the face?*

Then I remembered that Jim's timely appearance was a gift from the Almighty, and I needed to show my gratitude instead of complaining. I reached inside and pulled out half a pound of swiss cheese. "Here. The whole wheat bread's already out. I'll even make the sandwich for you, if you want."

"I'll do my own, thank you. You never offer to make my lunch." He gave me a suspicious look.

True. But let the record show that, for once in our almost 40-year marriage, I did offer.

My husband slathered enough mayonnaise on two slices of the bread to suffocate it, then said, "You're up to something. I can tell. You might as well tell me now and get it over with."

And I thought I was being so subtle. "I was just being nice," I said, "since we're having lunch together today. Like a mid-day date." I know, that was a real stretch, but I was desperate. I parked my keister in a chair, a container of low-fat peach yogurt in my hand. "But since you figured out I have something serious on my mind, maybe you can help me. I'd like to pick your brain a little."

Jim raised one eyebrow. "You're kidding. That's two things you've said in the past ten minutes that are surprising." He brought the sandwich fixings over to the table, sat down opposite me, and gave me his full attention. "My brain is at your disposal." A look of horror crossed his face. "You didn't dent your car again, did you?"

"Can't a woman want to talk to her husband about something without him assuming the worst?"

"Well, you did say it was serious," Jim countered. "Don't blame me if a new dent in the car was the first thing I thought of."

"This has absolutely nothing to do with the car," I said. "I want your advice about running a political campaign. I need your help."

Jim's face turned red. "Oh, for heaven's sake, Carol. I thought this discussion was over with last night. You can't be serious about this. You are the most a-political person I've ever known. You never pay attention to local issues, and if I didn't remind you to vote, I bet you wouldn't even bother. Did it ever occur to you that the reason idiots get elected is because so many people don't care enough to vote? And then they're the loudest ones to complain about who won." He shook his head and took a bite of his sandwich.

Forgive me, Lord, for the brief desire to commit husband homicide that just came over me. And give me the strength to overcome it before I do something I might regret.

"That's why I'm coming to you for help, dear," I said with as much sincerity as I could muster up under the current desperate circumstances. "Do you remember I told you about how Frank Bologna caused such an uproar at the memorial service yesterday, and how Sister Rose got rid of him after a terrible argument?"

Jim nodded, and spread mayonnaise on two more slices of

whole wheat bread. "So?"

"I also said that everyone there wanted her to run for town council against him, remember?"

"Those people weren't serious, though," Jim said, biting into his second sandwich. I tried to ignore the blob of mayo dribbling down his chin. *How the heck can you say that, since you weren't even at the memorial to see what happened?* But I didn't say that. Points for me, right?

"On the contrary, *dear*, they were very serious, but Sister Rose said she couldn't run because of her vows as a nun. Then another woman, Donna Trumbull, came up to congratulate Sister Rose on being so forceful. She's decided to run for Bologna's town council seat herself on a pedestrian safety platform, and she asked me to help her organize a campaign. Donna's a successful businesswoman in Fairport. She owns Mrs. T's Tasty Treats."

"Being successful in business doesn't mean she knows anything about politics," Jim said.

"Point taken," I said. "But she cares about what's happening in town, and wants to make a positive difference."

Jim mumbled something I didn't catch. Which was probably for the best, the way this discussion was going. I had to change my tactics, and quick. I searched my usual tried and true strategies and a sure-fire winner popped up. Read on and learn.

"You're right, Jim. I haven't cared about politics before. I've been Fairport's most apathetic citizen, and I'm embarrassed about it. I appreciate all the times you pushed me to get out and vote. My involvement in the community has been zippo for years."

"You're welcome," Jim said. "And I know you care about what happens in Fairport. You've just had other priorities."

"That's exactly right, Jim," I said, beaming. "I've had other priorities, just like you've had. But you're making a real effort to reinvent yourself since you retired, and I want to follow your example and do the same thing. Once again, you're pushing me in the right direction without even knowing you're doing it. I'm the luckiest woman in the world to be married to such a swell guy."

Jim gave me a big smile. "I'm glad you finally figured that

out, Carol. And if you really want to thank me...."

I pretended not to understand Jim's obvious hint. "Mary Pat Ryan's death hit me hard. I was actually thinking of running for town council, myself. If I won, maybe I could do something to make Fairport safer for pedestrians, so what happened to her wouldn't happen to another innocent person. I was going to talk to you about it at dinner last night, to see what you thought."

I paused and gave my poor husband a chance to catch up, then barreled ahead with my scenario. "When Donna Trumbull called and told me she was running, and her issue was pedestrian safety, I realized that helping her was the way I could make a difference in town and honor Mary Pat's memory at the same time. The crosswalks in this town aren't safe. Drivers speed through them all the time. Something has to be done. Don't you believe that pedestrian safety is important?"

"Of course I do. How could you even ask me that?"

"So, what if I was the candidate running for office instead of Donna Trumbull?" I asked, switching gears now that I had Jim focused the way I'd intended. "What advice would you give me?"

"But you're not the candidate," Jim countered.

"For the purposes of this discussion, let's pretend that I am," I said. "Oh, wait a second." I ran to my desk, grabbed a pen and pad, and prepared to take notes. "You know so much more about politics than I do. I'm anxious to hear what you have to say."

My goal in this exchange, in case you haven't figured it out yet, was to hook Jim into coming with me to Donna Trumbull's this afternoon, so I planned to keep my actual note-taking to a bare minimum. Not that it would matter how many notes I scribbled while Jim was talking. They'd be so illegible I wouldn't be able to read them, anyway.

"This is silly," he said. "I'll go along with this play-acting, just for the purposes of instruction." He gave me a skeptical look. "But you better not be plotting to pull the rug out from under me and announce your candidacy for town council after you've picked my brain."

"How could you think I'd be so devious?" I was shocked and

a little scared that Jim was catching onto my tricks after all these years. Even though, this time, he was wrong about the trick I was pulling, I realized I better be more careful in the future.

I put my right hand over my heart. "I hereby solemnly swear that I have no intention, ever, of running for elected office in Fairport. And if I break this promise, I'll forfeit babysitting privileges for my grandchildren forever. I can't think of a worse punishment than that. Now do you believe me?"

"That's good enough for me," my husband said. "Just be sure you stick to it." He cleared his throat, and I could tell he was finally ready to give me the Jim Andrews 101 Primer on Local Politics, a.k.a. Local Politics for Dummies. I hoped he'd hurry up or we'd never make the meeting with Donna Trumbull by 4 p.m.

"First, as a loving, supportive spouse, I'd tell you that I admire you for deciding to run for office," Jim said with all sincerity. "Most people say they loathe local politics and don't want to get involved. They don't realize that the candidate who's elected will have a direct impact on their own lives as long as they're residents of that town."

Jim stopped talking for just a minute, then said, "I don't see you taking any notes, Carol."

I waved my pen around. "Loathe, local, living. Got it. Go on."

"Are you sure you'll know what that means later? It doesn't make any sense to me."

"It's my own personal shorthand. Believe me, I'm getting all your important points down. They'll be crystal clear to me every time I go over them."

I guess that bluff was good enough for Jim, because he cleared his throat, then said, "Here's another important point. I believe that if a candidate has a life partner, it's crucial that the partner be openly supportive of the candidate right from the very beginning. I've seen some great candidates drop out of a race because of the negative impact the campaign has taken on their personal relationships."

I wasn't sure what Jim was implying. Did the hypothetical spouse open his or her mouth and stick both feet in it? Did the relationship suffer because the candidate's spouse didn't like the spotlight? Or resent that the candidate was out campaigning all the time, with no time for their personal relationship? I'd also heard rumors of campaign love affairs. Yikes. This could be getting into some dangerous waters. Good thing I decided not to run after all. Oh, wait a minute. I never was.

"Donna Trumbull is a widow," I said. "There's no problem about a supportive or resentful spouse because there isn't one."

Jim nodded. "Okay. Good to know. But continuing with the fantasy of you being the candidate in a local election, you'll be putting yourself out there personally, exposed to public scrutiny, every day of the week. You'll hear rumors, criticism, and cutting remarks everywhere you go. People will say you're too old, too fat, and the town busybody. They won't like your hair, your clothes, your car, your family, your dogs, your husband...everything."

"Oh, so you're worried about criticism, too," I shot back.

"No. Not me. But I'd be worried about you. I know how sensitive you are to the tiniest criticism."

Interesting observation, considering how much criticism comes from you. I didn't really say that, of course. But I filed it away for future use.

"It's certainly true that politics at all levels have become personal," I said. "All the campaigns for federal and state offices seem to be more shouting and name-calling than any real debate about issues. The television ads are terrible. Politicians are calling each other liars, cheats and thieves. They're not solving problems, only attacking each other." I looked down at my notepad, which was blank, and covered it so Jim couldn't see. It was time to get down to specifics.

"If I ran," I said, getting excited about the possibility of my pretend candidacy in spite of all the negatives Jim had pointed out, "even if I don't win, it'd be my chance to help turn the discussion back to real issues and bring more civility to town government. I think that's very important."

Hold it and focus, Carol. You're not the candidate, remember? Donna Trumbull is.

Reluctantly, I forced myself to abandon my fantasy of saving Fairport for future generations and concentrate on reality. Or whatever passes for reality in my peculiar thought process.

"I agree with you," Jim said. "And in this make-believe campaign of yours, I'd back you all the way."

"Great! How would we start?"

I'll spare you the details of the next excruciating hour, because I don't want you to suffer through it the way I had to. Confident that flattery would work to convince Jim to jump on the Trumbull campaign bandwagon, if only for this afternoon, I emphasized several times how impressed I was with his understanding of the political process. *"Oh, Jim, you are so smart."* Next, I pointed out that it was his civic duty to share his knowledge with Donna, who was a true neophyte in the local political pond. *"Jim, you owe it to the citizens of Fairport to help Donna Trumbull get elected to the town council."*

I was shocked when neither of those worked. But I didn't give up. Not me. I soldiered on, throwing argument after argument at him, but it was like talking to a brick wall. Or a man with selective hearing—take your pick.

I finally told Jim that, by sharing his knowledge with Donna Trumbull, he'd prevent a well-meaning local citizen from making a total fool of herself. I was so desperate at that point that I used myself as an example of how easily that could happen. That's what convinced him, reinforcing the male fantasy that they know everything and women know nothing. Ergo, when a female gets herself into a jam (that she can easily get herself out of all on her own, thank you very much), it's up to the man in her life to ride to her rescue on his white horse and save the day. I told him I needed his input at the campaign meeting in case I showed my ignorance.

As things turned out, I oversold my case and should have kept my big mouth shut.

Chapter 18

Being organized is highly overrated.

Nancy always says that you can tell an awful lot about people by the place they call home. In Donna Trumbull's case, the monstrosity she called home told Jim and me right away that she was awfully rich and had awfully bad taste. The house was an over-the-top mega McMansion set on what was previously two building lots with two perfectly nice colonial homes. I had a brief wave of sadness for the two houses that had been sacrificed to make room for this combination of Victorian and modern with more turrets and peaks than I had ever seen on a single structure. As if the style wasn't ugly enough, the structure was painted a garish blue with red shutters and white trim.

I couldn't look at Jim. I knew what he must be thinking, because I was thinking the same thing. Did Donna Trumbull have her house painted red, white and blue and then decide to run for office to match the colors? Or was it the other way around? I shook my head. The latter was unlikely, since she'd just gotten the idea after the argument between Sister Rose and Frank Bologna at Mary Pat's memorial service. Unless she kept a house painter on speed dial, nobody could get a house completely painted in just one day.

"I wonder if the inside is decorated with stars and stripes,"

Jim said, struggling to keep a straight face.

"Behave yourself," I said as I pressed the doorbell. I almost lost it myself when we were greeted by the first six notes of the "Star Spangled Banner."

"Interesting door chime," Jim said.

The front door flew open, revealing Donna Trumbull with a phone glued to her ear. She gestured us inside as she continued to bark orders at the person on the other end of the phone line. "Quite frankly, I don't care what your problem is, Sid. You figure out how to get the entire shipment of flour delivered to me by tomorrow morning at eight o'clock sharp or I'm cancelling your contract and using someone else. And not only that, I'll have my lawyers sue you. Got that?" She paused for a beat, then snapped, "Good. I'm glad you finally understand." And she ended the call.

I felt sorry for the poor person who was on the receiving end of Donna's wrath. Witnessing the call reminded me with a jolt that I'd seen an example of her temper before, when she'd yelled at the Fairport Garage owner for taking so long to fix her car. Too bad I hadn't remembered her temper before I promised to help her run for office and, even worse, roped Jim into her campaign, too.

You're overreacting, Carol. Give the woman a chance. She's under a lot of pressure. Every now and then you lose your temper, too.

In less than a millisecond, Donna's whole manner changed from Cruella de Vil to Mary Poppins. Okay, that's a slight exaggeration. She threw her arms around me, giving me a big hug. "Oh, Carol, I'm so glad to see you. Together we're going to do great things for the town we love so much."

Jim coughed, reminding me of his presence beside me. Not that I needed any reminding, understand. But I was glad he was still here and hadn't made a break for the front door yet.

"And who is this handsome man you've brought with you?"

"I'm Jim Andrews," Jim said. "Carol's husband. I'm only here to listen."

I took a deep breath. I knew what Jim was doing. He was distancing himself from Donna as much as possible, and putting the reason for his being here directly on my shoulders. Which, of course, was where it belonged. But please promise you won't tell anyone that I admitted that.

"Jim's just being modest," I said, shooting him a warning look. "He's an expert public relations professional. And he currently writes the State of The Town column for our local paper. I'm sure you've seen his by-line. I thought his expertise would be invaluable for this initial talk."

"This is so wonderful," said Donna, grabbing Jim's and my hands. "It's like getting two for the price of one." Releasing us, she started down the hallway toward the back of the house, me at her heels. I was dying to see as much of the house as possible, especially because I knew Nancy would want a full report. I fingered my cell phone, wondering if I could sneak a few pictures of Donna's living room, which was decorated in a style I'd term "early bordello."

"Let's sit in here," Donna said, indicating a well-appointed office, completely different from the rest of the house. "This was my late husband's study. After he died, and I bought the property next door so I could expand the original house, I decided to leave Mel's office intact, as an homage to him. If it wasn't for him, none of this would have been possible. I'm just a poor widow who got lucky."

Donna must have realized what she said, because she rushed to correct herself. "I didn't mean I got lucky because I became a widow. Mel and I started the business together. I miss him every day, even though it's been almost ten years since he's been gone. Mel always believed in me. He told me I could do anything I set my mind to. I think he'd be proud of my decision to run for town council in Fairport. I'm counting on you to help me, Jim." Donna favored my husband with another megawatt smile.

Jim leaned forward in his chair. "Well, I'm not sure how much time I can devote to your campaign," he said, "but this is where I think we should start." And the two of them began swapping ideas, ignoring me completely. What had I done? Jim was supposed to play a supporting role in Donna Trumbull's campaign. I was the one she'd recruited to take the leading role. I prayed Jim wouldn't accidentally out me as the neophyte political operative I was. Even though he was right, and I didn't know how to run a political campaign, I wasn't going to let my ignorance stop me. I'm a great believer in learning on the job. After all, when I had kids, I had no idea how to raise them, and look how great both Jenny and Mike turned out. Proof positive that I could learn to do anything.

A (tiny) part of me was glad to see Jim get excited about a new project for a change, instead of spending more and more time playing games on the computer or vegging out in front of the television. I remembered him admitting he was still having a tough time adjusting to retirement. But there was no way I was just going to sit back and let the two of them talk as though I was invisible. In a flash, I had the perfect approach to ensure my rightful place as the manager of Donna Trumbull's campaign.

"I knew the two of you would have a lot to talk about," I interjected, beaming at Donna and Jim like a proud mama who'd forced two squabbling kids to play nice with each other. (Oh, wait, that's really Jim and me.) I sat up straighter in my chair so I'd appear taller and more in charge.

I was pleased to see them both look at me with identical surprised expressions. Encouraged, I continued to assert myself. "One of the most important hallmarks of a political campaign is identity," I said, "and I'm not just talking about the candidate being a household name, either." I beamed my own thousand watt smile in Donna's direction. "You have that already. Your bakery business has made you a local celebrity."

Jim inched his chair closer to Donna's. "As I was saying...."

"Yes," I mused, moving to position myself directly in Donna's line of vision, "you definitely have Fairport name recognition, but it's not a name the public associates with politics. I think that'll work to your advantage in the upcoming campaign." I was warming to my subject now, as I realized I was onto something important. (Even if I took a circuitous route to get there.) Now was the time to expand on the ideas I'd shared with Jim.

"So many people in town are fed up with the status quo. I think it's the right time for a well-known, well-respected professional woman to run for local office. You can tout your business experience, and how you transformed what was a small local bakery into the giant success it is today. You've broken through the glass ceiling, and now you want to give back to the community that's embraced you and share your business expertise to make Fairport..." I searched for the right word. "You want to make Fairport safe again—for people pushing baby carriages, walking dogs, walking little kids to school, or riding bikes. You don't want what happened to a local woman recently to ever happen again. It's impossible for the Fairport police to patrol every single crosswalk, and every single intersection, twenty-four hours a day. If that's all they did, crime would run rampant in our town, and nobody wants that. We all have to participate, because making Fairport safe is everybody's job. It's an issue that affects every single resident, whether they realize it or not. Men like Frank Bologna have ignored this issue for years. It's time for a woman to get the job done."

I started to pace around the room a little. I was really rolling now. "And because you're a woman, the first woman to run for town council in Fairport's history, your campaign has to be woman-centered and women-driven. Only women out canvassing for the signatures that are needed to get your name on the ballot. Women making the phone calls to get out the vote. Women ringing doorbells all over town to convince people to vote for you. Women hosting fundraising brunches, cocktail parties, and coffee meet-and-greets to get your message out all over town. It's going to be great!" I paused to catch my breath. I don't think I'd ever been so passionate about anything before. (Well, I probably had, but the circumstances were completely different.) I shot a quick look at Donna, but her expression was unreadable. I wasn't sure if she thought I was brilliant or a complete idiot.

"I love it!" she finally said, surprising the heck out of me. "I really love it. Carol, you're a natural. No, even more than that. You're a political genius! This is a perfect strategy for my campaign." She jumped up and gave me a smooch on the cheek. "Thank you."

I gotta admit it. I was pretty proud of myself. Who knew that my hysterical stream of consciousness could produce such a positive response? I was so caught up with my eloquence and passion that when Jim spoke up, he startled me. I'd forgotten for a minute that he was in the room. "Carol's idea is certainly a new, unique platform for a local political campaign," he said. "Perhaps voters will respond to it positively, but only if it's conveyed the right way."

Donna's expression changed from one of interest to one of obvious annoyance. I guess Jim's subtle suggestion that she might not convey the campaign message properly didn't sit too well with her.

"Before we all get too carried away with such lofty goals," Jim continued, oblivious to the negative impact his words were having on the candidate, "there are more practical matters to be dealt with." Donna's eyes were narrow slits by now. I was afraid she was going to suggest the perfect place for Jim to stick his practical matters, and her choice of location would make a sailor blush.

I couldn't sit back and watch my husband continue to stick his foot in his mouth with his "I know what to do and you don't" attitude. "I think what Jim's trying to say," I said, flashing a warning glance at my clueless husband, "is that the campaign is going to be a learning curve for all of us. Speaking for myself, I've never done anything like this before, Donna. I really appreciate the faith you have in me to help you get elected. And I know that Jim's expertise will be invaluable to secure that goal, too." *Once he gets over his chauvinistic attitude.*

I didn't really say that last part, of course. But when we got home, Jim was in for a doozy of a lecture from me.

"I'm glad you said that, Carol. I was beginning to wonder if we could all work together," Donna said.

Thirty seconds of awkward silence followed. It was obvious (to me) that Donna was waiting for Jim to say something.

Finally figuring out what a huge gaffe he'd made, Jim said, "The issue of pedestrian safety applies to both men and women. It's a good choice."

"And children, too, Jim," I said, not letting him have the last word for a single second. "Think of all those children walking to school these days who have to cross streets in order to get there. Crossing guards are vigilant, but they're not on every corner. And all it takes is a single second for a driver to be distracted, probably by texting, to strike an innocent child." My eyes teared up as I thought about CJ on his first day of kindergarten, walking to school with Jenny, and all of a sudden, out of nowhere...well, it was too gruesome to think about. Nobody can conjure up an impending tragedy as well as I can, even if it was many years in the future.

"You've hit on another part of this campaign message we haven't even thought about," he said, speaking louder and more confidently now. "So many drivers speed through stop signs and yellow traffic lights without giving a second thought to the possible consequences. This issue also includes driver responsibility."

I looked at Donna to see how she was reacting to the Andrews husband/wife battle of words. It was important to include her in our conversation. After all, she was the candidate.

"What do you think, Donna?" I asked. "Is our brainstorming going in the right direction? Driver responsibility as well as pedestrian safety? They're two sides of the same problem."

"You've given me a lot to process," Donna admitted. I couldn't tell if she was pleased by that prospect, or not.

"AARP offers a safe driving course for older drivers," I said. "Wouldn't it be wonderful if we could get that organization to endorse your campaign?" Jim gave me one of his "Are you out of your mind?" looks, which you know I ignored.

"I just had another thought." My mind was bursting with ideas, and not even one of his famous looks was going to stop me. "When our kids, Mike and Jenny, were little, Fairport used to run a course called Safety Town to teach young children about, well...safety. I haven't heard about it in a long time. I wonder if it's still going on."

I turned to my personal font of knowledge. "Jim, do you know?" Before he could answer, the "Star Spangled Banner" began to play again, and Donna jumped up like the Energizer bunny. "Excuse me. I'll be right back."

Jim looked at his watch and mouthed, "How much longer?"

I shrugged. "I thought you were really into this. I'm staying, but you can leave if you want to. Better do it quickly, though. She's coming back."

"We're having quite a lively discussion. I'll be interested to hear what you both think," Donna said, ushering her two new visitors into the office. The first person was no surprise. It was Maria Lesco. But the second one was. An impossibly handsome man whom I'd met a few years ago named Tony Prentiss.

I wanted to swoon.

Chapter 19

Why do Americans choose from fifty candidates for Miss America and only two for President??

You'll be happy to know that I controlled myself. But the sight of Tony Prentiss, the hunky husband of my high school classmate, Neecy, and a former candidate for Connecticut State Senate (alas, he lost) certainly made my pulse quicken as well as my heart. Also my...never mind about that.

Neecy and I were both on the planning committee for our fortieth high school reunion. Her high school nickname was Nosy, not that any of us ever said that to her face. She was one of the people who made my life miserable way back then. But years passed and when we reconnected, we discovered life experiences that brought us closer. I'd never count Neecy as one of my BFFs, but she was still someone I thought of as a friend.

When her husband, Tony, a hugely successful (and gorgeous) local builder, ran for state senate, Jim and I supported him. I actually pitched in to get a campaign mailing out for him, something I'd never done before in my whole life.

Note to self: Remind Jim about my assistance in Tony's campaign the next time he suggests I have no political experience.

I have to admit that one of the main reasons why I was so willing to help Tony was...see above. Tony Prentiss was a man who took very good care of himself. Not too tall, not too short, with an athletic build (no evidence of the extra poundage Jim's been carting around). His gray hair neatly caressed his neck, and he was clean shaven, without a salt and pepper beard that some men grow in their later years to hide a sagging jaw line. Beautiful brown eyes. What we used to call, "bedroom eyes." Plus, the man simply exuded charisma. Why he lost the election, I'll never know. I was sorry I was only able to cast one ballot, and I was sure that most of the females in town felt the same way.

Focus, Carol. You're supposed to be professional, so for Pete's sake, act like it.

"Sorry I'm late," Maria said, looking a little flustered. "I had to wait until someone I trusted could cover for me. I started to powerwalk here from the restaurant, and then Tony was kind enough to stop and give me a ride. I invited him to sit in on the meeting. I hope that was all right."

"Of course it was. I should have thought of asking you myself, Tony. It's lovely to see you," Donna said, looking a little flustered, herself. It was obvious she was susceptible to the Tony Prentiss charisma factor, too. She gave Tony an adoring look, then added, "Where are my manners? Tony, this is Jim Andrews and his wife, Carol. They've agreed to help organize my campaign."

I couldn't help but notice that I'd been introduced as Jim's wife, not Donna's campaign manager. I allowed myself a brief spasm of annoyance, then reminded myself that if I acted like a professional, I'd be treated like one.

"Nice to see you, Jim," Tony said, giving my husband a manly handshake. Then he took both of my hands in his, giving me a smile that almost reduced me to a puddle right in front of everyone. "I've known this lovely lady since our high school days," he said to Donna. "I had a crush on you back then, Carol. I wonder what would have happened if I'd spoken up and told you so." And he winked at me.

I blushed a bright crimson (that was unprofessional but I couldn't help it, so please don't criticize me), not knowing how to react to Tony's declaration of unrequited love. Had he been worshipping me from afar for all these years, and I never knew it?

Then the sensible side of my brain, the part I rarely pay attention to, kicked in. Tony was at least two years ahead of me in high school, and a Very Big Man at Fairport Prep, the all-male Catholic high school in town. My school, Mount Saint Francis Academy, and Fairport Prep, did have joint dances back in those days, but the idea of Tony noticing me, a lowly underclassman, was absolutely ridiculous. I extricated my hands from his and quipped, "Neecy always said you had good taste, Tony. I guess this proves it."

Tony looked a little surprised, but then he burst out laughing, as did I.

"Perhaps we should get back on track and talk about Donna's campaign," I suggested, taking a seat next to my husband and giving his arm a little squeeze.

Donna immediately jumped in, happy to have the spotlight on herself once again. "Tony, since you're the only one here who's actually run for public office, perhaps you might give us the benefit of your experience. Some tips on what to do, and what not to do, to win an election."

I bit my lip to stop myself from saying aloud that, after all, Tony Prentiss did lose the only election he ran in.

"I have to admit that I learned more about what *not* to do, since I didn't win," Tony said, as if reading my thoughts. "But here's some basic advice." He turned his attention to Jim. "I know you've covered a lot of local politics, Jim. Feel free to jump in anytime with some thoughts."

"I'll take a few notes on my phone," I said. (You didn't think I was just going to sit there and not say anything, did you?)

I suddenly realized that, up to now, Maria Lesco had been sitting there quietly. She needed to be included in this strategy session, too. More than the rest of us, she had a personal interest in seeing that Donna's campaign for pedestrian safety was successful. "Why don't you take some notes too, Maria? We can get together later and compare what we have."

"Already prepared," Maria said, holding up a notebook and

pen. "I was a teacher, remember? I'm anxious to learn more about how a political campaign works, and how I can contribute. It's important to me that I'm involved." She dipped her head for a split second, but not before I saw tears glistening in her eyes.

For the next half hour—maybe longer—I tried to focus on the discussion and jump in whenever I saw an opportunity to contribute a suggestion. But I couldn't help feeling that Tony and Jim were lecturing the rest of us as though we were a trio of dim-witted women who didn't have a clue about how the political process worked, which made me mad. I looked at Maria, but she was scribbling notes like crazy. Even Donna was typing notes into her iPad like she was receiving the original Ten Commandments directly from Moses. She was the candidate, for heaven's sake. Didn't she even want to ask a question?

Oh, grow up, Carol. It's just another example of the man vs. woman dynamic that's been going on since the Stone Age. I had a brief vision of a man dragging some prehistoric prey back to the cave for supper, then lecturing his wife on how to cook it.

I sat there like a good girl, keeping my temper (and my big mouth) in check. I knew, even if nobody else in the room did, that the ideas I'd come up with just a short time ago were good ones, even if they were a little unusual. Donna Trumbull wasn't going to win this election using the same tired old methods that had been designed by a bunch of gray-haired (or balding) privileged men to elect more gray-haired, privileged men, so their beloved status quo would stay exactly the same way it always had. No more tired slogans like, "It's time for a change," which didn't mean a darn thing to the boys in charge. This was going to be a campaign run by women, to elect a woman. No men, gray-haired or not, would be allowed in the hen house. Then, maybe there'd be real change, for a change.

Hmm. I liked the sound of that. I typed, "Real change for a change," as a possible campaign slogan.

Oh, Carol, you are so brilliant. Don't stop now. What else?

I thought for a minute, and realized we needed a woman to be the honorary chairwoman of Donna's campaign. I knew the perfect person for the job, someone who could rally an army of committed volunteers like nobody else: Sister Rose. And I figured she'd say yes because, after all, Donna threw her hat in the ring (figuratively speaking) after Sister Rose declined to run for town council. I hoped that her vows as a nun wouldn't prevent her from accepting.

I began to type furiously on my phone as fast as my index finger would allow. (I never mastered the double digit technique the kids use.) Once Sister Rose agreed, we could start recruiting volunteers by using the invitation list from Mary Pat's memorial service. OMG. This was going to be great! And when Donna won by a landslide, I'd probably be recruited by a major female presidential candidate to run her campaign, too.

Oops. Bad idea. No way could I sandwich all those cross-country trips a national campaign would require into my already heavy babysitting schedule. CJ always came first. And I certainly wouldn't want to give The Other Grandmother the tiniest opportunity to muscle in and usurp my place.

I frowned. This was going to be tricky. I was lost in my own world when I heard Donna ask, "Do you agree, Carol?"

Yikes. I had no clue whether I should agree or disagree, since I had absolutely no idea what had just been said. Not that I planned to admit that, of course. You know me better than that. Instead, I waved my phone and said, "I've been making notes on the discussion. I need a little time to go through them."

Donna nodded. "That makes sense to me. I think we all need a little time to digest all this information. I know I do. There's a lot more to a political campaign than I ever realized before." She smiled. "But I love a challenge. More than anything, I just love a challenge."

"Great," I said, ready to head home. I had to figure out a sneaky way to get Jim to tell me what I should agree or disagree with, without risking another lecture about my limited attention span.

"We've made a good start, mostly thanks to Tony's valuable input," Jim said, interrupting my thought process as only he can.

"Let's plan a conference call tomorrow to hammer out specifics, Donna. I'll do an Excel spreadsheet tonight outlining the tasks we discussed and give assignments. That way, everybody will be clear about who does what, and there won't be any overlap. Specific job descriptions are going to be key. I'll also put together a timeline."

I almost laughed out loud. Job descriptions? Timeline? Who the heck was he kidding? I'd been fighting the losing battle of job descriptions ever since Jim retired. Who does what in our house? Who knows? I sure don't.

It suddenly dawned on me that, while I was zoned out in my fantasy of a woman-run campaign, there'd been an honest-to-goodness coup. I'd been usurped. No way was I going to let that happen. Even before I contacted Sister Rose, I needed time to brainstorm strategy with Maria. So I came up with the perfect plan.

"Maria, what's the special at the Trattoria tonight? Jim really loved the lasagna I brought home the other night." And before any of you rush to criticize me for not cooking dinner yet again, allow me to point out that the main reason I was ordering another takeout meal was to give me an excuse to talk with Maria privately. It was merely a lucky (for me) coincidence that delicious food I didn't have to cook myself was part of the plan.

"Tonight's special is ossobuco," Maria said. "We put that on the menu at least once a month. It's one of our most popular entrees."

Ossobuco is another one of Jim's all-time favorites. "Sounds yummy," I said, looking at Jim, who was trying to hide his interest and failing. "How about if I walk to the Trattoria with you and pick up an order to go?"

"I'd enjoy the company," Maria said. "And how about a pasta dish that you and Jim could share to go along with the meat course? Maybe Fettuccine Alfredo?"

"That's perfect," I said. "I'm salivating already."

I gave myself a high five, figuratively speaking. Because I knew I'd scored a home run. Correction: I'd scored three home runs. The first, of course, was another delicious dinner I didn't have to cook. The second was that I'd ordered it as takeout, meaning we'd eat at home, which Jim prefers (another thing we disagree on, but, oh well, choose your battles, right?). And the third was that I'd gained some private campaign strategy time with Maria Lesco.

I'm not asking for a round of applause or anything, but honestly, am I good or what?

Chapter 20

The only thing worse than a husband who never notices what his wife cooks or wears is a husband who always notices what his wife cooks or wears. And comments on it.

"Thank God that meeting is over," Maria said as we walked at a brisk pace in the direction of her restaurant. "I didn't count on another man being there when I invited Tony Prentiss. It was a spur of the moment decision, since he was nice enough to give me a ride. I thought he'd have some valuable insight, since he'd been a candidate himself."

"That's why I invited Jim to come," I said. "I was surprised when you walked in with Tony."

"Things didn't turn out the way I expected," Maria admitted. "I didn't plan on Tony taking over the meeting."

"He didn't do that all by himself," I said. "In retrospect, I shouldn't have invited Jim. But it seemed like a good idea at the time, since he's covered town politics for quite a while."

"I was ready to slug them both so they'd let us women get a word in. I could tell you felt the same way. Each one of them was trying to outtalk the other. It was almost comical."

I stopped and grabbed Maria's arm. "You're absolutely right. But how could you tell I was thinking the same thing? I never saw you look up from your pad. All you did was take notes. Lots and lots of them."

Maria laughed. "I wasn't taking notes on the meeting," she said. "I was planning next week's menus."

"You're certainly full of surprises," I said. "I thought you were hanging on every word that was said."

"Ha! No way. And remember that I'm a retired teacher, so I'm very good at reading a person's body language. It's a skill I developed over the years and never lost, like riding a bicycle. You should never play cards, Carol. Your face would give you away every time."

"I'll remember that, the next time Jim suggests a game," I said, hurrying a little more to match my pace with Maria's. "Hey, why are you turning left at this corner? The shortest way back to your restaurant is the other way."

"If we walk in that direction, it'll take us to the corner where Mary Pat was hit," Maria said. "I still can't bear to go anywhere near that intersection, whether I'm walking or driving my car. I don't know if I'll ever be able to. It's just too painful."

I'd used that intersection countless times since the accident and hadn't given it a moment's thought—except for being extra cautious, of course. But Maria was still grieving for the tragic death of her friend. "That should have occurred to me," I said. "I'm sorry. I understand why you feel that way."

"I don't normally share my personal feelings with anybody, but I know you saw me fighting back tears at one point during the meeting. Thanks for not handing me a tissue, or asking me how you could help. It would have embarrassed me."

"That's what I figured," I said, giving myself points that, for once, my better judgment had won the battle over my emotions. I groaned as I realized that Maria's Trattoria was still one long block ahead. I resolved to start my daily walking routine again first thing tomorrow morning, no matter what the weather was. Unless it was cold, rainy, or windy.

"The thing that made me the most angry about the meeting wasn't Jim or Tony lecturing us," Maria said, slowing down a bit so we were again walking at the same pace. "It was the way Donna reacted, hanging on their every word like they were so brilliant."

"I noticed that, too. For someone who has a reputation as a successful businesswoman, I found that very surprising. Jim and I accidentally overheard her screaming at a supplier when we got to her house this afternoon. She was so loud that we could hear her right through the front door. But when she opened it to let us in, she was nice as could be. A complete personality change. I've never seen anyone do such a total about-face in such a short span of time before."

"You must have heard Donna using her 'I'm the boss and don't you forget it' tone," Maria said. "Women in their own business have to develop a tough-as-nails attitude to be respected. I'd be mortified if you ever heard the way I've sometimes talked to a supplier who's given me an inferior cut of beef, for example, especially if I've already advertised it as our nightly special. That's not the real me."

As someone who'd had two children in Maria's class in the long-ago days when she was teaching, and had to endure excruciating parent-teacher conferences with her, believe me, I knew all about the "tough-as-nails" side to her personality. Not that I'd dare say that, of course.

"I guess you'd know more about that than I would," I said, giving her the benefit of the doubt. But I still didn't understand how a person could change personalities that rapidly. Which one was the "real" Donna Trumbull?

"Let me ask you a quick question before we go inside," I said, grabbing Maria's arm as we reached the Trattoria. "I guess I should have asked you this before I got myself all worked up about the campaign, but better late than never. What, exactly, do you know about Donna Trumbull?"

Maria turned around and looked at me like I was asking the most ridiculous question ever. "For heaven's sake, Carol, we just left the woman's house. Why didn't you ask her for a little background information?"

"How in the world could I have done that? She'd have thought

I was a little nuts. Or very rude."

"Exactly," Maria said, opening the door and ushering me inside. "Grab yourself a booth near the kitchen and I'll put your take-out order in. I'll be back as soon as I can. I'll ask a server to bring you something cold to drink. How about some Pellegrino with ice on the side?"

I nodded and slid into a booth. Swear to heaven, at that exact minute, my phone pinged with a text. It didn't take a genius to figure out that it was Jim, wondering how long I'd be. Honestly, when it comes to food, he's as impatient as both Lucy and Ethel combined. And that's saying something.

Me: *At Maria's. Order placed. Will text when it comes.*

Ping.

Jim: *How long?*

Ping.

Me: *Will text you!*

Ping.

"You really are too much," I said, laughing out loud. Perhaps a little too loud, as I startled the young server who had just arrived with my Pellegrino. "I wasn't laughing at you," I said as she beat a hasty exit, probably to tell her boss about the crazy lady who'd wandered into the restaurant.

I forced myself not to look at any of the "notes" I'd scribbled at the meeting. I hoped I could make some sense out of them. I've discovered that taking some time to ignore what I should be thinking about and instead take some time to think of things I have no business thinking about gives me a fresh perspective when I decide to return to what I should have been thinking about in the first place. Which makes perfect sense to me, even if it doesn't to you. I scanned the restaurant, and was surprised at how few diners were there. I checked my phone. It was now close to 6:00. That's dinnertime for the Andrews family, for sure. In fact, to hear Jim tell it, it's always dinnertime for us, unless it's breakfast time or lunchtime, of course.

I decided to amuse myself by making up stories about the other diners while I waited for my take-out order. For example, how long had the elderly couple at the corner table (even older than Jim and me) been married? Did they have children? Grandchildren? Or, maybe they weren't married at all, just dating. The idea made me smile. With all those senior dating sites Mary Alice says are on the Internet, that was entirely possible.

Moving along, I spotted another couple, younger, who were clearly married. Believe me, nobody fights like that in a public place without years of practice. And they didn't give a hoot if they were overheard, either.

"I'm not at all comfortable being here, Marty," the woman said. "With all the restaurants in Fairport to choose from, why in the world did you insist on coming back here? The last time, you made a complete fool out of yourself and we were told to leave."

"That wasn't my fault," the man answered in a loud voice. "I was provoked. We have just as much right to be here as anybody else does. I don't care if you're comfortable or not, Elaine. We're staying. I want another chance to confront that bitch and tell her what I really think of her and her dear friend, Mary Pat Ryan. Decide what you want to eat, but don't order anything too expensive. I'm not made of money, you know." He threw a menu across the table at his wife, but missed hitting her, thank God.

"You do that again and I'll hit you over the head with it."

OMG. It was Mary Pat's neighbor, the jerk who caused such a disturbance at the memorial service, and his long-suffering wife. If Maria came out of the kitchen with my order now, she'd probably dump my dinner on him.

This is a golden opportunity to find out why he hated Mary Pat so much. Don't waste it. You have to stall Maria.

It was lucky that the restaurant was reconfigured during a recent renovation, so the kitchen was now in the rear, not in the center of the room where Maria could see everything—and everyone. I fired off a quick text, hoping she'd respond.

Me: *Important u stay in kitchen for next 10 minutes. Can't explain.*
Ping.
Maria: *Are u crazy?*

Ping.

Me: *Yes. But please stay put. It's for MP.*

Ping.

Maria: *10 minutes.*

Okay, Carol, you better lie fast and make it good.

In a flash, I came up with the perfect cover story and approached the couple, who had positioned their chairs so they didn't have to look at each other. I pasted a fake smile on my face, pulled out my cell phone and tried to look like a professional news personality.

"Mind if I join you?" I asked, pulling out another chair before either of them had a chance to object. "I hope I'm not interrupting anything important, but I couldn't help overhearing your conversation. I'd like to talk to you about Mary Pat Ryan for a story I'm doing for my blog, the Fairport Snitch." I flashed my fake smile again. "I'm sure you've heard of it. We have over ten thousand followers."

The woman looked uncertain, and the man looked angry. I was getting nowhere fast.

I took a deep breath and kept going. "You may follow the Fairport Patch," I said. "But that site only talks about the good things that are happening in town." I snorted. "It might as well be written by the Chamber of Commerce. What a joke. My blog, the Fairport Snitch, is all about the dark side of what goes on here. I think you two would make a perfect interview to tell what you know about that hit-and-run victim, Mary Pat Ryan. From what I couldn't help but overhear, you weren't exactly admirers of hers."

The man's expression changed to one of triumph. "You see, Elaine, I told you coming here was a good idea." He pumped my hand. "I'm Marty Lambert. Glad to meet you."

I pulled my hand away and resisted the urge to wipe it on my chinos. Ugh. Clammy.

"Carol Kerr," I said. "Fairport Snitch Editor-in-Chief. When can we talk?"

"How about right now?" Marty asked. "We're all right here."

I shook my head. "Pretty soon the restaurant will be too

crowded and noisy. How about tomorrow morning at your house?"

"Are you going to video us?" Elaine asked, looking nervous. "I need time to clean."

"Don't worry about that. I'm sure the house will be fine for my purposes. How's ten o'clock?"

Marty scowled. "I have to work then."

I smiled. Again. No way was I letting this golden opportunity get away, no matter how difficult Marty made it for me. I pretended to think for a minute, then said, "Interviewing you right now is fine for me, but not here. We won't have any privacy. I'm sure what you have to say is confidential." I grinned. "At least, until I share it on the Snitch."

I looked at Elaine, who was fidgeting in her chair. Poor woman. She was already uncomfortable, and I was about to make it worse. "Can we go to your house now? I'd also like to see where Mary Pat Ryan lived, and take a few pictures of both houses." I waved my phone around and said, "If we leave right now, it'll still be light outside. What do you say, Marty? Are you game?"

I decided to go for broke and stood up. "Or maybe what you have to tell me isn't as dramatic as you say it is. Let's just forget it."

I turned to go, and Marty grabbed my arm. "It's dramatic, all right." He scribbled something down on a napkin and shoved it in my hand. "Here's our address. See you there." He jumped up, turning over his chair in the process. "Come on, let's go."

Elaine called out over her shoulder, "Please don't rush. Give me at least half an hour to tidy up."

I nodded. Been there, done that. Thank heavens for large closets with secure doors.

According to Marty's scribbled note, he and Elaine lived about five miles north of Fairport Center, near the Bridgeport city line. I calculated it would take me about 15 minutes to get there if I didn't hit any traffic, which would give me plenty of time to drive home and drop off dinner first. Assuming that Jim didn't cross examine me about where I was going and why, which was par for the course with him. He has lots of trouble keeping up with all my comings and goings, and it's even tougher when he doesn't hear what I'm saying half the time. Oh, well.

I texted Maria the "all clear" and she appeared in a millisecond carrying two shopping bags. "I hope your food is still hot when you get it home," she said in the same scolding tone she used in her teaching days. "And what were you up to out here? It's a good thing we've gotten to be good friends, or I would have ignored your text. After all, it is *my* restaurant."

Being a veteran of many withering looks from Sister Rose, Maria didn't scare me. Compared to the good sister, Maria was an amateur.

"Mary Pat's nutty neighbor, the one who disrupted her memorial, was here. I figured that if you caught sight of him, you'd go ballistic and throw him out. But I was able to convince him to talk to me about his problems with Mary Pat. I'm going to his house right after I drop off the food."

Notice I spared Maria any details about my creative thinking process. We were friends, but only members of my immediate circle understand it, excluding my husband.

"I'll go with you," Maria said. "I want to give that jerk a piece of my mind!"

"No!" I said, grabbing the bags. "That's the worst thing you can do. If you come along, I'll never get any information out of him. And..." I held up my phone, "I plan to record what he has to say. I'll share it with you later. Promise."

"All right," Maria agreed. "Be careful with these bags. I tried to pack them light. That's why I split the order in two."

"I'll put them on the floor in the back," I said. "That way, they won't move around. And it's a short drive home from here. Don't worry about that." I checked my small purse for a credit card and my car keys, came up empty, and panicked. "Oh, my God, where's my wallet? And my keys? Jim'll kill me if I lost them."

"Carol, we walked here, remember?" Maria said. "I don't know if you even brought your wallet with you. Did you walk to the meeting, too?"

OMG. How stupid I was. My purse was big enough to hold my cell phone and lipstick, my two priorities when I'll be seen in public. I hadn't bothered with a wallet or keys, because I was with Jim. Now my chances of making a quick getaway without being interrogated by Jim were nil. Plus, I had no idea which purse my keys and wallet were in, because I always change purses to coordinate with my outfit. (Well, don't you?)

This is what usually happens to you when you tell a lie, Carol. You get caught. Don't you ever learn? And the fictional Fairport Snitch lie is really a whopper.

Think, Carol. You can deal with this situation somehow, without Jim catching on.

I needed to find someone who'd drive me home, run inside and drop off the food, then drive me to Marty and Elaine's. Someone I could trust to keep her mouth shut and go along with me on this adventure without questioning why we were doing it. I reviewed my besties list: Nancy was probably showing a house, so forget her; Claire would give me a lecture about how I was being stupid coming up with such a ridiculous idea as the Fairport Snitch; Mary Alice was probably doing special duty nursing at the hospital. Besides, when I'd contacted each of them earlier today and begged them to come to the meeting at Donna's, they'd all (politely) blown me off. I didn't dare call Jenny, for obvious reasons. I was doomed.

I closed my eyes and sent up another short prayer to the Good Lord, asking Him to please find me someone to be Watson to my Holmes. Just for good measure, I promised if He helped me out this time, I'd never, ever ask for help again. I hoped He wasn't keeping track of how often (and recently) I'd sent up the very same prayer.

When I opened my eyes, the perfect person, someone I'd trusted with all my secrets (and what my real hair color was) for umpteen years, walked into Maria's Trattoria. My hair stylist, Deanna.

Chapter 21

A clear conscience is usually the sign of a bad memory.

"You saved my life today. I was in a bind and didn't know how to get out of it."

Deanna gave me a quick look and laughed. "You must be kidding. You've saved me from another boring evening watching the Hallmark channel. I've been binge-watching sappy romance movies all week. Can't seem to stop myself." She gestured at her takeout bag from Maria's. "I'm a sucker for Italian food and Italian men. And since there's no man, Italian or otherwise in my life right now, I'm consoling myself with a carb overload."

Since Deanna's tummy was as flat as the proverbial pancake, I was sure she was exaggerating about the overeating. But I never realized before how lonely she was. Her whole life revolved around Crimpers, and I couldn't recall a single time that she'd turned me down when I'd had a hair emergency that needed immediate repair, even if it meant she had to work late to fix it. Boy, was I a selfish person. I gave myself a mental slap and vowed to be more considerate of her schedule in the future.

"You should compare notes with Mary Alice sometime," I said. "She's tried a few of the online dating services for people over fifty, but she hasn't met Prince Charming yet. She's kissed a lot of frogs, though."

"I'll think about it," Deanna said. "I'm uncomfortable sharing details of my private life with anyone else. And speaking of Mary Alice, how come you didn't ask her or your other posse members to join you in your latest escapade? How did I get so lucky?"

I wasn't quite sure how to take that remark. Was Deanna being sarcastic?

"I figured that as soon as I told any of them what I was up to, they'd all refuse. And probably give me a lecture on my outrageous plan, besides saying no." Which was at least partially true.

"I only hear about your adventures after they're over, when you come into the shop and share them," Deanna said. "I've always been a teensy bit jealous of Nancy, Claire and Mary Alice, because they get to share in the fun first-hand. You've certainly piqued my interest."

"Then I guess my timing is good," I said. "I really appreciate your driving me to drop off dinner first. If you hadn't come inside too, it would have been a lot tougher to make a speedy exit. Jim asks a lot of questions at the worst possible times. You'll probably have to heat up your dinner when you get home. I just hope the food doesn't spoil."

"The weather's cool, so I'm sure it will keep," Deanna said. "Besides, having to nuke my dinner is a small price to pay to be part of one of your fun adventures."

I squinted at my phone. "Turn right at the stop sign onto Black Rock Avenue."

Deanna came to a full stop at the corner, looked right and left to be sure there was no traffic or bikers or—even worse—pedestrians coming, then turned as directed. "When you said 'outrageous' plan, Carol, what exactly did you mean? We're not going to do anything illegal, are we?"

"Of course not! I'd never do anything illegal myself, much less ask anyone else to. We're going to pretend to interview someone for a non-existent local blog, the Fairport Snitch."

"I never heard of it."

"That's because it doesn't exist," I repeated. Sheesh. Maybe

Deanna was the wrong choice, after all.

She was the only choice. So be patient with her. Not everyone's a natural born liar. I mean, creative thinker.

"We're going to meet the couple who live next door to Mary Pat Ryan," I explained. "Or, I guess I should say 'lived' since Mary Pat is now deceased. The husband said some terrible things about Mary Pat at her memorial, and Maria Lesco made him leave. She and Mary Pat were really good friends." I looked at my phone again. "Turn left here. We're looking for a gray house halfway up this block on the right side. But before we get to the house, pull over for a sec and we'll figure out a plan of action."

"You mean you don't already have a plan, Carol?" Deanna asked, now looking nervous. "I figured you'd just tell me what you wanted me to do, and I'd do it. But I have to warn you, I'm not much of an actress. I'm much more comfortable listening to a person's story and saying 'uh-huh' at appropriate intervals. I guess I'm sort of a therapist, in my own way."

"That's a perfect analogy," I said, relieved to find a role Deanna was comfortable playing. "You're the therapist who looks sympathetic and interested, and nods her head now and then. Feel free to add an 'uh-huh' or two now and then, whenever you feel like it. I'll ask the nosy questions. Our goal is to find out why this guy hated Mary Pat so much, and if he had anything to do with her death. What you're really there for is to be another set of eyes and ears for me, to be sure I don't miss anything important. It shouldn't take too long."

Because once the guy and his wife catch on to what we're up to, they'll probably throw us out. I didn't share that with Deanna, of course.

"Afterwards we'll go back to my house, have our dinner, and compare impressions and notes. Does that sound okay to you?"

"Now that I know my role, I feel a lot better," Deanna said, cruising down the street and parking in front of 333. "This is my first time as an accomplice. I hope I pass the audition."

I laughed and pointed the camera app on my phone at Marty and Elaine's house. It looked well kept, although the shutters could have used a fresh coat of paint to spruce them up. I snapped a couple of pictures before the door opened, revealing the odious Marty and the biggest white cat I'd ever seen. I did a double take. Were my eyes playing tricks on me? At my age, if I'm not wearing my glasses, I can't always be sure of what I'm seeing. Nope. I wasn't hallucinating. The cat was wearing pink, sparkly fairy wings.

"This is my associate, Deanna," I said, not daring to look at my partner-in-crime to check out her reaction to the cat's unusual attire. "She always comes along on interviews with me. Sometimes they get pretty intense. Our boss doesn't want any lawsuits."

Marty nodded as though that made complete sense to him. No surprise there. Anyone who'd play dress-up with a cat was obviously open to unusual experiences.

"Is your cat pregnant?" I asked, stepping around Marty to get further inside the house in case he'd had any second thoughts about our chat. There was no sign of Elaine anywhere.

"Nope. Princess Piggy just has a healthy appetite. But she's not fat, she's fluffy. That's why her name is Princess Piggy. Funny, right?" Marty laughed, a sound that resembled a donkey braying, and revealed a set of teeth that could have used a good flossing.

"Hilarious," I said, hoping the poor cat didn't have an inferiority complex. "And what happened to her tail? Why is it so short?"

Marty's face darkened. "That damn dog next door," he said. "They got into a fight and she bit it off. Damn, I hated that dog. I hated her owner even more."

"Poor kitty," Deanna said, reaching down to give the cat an affectionate stroke on her head. The cat immediately bared her fangs, hissed, and bit Deanna's index finger. Good lord.

I rummaged in my pocket and found a clean tissue. "Here," I said, pressing it into her hand. "Your finger's bleeding a little."

"It's no big deal," Marty said. "She bites people all the time." How charming.

"I hope your cat is up to date on her shots," I said. *And that you take better care of your cat's teeth than you do your own.* I didn't say that last part out loud, of course.

I walked into the living room without any invitation from Marty. Deanna followed close behind, still dabbing her finger to stop the bleeding. I sat in what I figured was Marty's chair—a leather recliner—and set up my cell phone to record our conversation. "I'm going to record you so I can play it back later when I write the blog post," I said in the interest of full disclosure. Well, as much full disclosure as I was prepared to give without telling Marty there was no such blog as the Fairport Snitch. I gestured toward Deanna. "She may snap a few pictures with her phone, and add a few questions. Okay?"

"Fine with me."

"So," I said, smiling and looking encouraging, "tell me your impressions of Mary Pat Ryan. How long were you neighbors? What was it like to live next door to her?"

"She was a real pain in the ass," Marty said, making himself comfortable on a tattered sofa that Princess Piggy obviously used as her scratching post. "Elaine and I thought we were moving into a nice neighborhood, with the perfect backyard setup for our beautiful Princess Piggy to play. Ha! What a laugh. The first night we were here, we let Piggy outside for a little while, to kind of get to know the area. You know what I mean?" He picked up the cat; she hissed at him and bit his hand. At least Piggy disliked him, too.

"In less than a minute," Marty continued, oblivious to the fact that his hand was now bleeding, "this vicious dog came out of nowhere and attacked our sweet kitty. But you fought back, didn't you, sweetheart?" Marty asked, stroking her head and ignoring Piggy's efforts to bite his hand again. "You were so brave. Poor Piggy. Poor baby."

I couldn't believe what I was hearing. I knew for a fact that Mary Pat's dogs were all extremely well trained. I couldn't imagine one of them attacking another animal.

"It just got worse and worse. That damn dog was outside all the time, night and day, barking like crazy, waiting for another chance to attack poor, innocent, gentle Piggy. My poor sweetheart would go outside to take a stroll around her own yard and that dog would pounce on her. A cat's got the right to prowl around her own yard. Don't you think so?"

Without giving me a chance to answer—which was a good thing under the circumstances, because I had no idea what to say—Marty continued listing his ridiculous grievances against Mary Pat. "But I finally got lucky. Somebody nailed her and that dog while they were out walking. What a break. I'm glad she's dead. I hope her dog's dead, too. Good riddance. We finally got some peace and quiet around here."

"Marty!" Elaine screamed. "Don't say that." She ran into the living room carrying a broom, which she shook at her husband. "Don't speak ill of the dead. She'll come back and haunt us."

I could see from the look on Deanna's face that this so-called interview wasn't going the way she expected it to. There wasn't a single opportunity for her to look sympathetic or say, "uh-huh." Instead, she looked shocked. Truth to tell, I was pretty shocked, myself.

"That's a very interesting story about the two animals," I said. "Did anyone else see the dog attack your cat?" I looked at Elaine. "What about you?"

She looked down at her hands and didn't answer. Which told me quite a lot.

"Are you suggesting I'm lying?" Marty said, jumping up from the sofa so fast that the cat landed on the floor. And, of course, hissed at him some more.

"Nobody calls me a liar! Not in my own house or anywhere else!" He loomed over me, his face red and the veins in his neck pulsating. "You're sitting in my chair. Get up and get out. If I see anything I've told you on the Snitch, I'll sue you." He scooped up Princess Piggy and cuddled her to his chest. This time, the cat didn't seem to mind. In fact, I could swear she was smirking.

Chapter 22

Give a man a fish and he eats for a day. Teach him to fish and you can get rid of him for the whole weekend.

"You certainly provided me with an interesting way to end the day," Deanna said, pulling into my driveway behind another car. "That man is a little unhinged about his precious cat."

I realized the other car was Jenny's. *Please don't let this mean she and Mark had another fight. What would I do if she told me they were getting a divorce? OMG, poor CJ, growing up being ferried back and forth between his parents, not knowing where his primary home was. Jim and I would have to step in. Although, we could put an addition on the house and Jenny and CJ could live with us. What a wonderful idea!*

Deanna prodded me, bringing me back from my worst-best-case fantasy scenario. "We're here and I'm hungry. If it's okay with you, I want to go home and have my dinner and we can compare notes another time." When I didn't respond, Deanna poked me again. "Carol, I'm talking to you. Didn't you hear me?"

"Sorry, I was thinking of something else. Thanks so much for coming with me. And you're right about that man. He's a little obsessed about Princess Piggy. If I didn't have you as a witness, nobody would believe me. I just wish I had a picture of that damn cat in all her glory."

Deanna waved her phone. "I took a few. I'll email them to you later tonight."

"Great," I said, relieved. I gave her hand a quick squeeze. "Maybe we can talk tomorrow. And thanks again."

I ordered myself to take several deep breaths before I faced my family. If something was really wrong, my getting upset about it (in advance!) wasn't going to do anybody any good.

Courage, Carol!

Imagine my surprise (and relief) when Jenny greeted me at the kitchen door with a smile on her face and a sleeping CJ in her arms. "Surprise! Mark's working late again and CJ was a little fussy. I thought a car ride might calm him down, and figured a visit with my favorite parents would calm me down." She kissed the most beautiful grandbaby in the world on the top of his head, then kissed me. "It worked for both of us!"

I let out the breath I didn't realize I'd been holding and laughed. "You know we're always glad to see you, sweetie. Have you eaten? Where's your father? Did he tell you about our little adventure today?"

"The one you two shared?" Jenny asked, cradling CJ carefully as she made herself comfortable at the kitchen table. "Or the one you just had? I can tell by the look on your face that you've just been up to something you don't want Daddy to know about."

Busted. My darling daughter knew me far too well.

Not wanting to involve Jenny in any way, although I knew she'd find my recent encounter with Princess Piggy hilarious, I fell back on one of my favorite tactics and immediately changed the subject. "You look uncomfortable holding CJ that way. I have a surprise for you. Come into the bedroom and see what I bought this week."

"Does Daddy know you've been shopping?" Jenny asked as she followed me. "Or did you...? Oh, wow, Mom! It's a porta crib.

What a great idea!"

"And you thought I was going to show you a new outfit I bought and had to sneak into the house so your father wouldn't find out," I said, grinning. "I bought the crib for purely selfish reasons. Since CJ now has his own bed here, I'm hoping we can have lots and lots of sleepovers. And, yes, this was a Jim Andrews-approved purchase."

Jenny gave me a big kiss. "Thanks, Mom. This is so great. Let's try it out and see how he likes it."

Miraculously, CJ didn't utter a peep as Jenny lowered him into the porta crib. "I'll leave the door open, in case he wakes up," she whispered as we tiptoed out of the room.

"Let's see if your father left me any dinner," I said, continuing my efforts to halt Jenny's curious questions about my most recent adventure. There was no way I'd take a chance and confide in her again, risking possible backlash from Mark. Being a mother-in-law often involved navigating tricky waters, especially for someone with a big mouth and an even bigger imagination, like me.

"To answer your first question, Mom, Dad's on his computer working on something for Mike. We'd Skyped him a little while ago so he could see his nephew. Mike had some financial questions, and Dad offered to help by doing some research. You know how he loves doing that."

I felt a pang in my heart. I'd missed the chance to connect with my only son because I'd been nosing around playing detective again, inserting myself into other people's business. Which was probably the Good Lord's not-too-subtle way of telling me I should try minding my *own* business more often.

Oh, get over yourself, Carol. Even you can't have everything. Stop being so selfish. It's not like the rest of the family plotted to deliberately exclude you. It just happened.

"When CJ and I got here, I hadn't had any supper. I confess that I had a few bites of yours. I did save some for you, though. I hope that was okay."

"Honey, of course it's okay. You need to keep up your strength to nurse CJ. No skimping on meals for you. If you're still hungry, feel free to finish my share, too. I can always find something else to eat."

Jenny patted her tummy. "Thanks but no thanks to any more of Maria's yummy food. I'm trying to lose the weight I gained when I was pregnant. Now," she pulled out a kitchen chair and gestured me to sit down, "it's time for you to quit stalling and tell me what you've been up to. Don't try to deny it, either. You've got that gleam in your eye that I know all too well. I'll heat up your dinner and you talk."

"You must be practicing for when CJ gets older and does something naughty," I said. "I can tell already that he won't be able to put anything over on you."

"You're stalling again," Jenny said.

"Yes, I am," I admitted. Being bossed around by my own flesh and blood was a new experience for me. Except for you-know-who, and he only thinks he's in charge.

"Okay, here goes. I've got to make this quick, though, in case your father walks in." I proceeded to give Jenny the highlights of my adventure with Deanna. She didn't look the least bit surprised at how I made the snap decision to "interrogate" Marty and his wife. Grinned when I told her about the Fairport Snitch. And laughed out loud when I got to the part about Princess Piggy.

"I can't believe anyone would spoil an animal so much," Jenny said. "Present company excepted, of course." Lucy and Ethel had stationed themselves in their favorite spot, under the kitchen table, in case any morsel of food happened to drop their way. Jenny gave each dog a quick pat. "You two are the undisputed queens around here. We only live to fill your food bowls."

Lucy licked her hand, then gave me a reproachful look. I guess I didn't measure up to Her Majesty's demanding standards as well as my daughter did.

Jenny's expression turned serious, and she shifted in her chair. *Uh, oh. Here it comes. Brace yourself for some bad news, Carol. And whatever you do, for Pete's sake, let her talk and don't interrupt.*

"I really came tonight because I need your advice about something. I wanted to bring it up last night, but then I chickened out. I may be wrong. It may not be true. But it may be. I don't know. Why is this so hard?" She started to cry. "I just hope Daddy doesn't come in the kitchen now and hear me. I don't want him to know. He won't understand."

Oh, my God. This must be worse than I imagined. And you all know what an active imagination I have!

I grabbed her hands. "Honey, you can tell me anything. I promise, I won't breathe a word to anybody, even your father. Is it about you? Are you sick?"

"No, Mom," Jenny said, her eyes now swimming with tears. "It's Mark."

"Mark?" I repeated, trying to comprehend how my straight-as-an-arrow, play-by-the-rules son-in-law could do anything that would upset Jenny this much. I prayed there hadn't been another argument. I knew how sleep-deprived young parents can be, and that can make every situation worse than it actually is.

"I can't tell you anything else," Jenny said. "Forget what I said. Everything's okay." She jumped up from her chair. "I have to get CJ and go home. I shouldn't have come."

"Now you listen to me, young lady," I said in my most "don't mess with me" tone of voice, "you're not going anywhere until you tell me what's going on."

"That's the problem, Mom," Jenny said, her eyes threatening to spill over. "I don't know what's going on. Mark claims that he and Paul are working on a top-secret case that nobody else in the department is supposed to know about. He's been out most nights, and when I called him at the station, the dispatcher said they weren't listed on the duty roster. What if he made up a story about a top-secret case and he's really having an affair? Paul could be covering for him."

Oh, for heaven's sake. My darling daughter had inherited one of my least attractive personality traits—jumping to conclusions. I knew I had to stop her train of thought right away, before she confronted Mark with her suspicions (which I was sure were completely wrong) and things got even worse between them.

"The fact that Mark wasn't on the duty roster when you called makes perfect sense because he and Paul are on a top-secret assignment," I pointed out. "You realize that, don't you, honey? Please don't jump to any conclusions. Whenever I do that, I always regret it later." I was exaggerating to make Jenny feel better, of course. I rarely regret my rush to judgment, because more times than not I'm right and everyone else is wrong. Just sayin'.

I took a bite of the ossobuco, which was now cold. Yum. It was just as delicious this way as it was piping hot. Who knew?

"Mark is so completely bonkers about you that the idea of him having an affair is absolutely ridiculous," I continued. "So why don't we put our heads together and try to figure out what top-secret assignment he and Paul could be working on?"

I know. I know. I had no business trying to nose into my son-in-law's official business. But my daughter's happiness was at stake, so how could I not jump in and help her? And if Mark had a problem with that, too bad.

"I do know there's been an upswing in petty thefts, break-ins, and domestic abuse cases recently," Jenny said. "There are more drug overdoses than ever, and people are dying. The department is short-staffed because of additional budget cuts, and they're dealing with so much."

My goodness. It sounded like Fairport was in the middle of a crime wave. I made a silent promise to be sure that all the windows and doors in the house were locked before we turned in for the night. "Should your father and I worry about being mugged on Fairport Turnpike?" At Jenny's startled expression, I added, "Only kidding." *I hope.*

"Here I go again, talking about confidential police business with you after Mark told me not to," Jenny said, looking miserable. "But I have to talk to somebody or I'll spend all day and all night crying and worrying. And some of these things do make the local paper or Fairport Patch, so they're public knowledge. Anybody who monitors police calls can easily find out what's going on."

"Like my dear neighbor Phyllis Stevens," I said, laughing. "I can't count the number of times I've seen her at her picture window with binoculars. She claims she's taken up bird-watching, but I don't believe that for a single second."

"Neighbors can be tough," Jenny said, returning my thoughts to my earlier visit with Mary Pat Ryan's nutty one. "I guess Mark and I are lucky that people come and go so often in our condo complex that we rarely have time to get to know them. Not that we're unfriendly. We're just...what did you used to call it? Supermarket friendly. A quick hello or a smile, and that's it."

"How about if we work backwards to try and figure out what's going on with Mark?" I suggested. "Do you remember when he first mentioned this top-secret assignment? Maybe if we can figure out what was going on in town then, that will get us somewhere. But don't tell me anything you're uncomfortable with. How does that sound?"

I had a sudden brainstorm. "Do you think this top-secret assignment could have anything to do with Mary Pat's hit-and-run accident? Nobody's been arrested yet, right? And what about her dog?"

Jenny looked surprised. "Everything's fine now and the police are releasing Harriet as soon as they can find her a new home. Mark explained everything to me yesterday, and I insisted he tell you right away. He said he called you."

OMG. Did my son-in-law and I have a conversation that I'd forgotten about? Maybe I was losing my memory. At my age (and it's none of your business what age that is), I worry about that a lot. I confess there are more and more times I walk into a room and completely forget the reason why I went in there. Bet that happens to some of you, too. But don't worry, I won't ask you to share. But to forget a conversation about something this important was a major cause for alarm. Maybe it was time to schedule that physical I'd been procrastinating about for months. A doctor should be able to test for memory loss, right?

"Do me a favor and remind me about the specifics," I said as calmly as I could. "You know how crazy things have been around here. Sometimes I wish I had a delete button in my mind so I could get rid of all the unnecessary stuff I stress about and concentrate on the important things."

"I feel the same way," Jenny assured me. "I bet you were glad when Mark told you that the person who'd been sending threats to Mary Pat Ryan about her dog was finally found."

"Threats?" I repeated. "I don't know anything about threats."

You're really losing it, Carol. Call the doctor first thing in the morning to schedule an appointment. Tell the office it's an emergency.

"That's weird," Jenny said. "Maybe you forgot."

She stopped herself and her eyes filled with tears again. "Or maybe the conversation with you is another thing Mark hasn't been honest with me about. He could have lied to me about this, too."

Oh, no. This was getting way out of control.

"Stop this behavior right now, young lady," I said. "It's entirely possible I did forget. So fill me in now, and dry your eyes." I handed Jenny a paper napkin, which she balled up in her fist.

"You're right. I'm being stupid. Let me tell you what I know without being emotional." Jenny took a deep breath. "Before the hit-and-run accident, Mary Pat had been receiving anonymous letters threatening her and her dog. Remember, Harriet is a valuable show dog and was insured for thousands of dollars. That's why Paul Wheeler took her to live with him right after Mary Pat died, to protect her."

"You're kidding," I said, trying to wrap my head around this new information. "You mean there were threats to harm Harriet? And Mary Pat?"

"Yes, Mom. The police found several letters when they searched Mary Pat's home after the accident. She hadn't reported the threats, which was a big mistake on her part. The police thought the person who was sending the letters was also the hit-and-run driver."

"I'm shocked," I said. "But fascinated. What happened next?" I thanked my lucky stars that Deanna and I were able to beat a hasty retreat from Marty's house without being attacked.

I suddenly realized I'd done it again. Despite my good intentions, I was encouraging Jenny to share what was probably confidential police business with me.

Smarty pants that she is, Jenny saw the expression on my face. "It's okay, Mom. Mark wanted you to know about this."

Thank goodness.

"So, did Mark and Paul zero in on Mary Pat's neighbor as a prime suspect?"

"Right away," Jenny confirmed. "He may be a little unbalanced when it comes to his precious cat, as you saw tonight, but Marty had an alibi for the hit-and-run accident. He and his wife were at a relative's funeral in Chicago when it happened."

"But what about the threatening letters?"

Before Jenny could answer, I was conscious of my dear husband standing over me, scaring me to death. "Mind if I join this conversation?" he asked.

"Why do you always sneak up on me like that?" I snapped.

"Maybe I'm not the only one in this family whose hearing is going," Jim said.

Humph.

"Have a seat, Dad," Jenny said, before I had a chance to respond to Jim's goading with one of my usual zingers. I was relieved to see that she was calmer now. Or maybe she was just putting up a brave front so Jim wouldn't suspect how upset she was. He hates to see his little girl cry.

"What's this about an alibi?" Jim asked. "I hope it's not you."

I looked down at my hands, because I knew what was coming next. "Are you meddling again, Carol? Don't we have enough to do working on Donna Trumbull's campaign? I only agreed to help out because I thought that would keep you out of trouble for a while. At least until Election Day."

Double humph. Now I was really angry.

"Oh, wait a minute. I think I get it," Jim said. "Marty is Mary Pat Ryan's neighbor, right? And for a while, the police thought he was the person writing threatening letters about her dog. Am I right?"

"You're right, Dad," Jenny said. "But how did you know?"

"Mark called yesterday and told me about the threatening letters Mary Pat Ryan was getting," Jim said. "He suggested we insure Lucy and Ethel, because they're also pure bred dogs, in case someone decided to go after them. I didn't tell you, Carol, because I didn't want to plant any outlandish ideas in your head. He said the police had traced the source of the letters to a rival dog breeder, who was trying to intimidate Mary Pat so she would stop showing her dog. Lucy and Ethel aren't show dogs, so there's no reason to insure them. I never knew dog shows could be so vicious."

Knowing Jim, he also didn't mention Mark's call to me because he didn't want to spend the money that pet insurance would cost. But at least I knew now that I hadn't forgotten such an important conversation. I'd never had it in the first place.

"Mark also told me...." Jim clamped his lips shut. "I can't tell you about that. You'll find out eventually. But I'm glad Mark knows that he can trust me with sensitive police business."

Jenny and I sat there in angry, bonded silence. I knew she was mad that Mark had talked to Jim about confidential police business when she'd been forbidden to do the exact same thing with me. And I was mad because Jim hadn't told me about Mark's phone call until he absolutely had to.

Switching conversational gears with warp speed that rivaled my own, Jim added, "Mike sends his love. He's sorry he didn't have a chance to talk to you, Carol. And Donna Trumbull wants you to organize a kickoff rally for her campaign this weekend."

"Anything else, *dear*?" I asked, hoping that, this time, my frequently clueless husband caught the sarcasm dripping from my voice.

Jim shook his head. "Nope. That's all." He yawned. "I'm beat. This has been a busy day. I'm going to bed."

Jenny was up in a flash. "Wait a minute, Dad. CJ's asleep in your bedroom and I don't want to wake him. He was extra fussy for most of the day."

"Fine. Let me know when the coast is clear," Jim said, being agreeable for once. "I'll watch the Weather Channel for a while."

I waited until I was sure Jim was safely out of earshot, then proceeded to give my daughter some wifely advice. "I know you're angry, sweetheart. So am I. But I know from years of experience that the best way to handle this kind of situation is to get a good night's sleep, and then look at the situation again in the morning."

"But, Mom...."

"No buts, young lady. Believe me, I know what I'm talking about. If CJ's sleeping soundly, with any luck you'll be able to get him home and in his crib without him waking up."

"But...."

"We'll talk tomorrow," I said, pushing my daughter toward the bedroom and my sleeping grandchild. "Mother knows best."

Once I sent a still protesting Jenny and sleeping CJ on their way, I stored the remnants of my dinner in the refrigerator for tomorrow, had a low-fat yogurt, took a quick shower, and managed to climb into bed and fall into a deep sleep before Jim and his snoring could join me. Which is why I missed three texts—one from Jenny, another from Sister Rose, and a third from Maria— telling me someone had been arrested for Mary Pat's hit-and-run accident.

Chapter 23

The secret to happiness is good health, good friends, and an awesome sense of humor.

What a pleasure to wake up from a good night's sleep feeling alert and refreshed. A gift to myself that didn't cost me (or Jim) a single cent. Note to self: Resolve to get to bed earlier than husband and dogs as often as possible.

I was brushing my teeth when I noticed my phone, perched precariously on the edge of the sink. I'd left it charging in the bathroom last night, but I'd never put it so close to the edge that it could easily fall and get damaged. And, since I didn't do it, and the dogs aren't tall enough to reach the top of the sink, that left only one other possibility. An additional item on my list of things to "discuss" with Jim, should I so choose. He's always moving my things around, and yet he gets mad at me if I should innocently do the same thing. Presto—my good mood evaporated, just like that.

Sighing, I unplugged the phone and apologized for any ill treatment it had received from you-know-who. I've found it's a good idea to keep on my phone's good side, so when I need it in a hurry, it's always there for me. It's possible that I'm atoning for the time, years ago, when I lost the darn thing for several days, and my carelessness contributed to Jim's almost being arrested for murder.

I usually start my day by checking the latest news on my phone while enjoying my first cup of coffee. But today, I had other things on my mind as I marched into the kitchen. The other half of my marriage sat at the kitchen table wearing his favorite ripped sweatshirt, his unshaven face partially hidden behind the local paper. Without speaking, he acknowledged my presence by pushing a thermal mug of coffee, lid on to keep it hot, in my direction.

It's hard to be mad at a guy like that. But not impossible.

"Thank you," I said, acknowledging his attempt to get on my good side.

"I figured we'd have a special breakfast today," he said, folding the paper carefully so the front page was visible to me. "Do you want to go out to celebrate at the Fairport Diner? You know how you love their omelets."

I had no idea what Jim was talking about, but in my current mood, I was loathe to admit it. What did we have to celebrate? And why was Jim grinning at me that way?

Stalling for time, I grabbed the paper and the pair of cheater specs I now keep handy. The banner headline across the top of the front page was big enough for me to read even without them. **SUSPECT ARRESTED IN HIT-AND-RUN ACCIDENT by Jim Andrews. Exclusive to the _Fairport News_.**

"The police actually found the driver? That's wonderful. I can't believe it." Tears of joy pricked my eyes. "How did you get the exclusive story?"

"Mark," Jim answered. "I wanted to tell you last night, but I couldn't until the news officially broke in the paper. He and I made a deal that, when an arrest was made in the hit-and-run, I'd get the story first for the local paper. Naturally, he checked with his boss first to be sure it was okay. He got the go-ahead this one time. It'll probably never happen again."

"I'm so relieved someone has finally been arrested. Mary Pat will get the justice she deserves."

"I hope you're right, Carol." Jim's face was troubled. "The police have a confession, but despite that, it doesn't sound like they have a very strong case. A lot of the guy's story doesn't make sense. I wonder if he had legal counsel before he pled guilty."

"Honestly, Jim, you know that if Mark was involved in the arrest, the driver would have been read his Miranda rights and offered the chance for legal representation. He obviously declined. His conscience was probably killing him. I know mine would be if I'd ever done anything so heinous."

"I guess you're right. I'm not a crime reporter, but since Mark gave me the exclusive, I was the only one who could write the story. The tight deadline to make today's paper was too much for me. I'd rather concentrate on my weekly column. And, to tell you the truth, I feel sorry for the driver. He's very young, and he doesn't speak English very well. He must be scared to death."

This was too much. "Wait a minute," I said, glaring at my husband. "Are you telling me that you feel sorry for a person who mowed down an innocent woman who was just out taking her dog for a walk? And as if that wasn't bad enough, he then drove away and left her to die without trying to help her? You can't be serious."

"Don't blow your top at me," Jim said, looking defensive. "I don't know why I feel so uneasy about the way the case wrapped itself up in a nice little bow after so long. Maybe I'm tired, and that could be affecting my judgment. After I filed the story last night, I was wide awake. Instead of coming to bed and waking you up, I tried to snooze in the recliner." He rubbed his neck. "And got a pain in my neck. Maybe we can go out to eat later. Right now, I'm going to bed. I hope some sleep will clear my head."

I kept my mouth shut, for once. Now I knew why I'd gotten such a good night's sleep, and I felt a little guilty about it. I was also probably the person who'd left my phone in such a precarious position on the bathroom sink.

"And for heaven's sake, contact Donna Trumbull right away," Jim said. "She called four times last night after you turned in, wanting to talk about this kickoff rally. You'd think she was running for president, instead of town council."

"It's important to her," I said, automatically rising to the defense of another woman. "And she's a late entry in the race.

She needs to make up for lost time."

"I suppose," Jim said, not looking convinced.

"Yesterday afternoon you were all hot to get her elected," I reminded him. "Today, you're brushing her off like lint."

"Not true," Jim said. "I thought about the meeting at her house while you were out doing heaven knows what with Deanna." He looked at me over his glasses, which had slid down on his nose. I knew he was waiting for me to fill him in on what we'd been up to, which I had no intention of doing. I just sat there, mute, and sipped my coffee.

Finally catching on that I wasn't going to respond, Jim continued, "I realized that I was horning in and taking over, something you always accuse me of doing. I decided to step back and let you run Donna's campaign. It'll be a good learning experience for you. But I'll be here, ready to step in and help you, whenever you need me. How does that sound?"

"That sounds fine to me, as long as you're sure," I said, trying to mask my surprise (and relief) at Jim's sudden change of attitude. After almost forty years of marriage, I knew Jim had the best of intentions, but he wouldn't be able to resist horning in and "helping" me for very long. I held out my coffee mug. "Right now, you can help by pouring me more coffee. I need a lot more caffeine before I talk with Donna."

"Carol, it's about time I heard back from you. If we're going to work together, you need to know that I must be able to reach you twenty-four/seven. No exceptions."

It had been quite a while since somebody talked that way to me, and I wasn't going to let Donna get away with it. Even Sister Rose didn't use that tone of voice with me. Not often, anyway.

I opened my mouth to set the record straight, without losing my temper, but before I could utter a single syllable, Donna said, "Hold on." The next thing I heard was her berating someone I assumed was an employee about the way a truck was being loaded.

"Sorry for all that, Carol," she said in a more reasonable tone. "I'm having trouble getting orders out today and I'm taking it out on you. We have two new drivers starting, and my warehouse manager is out sick. I have to supervise everyone all by myself, and it's frustrating."

I was mollified. Slightly.

"I understand that you have a private life and family responsibilities," Donna continued. "I hope you'll be able to give the amount of time and attention to my campaign that I need to win the election. It's my first foray into politics, and I'm not good at losing." She laughed. "I suppose nobody really is."

I let that comment slide, and instead chose to focus on something positive. "Did you see this morning's paper about the hit-and-run driver being arrested?"

"Of course I did, Carol. That's why I've been so frantic to reach you. What a lucky break to have the police finally arrest the driver. The timing is absolutely perfect."

"The timing is perfect? I don't understand. Perfect for what?"

"Why, for my campaign, of course. Since pedestrian safety will be my major campaign issue, we can capitalize on how the police finally got their man, and also remind voters how senseless that accident was. An innocent woman, out walking her dog, mowed down at a pedestrian crosswalk and the cowardly driver speeding away. Why, it almost sounds like the beginning of a movie, doesn't it? Oh, I just love it. Don't you?"

"I don't feel comfortable exploiting the tragic death of—"

"We're not exploiting anything, Carol. It's a fact. The hit-and-run accident actually happened. A woman died. Although...maybe it would make more of an impression on voters if we recreated the accident and used it for a campaign commercial to promote pedestrian safety. I wonder how much that would cost? Maybe you could find that out. Would Jim know? And we'd have to find a dog to use. Maybe one of yours?"

Are you out of your mind? I didn't really say that out loud, of course. "I think that's in very poor taste," I said, finally finding my voice.

"I don't agree," Donna said in an icy tone. "I run commercials for Mrs. T's Tasty Treats all the time. What's the difference? The baked goods are a product I want to sell, so I pay actors to convince people to buy them. This time, I want to win an election, and I'm the product I want people to buy. I mean, vote for. There's nothing wrong with my paying actors to convince people to vote for me. Those election commercials are all show business, anyway. Everybody knows that. I'm sure that most of the perfect-looking so-called families of the candidates are really hired actors."

"I don't think that's true," I said.

"Maybe I'm wrong about that," Donna said. "But we're getting off the main subject, which is my own campaign commercial."

"You wouldn't want to show the actual accident, would you?" I asked.

"Of course not, Carol. What a silly question. Besides, I doubt we could find an actress willing to play the part of someone being hit by a car, don't you agree? Although..." she paused for a beat, "I suppose we could hire a stunt woman."

"If you plan to hire someone to portray Mary Pat Ryan being hit and killed by a car, count me out," I said. "I want no part of it. It's becoming apparent that you've picked the wrong person to run your campaign. You've already made up your mind about what you want to do and what I think is obviously irrelevant." I was itching to add some colorful language to emphasize my point, but held back because I am a polite, well-mannered woman, known for impeccable social graces under the most trying circumstances. Just ask any of my friends, and they'll tell you the same thing.

"Please tell me you don't mean that," Donna said, sounding panicky. "I'm used to ordering people around in order to get things done in business, and I realize now that I'm using the same tactics on you. It's not intentional, believe me. I really do value your opinion, and I've been told by many in Fairport that your organizational and people skills are superb. Please speak your mind any time you want. Just promise that you won't leave the campaign. I really need your help. I want to honor the memory of Mary Pat Ryan and protect the citizens of Fairport from a senseless accident like hers."

I had to hand it to Donna. Her impassioned plea was like a sledgehammer blow to my most vulnerable spot—my emotions. If she gave speeches this powerful during the campaign, she'd have every woman in Fairport lining up to support her. Heck, she'd probably convince people to sell their homes in neighboring towns and move here. I made a mental note to check out that thought with Nancy, to see if she thought other Realtors could be approached with that pitch. Despite my mixed feelings, I was beginning to get excited again about being involved in a campaign that could change my town for the better.

"I could tell from yesterday's campaign meeting how simpatico you and I are," Donna continued. "I saw you shooting daggers at your husband when he took over the meeting and effectively cut you out of the conversation. But you didn't let him get away with it. You spoke up and took control right back. I was proud of you for that. You're really a lot like me. I didn't let my husband push me around, either, although he certainly tried to on enough occasions. Then my problem was solved. Conveniently and permanently. Maybe you'll solve your problem the same way."

Before I had a chance to ask her what the heck she was talking about, Donna said, "One thing we haven't discussed yet is your salary, Carol."

Salary? I'm going to be paid for this? Holy cow. I figured I was signing on for another volunteer job.

"Do you have a dollar figure in mind?" Donna continued. "I understand it's hard for you to put a price tag on all the work you're prepared to do to help me win this election. So why don't we say...." And she mentioned a sum that would keep me in designer duds for the next year. Lucy and Ethel, too.

In a daze, I said, "That's fine, Donna."

"Great. I'll email you a contract to sign so it'll be all nice and legal, along with a list of tasks for you to start on immediately. I've already requested a permit to use the Town Hall green near the gazebo for my kickoff rally next Saturday. Your first job is to contact Sister Rose and get the list of women who attended the memorial service. We want to recruit them as volunteers as soon as possible."

The next thing I heard was the dial tone.

"Donna Trumbull needs a lesson in personal relationships," I said to a snoozing Lucy and Ethel. "Barking orders isn't the way to get me to do her bidding, even if she's paying me."

Lucy gave me a disdainful look, reminding me loud and clear that barking orders has always worked for her. "Present company excluded, of course."

I checked my phone again and read the texts I'd missed, which now numbered eight, including Nancy, Claire, Mary Alice, and Deanna. (I shouldn't have to tell you that Sister Rose and Maria had texted me twice.) I realized that my next step had to be gathering my posse together, ostensibly to celebrate the arrest of the hit-and-run driver. But my ulterior motive, of course, would be to recruit everybody as volunteers for Donna Trumbull's campaign.

I was feeling a little guilty about exploiting my friends that way when another text from Maria arrived. It was short and to the point, reminding me of the ones I frequently receive from the not-so-fun nun.

10:30 A.M. mandatory meeting here 2day. See you then.

Chapter 24

I have good news and bad news. The good news is that I have everything I had thirty years ago. The bad news is that it's a lot lower now.

"I never thought I'd see this day," Maria said. "I know everyone here is as happy as I am that Mary Pat's hit-and-run driver has finally been arrested. If there's any justice in this world, he'll be in jail for a long time for his cowardly act. But his fate will be decided by a jury, not me." She pointed to a tray of freshly baked biscotti in the center of the table. "This is the best I could do to celebrate on such short notice. I really wanted to serve prosecco, but I figured it was a little early in the day for that. There's also cappuccino and regular coffee. Please, help yourselves."

"You don't have to ask me twice," Nancy said. "I just came from the gym and I'm starving." She broke a biscotti into four pieces and offered me the three biggest ones. Weakling that I am, I grabbed them all and immediately popped one in my mouth. So, sue me. It was a crazy morning and I was hungry, too.

Sister Rose, true to form, declined any of the refreshments and got right to the point. "Maria, dear," she said, "everyone here feels the same way you do, and this is a cause for celebration. But..." she checked her watch, "in order to be here this morning, I had to call additional volunteers to cover the thrift shop while I was gone. Perhaps I could take some biscotti with me, as a thank you for them. I really should get back. If there's anything I need to know, you can always send me a text."

"Please, Sister, don't leave yet," Maria said. "We have other business to discuss, and you're an important part of the discussion." She beckoned to me. "Carol, you should be sitting at the head of the table. Even though I called this meeting, it's really your show."

Oh, I finally got it. Maria had taken the burden of calling the first volunteer recruitment meeting for me, figuring that I'd be uncomfortable with my sudden mantle of responsibility. And she was right. The only ones in my life I give orders to are Lucy and Ethel, and they usually ignore me.

But this time, I was emboldened by the realization that I had actually been hired—for money!—by someone who believed in my professional ability to get the job done. Not that I planned to share the news of my newfound riches with any of my friends. They'd probably think I was exaggerating, anyway.

"I'm fine where I am, thanks," I said. I was self-conscious about the spotlight suddenly shining on me, even though everyone in the room was someone I considered a friend. (Even Sister Rose under most circumstances, which shows how far I've come on my road to mature adulthood.)

I cleared my throat, unsure how to begin.

"For heaven's sake, Carol," Nancy said, "I'm on a strict timetable like Sister Rose. I have a house showing at noon, and I have to get home, shower, and figure out what to wear. So, what's going on?"

"Is this an idea about improving pedestrian safety in Fairport?" Mary Alice asked. "No matter what crazy scheme you have in mind, count me in."

"It's not a crazy scheme at all," I said. "Maria and I were invited to Donna Trumbull's home yesterday to start organizing her campaign for town council. Her primary issue is making our town safer for pedestrians. She's asked Maria and me to start recruiting volunteers to spread her message and help get her elected. So, are you all in?"

"Carol's just being modest," Maria said. "Although I was included in yesterday's meeting, Donna's asked Carol to run her campaign. We're all going to help, any way we can. Right?"

"I agree that pedestrian safety is an important issue," Claire said, looking troubled. "But before I agree to sign on to anybody's campaign, I need to know more about the candidate I'm supporting."

"Spoken like the wife of a lawyer," I said. "So, what do you want to know?"

"For starters, what's her background? What's her political affiliation? Has she been involved in any local organizations? All I know is that she and her husband started a bakery business, he died, and she took it over. That's not enough for her to win my vote. I doubt it's enough to win anyone's."

I realized I didn't know the answers to any of these questions. I shot Maria a panicked look, and fortunately, she stepped in and saved me from looking ignorant. "That information is certainly important, and I'm sure Carol will prepare a biography of Donna for everyone to read. But what's even more important for me, is that Donna Trumbull *cares*. She cares about our town and she wants to do everything she can to make it a safer place for all of us to live in. And walk in. When she heard about the memorial service for Mary Pat, she contacted me and offered to provide all the baked goods free of charge. In fact, a lot of the other items that were served that day were provided by her company. Even though the Trattoria is a restaurant, I was grateful for the extra help. It took a big burden off of me."

"I think it's important for women to be represented on our town council," Mary Alice said.

"Mary Alice is right," Sister Rose said. "As the council is currently configured, all the members are men. If Donna Trumbull doesn't run, all the candidates will be men, too. Women's voices need to be heard. There are so many issues in addition to pedestrian safety that are being ignored. Domestic violence is another one. I can't count the number of times I've approached the town for some small grant for the domestic violence program the thrift shop supports and been turned down. The shop is an important revenue stream for our program, but we need much more financial support to keep serving our clients. The number of victims who come to us for help is increasing rapidly. We're in a real crisis, and if we don't get help, we may have to close our doors." She looked at me. "Count me in to help you on Donna's campaign. Tell me what you want me to do."

Wow. I couldn't have asked for a better endorsement if I'd planned it myself.

"It's our time, and this is our opportunity to make a real difference in Fairport," Sister Rose added, looking around the table. "Donna Trumbull is willing to take up an important cause. So, are we all going to help her?"

And, just like that, I had the first campaign volunteers.

I sat back in my chair and relaxed, happy to have Sister Rose take over the meeting, because I knew that she'd be a lot more successful getting everyone on board than I'd be. I pushed back the niggling feeling of guilt that crept into my mind, reminding me that she was doing my job, for which I was being handsomely paid.

Funny how you don't seem to mind Sister Rose taking over, when yesterday you were mad at Jim for doing the exact same thing. I made a mental note to think about that later, once the campaign was over. Or not.

"I have the list of alumni who were invited to Mary Pat Ryan's memorial service," Nancy announced. "I think we should use that list to start recruiting more volunteers."

I sat up straighter in my chair. It was one thing to have Sister Rose take over my job, but quite another to have my BFF, who was, after all, a peer, take charge. "I have that list too, Nancy," I said.

Ignoring me completely, Nancy continued, "Before we begin contacting other people, I think the list needs to be pared down to people who actually live in Fairport. They're the ones who'll be voting in the election, after all."

"I don't agree," Claire said. "Anyone can volunteer in the campaign, whether they live here or not. Anyone can help spread the word and, even more important, contribute financially to

Donna's campaign. Larry says a candidate needs lawn signs and handouts, all of which have to be printed. Plus a webpage that looks professional, which needs to be constantly updated. Maybe even a billboard or two on major roads. Email addresses have to be collected, too, in order to build a mailing list. That's a lot of work. We'll have to hire people to get those jobs done, and it'll cost a lot of money. So Donna's committee," Claire gestured around the table, "meaning *us*, will have to raise money, too."

At the mention of money, everyone started talking at once. "I'm not comfortable at all asking people for money," Mary Alice said, looking troubled. "I'm happy to do some canvassing and hand out flyers, but I draw the line at asking people to donate. If I have to do that, I'm resigning right now. Sorry, Carol. Nothing personal."

Time to take control back, Carol, before there's a mutiny and everybody walks out.

I stood and willed myself to appear taller than my current height of 5 feet 2 inches. Grabbing a teaspoon, I banged it against my coffee cup. "Let's try and discuss this rationally. First things first."

I could have heard a snort coming from Claire's direction, and a muttered, "That'll be a first." But, on the other hand, I could be mistaken. Either way, I refused to allow that to deter me. I had a brief vision of Jim checking our bank balance online (as he does on a daily basis) and finding a hefty deposit from Donna Trumbull added to our checking account, earning me huge kudos from my surprised husband. Onward!

"Don't worry about raising money," I said, taking a huge leap of faith and praying that I was right. "Donna is funding her own campaign. She's so committed to making Fairport a safer place for everybody that she's investing her own money in its future."

"Why didn't you make that clear in the first place, Carol?" Claire asked.

"I'm making it clear now, and that's all that counts," I said, giving her an icy look. "Now, let's get down to business without any further interruptions. The first thing we have to do is be sure

Donna's name gets on the ballot," I continued, speaking with the confidence my about-to-be-increased bank balance gave me. "We have to collect a certain number of signatures to make that happen. We don't want her to be a write-in candidate. That'll doom her candidacy before it has a chance to get off the ground."

Claire nodded her head. "That makes sense. So, how do we make that happen?"

"Good question," I said. "According to our town charter, a thousand signatures from registered Fairport voters are needed to get a candidate's name on an election ballot. All of those signatures must be certified as genuine by the town clerk's office. In case some signatures can't be validated, we need to collect fifteen hundred, just to be on the safe side."

I looked around the table. "That's where the list from the memorial service will come in handy. We need as many people as possible to canvass the town collecting signatures. Are you with me so far?"

"I guess so," Nancy said. "I'm certainly willing to canvass for signatures. And who knows?" she added with a mischievous grin. "Maybe I'll pick up a new real estate listing while I'm at it."

Now it was Sister Rose's turn to look troubled. "I don't think that's such a good idea," she said. "It's like mixing apples and oranges, if you'll forgive me using an old cliché."

"I agree with Sister Rose," I said, ignoring a dirty look from Nancy. "For all we know, that might be illegal. A conflict of interest. But..." I paused as a brilliant idea popped into my mind, "maybe you could wear your Realtor badge while you're collecting signatures. That way, people would know who you are and what you do. And they could follow up with you at a later date if they wanted."

"That's perfect," Nancy said. "I'll just have to be sure I'm wearing an outfit that coordinates with my badge. I wouldn't want to clash."

Heaven forbid.

Maria raised her hand. "I have a suggestion to throw into the mix," she said. "How about if we have t-shirts made with Donna's name and something about pedestrian safety to wear when we're collecting signatures?"

"A uniform," Mary Alice said, smiling at Sister Rose. "Just like the old days at Mount Saint Francis."

"That's fine, as long as I get to pick the colors," Nancy said. "Dream Homes Realty colors are green, blue and white. I'm not sure what the exact names of the colors are, though. I'll find out and let you know before you order the shirts, Carol."

Give me a break. Now we were veering off into a discussion of campaign fashion. How I wished I'd learned to whistle with my fingers, the way people do in New York when they want to hail a cab. Sadly, my education skipped any kind of activities that weren't considered "ladylike." I banged my spoon on my coffee cup again to get the group under control, but nobody paid the slightest attention. They were too busy discussing Nancy's t-shirts.

In a split second, a piercing whistle shattered our eardrums, and probably a few sets of china and glassware in the restaurant, too. "I've always wanted to do that," Sister Rose said, sitting back in her chair and looking extremely pleased with herself. "That was fun."

That got everybody's attention, all right. "You really are full of surprises, Sister," I said, laughing.

"You have no idea," Sister Rose said, her eyes twinkling. "Just because I'm a nun doesn't mean I don't like to cut loose every now and then." Her expression turned serious. "Carol, dear, I know you're doing your best to organize the group, but as I said a little while ago, I really have to get back to the thrift shop. So how about I volunteer to contact everyone on my alumni email list about Donna Trumbull's campaign and see how much interest I get?" She whipped out her smartphone and made a few quick notes to herself. "I need the campaign rally details, however." She looked at me expectantly.

"Donna has already requested a permit to use the Town Hall green for the rally next Saturday."

I started to add that the permit had yet to be issued, but Maria interrupted me. "I have the invitation list for Mary Pat's colleagues, and I can contact all of them. Doing the campaign rally in front of Town Hall means we should get good attendance. We're bound to attract media attention, too."

Good grief. Maria was looking directly at me when she used the word "media." It was obvious she expected me to get the *Fairport News* to cover the event. That meant a direct appeal to Jim, who now didn't want to be involved in Donna's campaign at all.

When in doubt, create a diversion, Carol.

"I know the Patch will be all over this event, and that's what really counts these days," I said. "Jim says more and more traditional newspapers are going out of business, since most people get their news online. Advertising revenue is down, too, and the paper isn't covering a lot of local events. Jim's worried our little local paper will fold because nobody's reading it anymore."

Okay, maybe he never actually said that, but I figured he must have thought about the paper's possible closing at least once, and that's the same thing. At least, by my creative standards.

"I hope that doesn't happen," Mary Alice said. "I love our local paper."

"I'm just saying we can't take local media coverage for granted," I said. "I hope you all understand that."

Maria was now typing furiously into her phone. In a matter of seconds, all our phones pinged. "I just texted a to-do list and assigned tasks to each of you," she said. "I hope you don't think I'm treading on your position as campaign manager, Carol, but we need to get this show on the road as soon as possible. You'll still be the only contact between us and the candidate, though. All right?"

You have no idea how thrilled I am to be off the hook as much as possible. I didn't really say that out loud, of course.

"Fine with me," I said. "I'll be back in touch as soon as I confirm the time of the kickoff rally."

"I'll send out a preliminary email to my list, and tell them specific details will follow," Sister Rose said. I was relieved to see that she wasn't giving me grief because I didn't have the final details yet.

Nancy sprinted toward the door, then called out over her shoulder, "Don't forget to order the t-shirts, Carol. White shirts with green and blue letters. And you better put a rush on the order so we'll be sure to have them for the rally."

"As long as Donna approves of the shirts," I called out. "Remember, she's paying the bills."

But my BFF had already vanished. Honestly, that Nancy.

Chapter 25

You're only as old as you feel, but not nearly as important.

"There's no way I'm spending my good money on t-shirts! Have you lost your mind, Carol? If this is all you've come up with to help me win this election, I think I made a mistake hiring you."

I could feel my cheeks flame, and I knew my eyes were filling up and would spill over if I didn't control myself right away. Unfortunately, Donna and I were FaceTiming, so she could see my expression.

You could terminate the call and blame your cell phone for a bad connection. Or just quit the campaign and let somebody else deal with Donna the Prima Donna.

I banished the second thought as quickly as it came into my head. No way was I quitting. As Harry Truman once famously said, "If you can't take the heat, get out of the kitchen." And since I was in my own kitchen, with Lucy and Ethel and their favorite chew toys at my feet, if either Donna or I had to leave, it sure as heck wouldn't be me. Sensing my distress, Ethel dropped her toy in my lap, which made me smile.

"Carol? Carol? Are you still there?"

Fortified by the gesture of canine support, I gritted my teeth and said, "Of course I'm still here, Donna. Or maybe there's something wrong with your eyesight as well as your people skills."

OMG. I couldn't believe I actually said that out loud. I braced myself for the outburst that was sure to come my way, and wondered if I could collect unemployment for a job I'd been on for less than a week.

To my complete surprise, Donna burst out laughing. "It's been a long time since somebody's had the nerve to call me out like that," she said. "And you were right to do it. I was way out of line. I just found out that another female candidate is running for a seat on the town council. She's some young hedge fund genius who works in New York. She managed to get all the signatures she needed to get her name on the ballot just by canvassing other commuters on Metro North. Can you believe it?"

I thought that approach was pretty clever, but I didn't dare voice that to Donna when she was just calming down.

"What's her name?" I asked. "Maybe she's not a serious candidate."

"Her name's Carla Grimaldi," Donna said. "She went to The Campaign School at Yale. She's definitely a serious candidate, even though she's only lived in Fairport for a year. She's running on a platform of fiscal responsibility. She's even got a slogan for her posters. 'Don't hedge your bets. Vote for Carla Grimaldi.' How stupid is that?"

I was getting more and more impressed with Carla Grimaldi. Maybe if Donna fired me, I could get a job with her.

"Her last name ends in a vowel, just like Frank Bologna's, so she must be Italian, too," Donna continued. "They're probably related. In fact, I bet he convinced her to run so she'd take away votes from me. Fairport needs a real American on the town council with a real American name, not some foreigner."

"I'm sure she's an American," I said, shocked at what Donna had said. "In fact...."

"As if that isn't bad enough," Donna said, paying no attention to what I'd just said, "using Town Hall green for my kickoff campaign rally is out. I'm sure Frank Bologna had something to do with denying me a permit, but I can't prove it. I followed up on this myself, Carol, since you didn't bother to do it." Heavy sigh. "I hope I don't have to do your job as well as run for office. Lord knows I'm paying you enough."

That accusation was completely unfair, because Donna was the one who applied for the permit in the first place. I knew it would do no good to remind her about that. To say nothing of the fact that, so far, she hadn't paid me a single dime.

She's stressed about this new candidate, and she's taking it out on you. Ignore that outburst and tell her about today's meeting so she won't stop payment on your first check. Assuming she gives you the contract to sign, so your job is official, and you really will get paid.

"I've already held the first volunteer meeting," I said. "People are starting to canvass for names to be sure you get on the ballot. That's how the subject of t-shirts came up in the first place, as an official way to identify your volunteers."

I could see Donna scowling at me and vowed I'd never use FaceTime again. "By the way, I haven't received the contract you promised to send me to make my position official. And so there won't be any more misunderstandings on what I am being hired to do, the contract should include a specific description of my job responsibilities. The sooner I receive that, the better. I'll sign it and get it back to you as soon as I've had a chance to look it over, assuming there are no problems with it. I prefer to have everything spelled out in writing. I'm sure you understand."

Wow, Carol, you sound so professional. Where did all that come from?

"I'll have it to you by the end of the day today," Donna said. "How about bandanas for the campaign volunteers instead of t-shirts?"

What I wanted to answer was, "With all your money, you can certainly afford a few t-shirts. Boy, are you cheap." But since some of that moolah was going to enrich my own bank account, I kept that thought to myself and agreed to the change.

"Great. Order them right away, so we'll have them in time for the campaign rally. We're holding it at Neecy and Tony Prentiss's home now, which is even better than Town Hall. People will attend just to see the house. Noon sharp on Saturday. I'm counting on you to get a huge crowd to attend with lots of press coverage. Not just the local one. I want national coverage. Get on it right away."

I resisted sticking my tongue out at her, even though I knew she could see me. Two things stopped me. First, I imagined the joy of caressing the first salary check I'd earned in a long time, and, even better, waving it in Jim's face. And, second, Donna had already clicked off.

For the next few hours, I worked like a demon, figuratively speaking. I was determined that, just once, Donna would praise me for all I'd accomplished, rather than pointing out all the things I hadn't. I didn't even take a break for lunch, nor check the fridge to see what I could whip up that would pass for dinner in Jim's eyes. And stomach.

My primary goal was to be sure there was a huge crowd of enthusiastic supporters at the kickoff rally (and that everyone went to the right place, of course), so I sent off texts to the committee about the new location, adding how thrilled Donna was with all the work we'd done so far to get her elected. Of course, that was a complete lie (the latter, not the former), but I had to keep the team's spirits high. Even though I tried to spin substituting campaign kerchiefs for t-shirts as a fabulous idea, Nancy immediately texted back that t-shirts were much more fashionable and would cost the same. I ignored her.

To be honest, I was feeling overwhelmed with all the things I was supposed to take care of. And only heaven knew how many others Donna would toss in my lap before the election, despite her agreeing to spell out my job description in our contract. I needed to talk to someone who'd been involved in a political campaign before.

No, correction. I needed to talk to another *woman* who'd been involved in a political campaign. No roosters in this chick's henhouse.

Then I had one of my truly brilliant ideas. I would reach out to Neecy Prentiss, to thank her for hosting the kickoff rally at her home. And because I am a person who's known for her impeccable manners, I'd also ask if there was anything I could do to help her with the rally. While we were having a nice chat, one Mount Saint Francis alumna to another, I'd oh-so-casually ask if she had some tips about a political campaign to share with me.

I don't like putting people on the spot, though. Maybe an email would be the best way to start this conversation. I don't use my phone to send emails if I can help it, because my email messages are usually longer than my texts. I decided to give my phone a chance to rest and recharge while I used the computer for a change.

I hoped my computer wasn't mad at me for neglecting it for so long. Just to be sure, while I powered it up, I sent a quick prayer to St. Isidore of Seville, proclaimed the patron saint of the Internet in 1997 by Pope John Paul II. St. Isidore was a bishop and scholar who lived in the sixth century AD, and tried to record everything known at that time in a 20-book opus, "Etymologies." He's also the patron saint of computers and their users, and computer repair people. (I hope you're all impressed with my wealth of knowledge.)

Call instead of sending an email, Carol. It's more personal.

I realized I was getting a personal message from St. Isidore saying he was busy solving somebody else's computer crisis, and was referring me to the Archangel Gabriel, the patron saint of telephones and telecommunications. Gabriel's always been the official messenger between the Good Lord and humans, and his job is probably even more demanding now that we have text messaging. My phone suddenly pinged, which scared me to death. OMG. Was I getting a text from Gabriel now?

I squinted at the text and relaxed. It was Jim, not Gabriel, announcing that he'd be gone all day. I'm embarrassed to say I was thrilled. Now I'd have the whole day and evening to myself.

Don't waste it, Carol. Quit dithering and get back to work.

After a short break for canine and human needs, I punched in Neecy's cell phone number. After four rings, I heard a dog barking and then my classmate's voice. "Hi, Carol. Hang on a second. Down, Porter. I'm getting your water. Just be patient."

"It's nice to know that my house isn't the only one in town that's run by a dog," I said, laughing, when Neecy came back on the line.

"I swear, sometimes Porter is more demanding than Tony," Neecy said. "But she's so sweet, and works so hard as a therapy dog, that I just have to spoil her. You know she's my baby, now."

Indeed, I did know that. In fact, I was one of the few people who knew that Neecy and Tony's son had died tragically several years ago, and Porter, quite literally, saved Neecy's life.

"So, what's up, Carol? I hear from Tony that you're involved with Donna Trumbull's run for town council. What can I do for you?"

"I called to ask what I could do for you," I said, guilt washing over me at my scheme to take advantage of our friendship to save my sanity and my job. "And especially to thank you for agreeing to host Donna's kickoff campaign rally at your house. It's so nice of you."

"It's really no big deal," Neecy said. "Believe me, I'm not being nice. When Tony first said he wanted to do it here, I said no. Donna Trumbull isn't one of my favorite people, although I really liked her late husband a lot. Mel was a wonderful man. He just adored Donna, and gave her everything she ever asked for. I'm not sure the feeling was reciprocated, though. She always was a self-centered woman. Tony says she's changed now, and I hope he's right. She has a chance to do something important for Fairport. But I'm betting she has a personal agenda, too."

Wow. Coming from Neecy, this was pretty surprising. She and Mary Alice were two people who never said a mean word about anyone.

"I'm beginning to realize that I don't know Donna very well," I admitted. An understatement, for sure. "But she really saved the day at Mary Pat Ryan's memorial service."

"Yes. I was surprised when I heard that she'd donated all the baked goods. The old Donna never would have been so generous."

"She's obviously changed," I said, blocking out the memory of our most recent phone conversation. "She's running on a campaign to improve pedestrian safety in Fairport. It's an important issue to her, and to me. It scares me to think that I could be taking one of my dogs for a nice walk around town and be hit and killed by a car, the way Mary Pat was. I always took my personal safety for granted, but not since Mary Pat's accident. We need more crosswalks and stop signs. Don't you ever worry when you're out walking Porter?"

"She's a Lab, so she's pretty big and easy to see," Neecy said. "But you're right, of course. We do need more crosswalks and stop signs. Traffic lights, too."

I wasn't about to let a golden opportunity to probe into Donna's past go by, especially since I was having some prickles of doubt about her, myself. "I have to write Donna's biography for the campaign literature and the webpage," I said. "I'd like to have something drafted for her approval by the end of today. Since you and Tony knew her and her late husband, maybe you could share some personal stories with me. I'd really appreciate that."

"I've already said too much," Neecy said. "If Tony overheard me, he'd go through the roof. One of his favorite sayings is, 'Loose lips sink ships.' And my lips have certainly been loose during this phone call."

Rats. Just when we were getting somewhere.

"I will say one more thing, though, before we get into the logistics of the event. But it's just a personal impression, and certainly nothing you could use in her biography."

I held my breath and my tongue. A real effort, let me tell you.

"Tony and I went to Mel's funeral," Neecy continued. "In fact, Tony was one of the pallbearers. Donna didn't shed a single tear. In fact, she didn't look sad at all."

I was stunned. I couldn't imagine anyone being so cold. If Jim pre-deceased me, I knew I'd be a blubbering idiot at the service, despite Jenny and Mike's efforts to calm me down. Jim and I have had our differences over the years, and there've been times that I've been furious at him because of some stupid (in my opinion) thing he'd done, but I couldn't imagine life without him.

Then I remembered Jackie Kennedy, one of my all-time idols. She was able to keep her emotions in check during JFK's funeral, and became a model of courage for our entire country. Perhaps, instead of being cold and unfeeling, Donna was able to keep her emotions in check and grieve in private, for which she should be applauded, not criticized.

I bit back the negative comment I was about to make and reminded Neecy about Mrs. Kennedy. She remained unconvinced, however. "I understand what you're saying, Carol. But remember, I saw the Trumbulls' marital relationship myself. You didn't. Donna's behavior at Mel's funeral is only one example of a pattern that had been going on for years."

This conversation wasn't going the way I'd expected at all. Even I wasn't naive enough to think Neecy'd give me any advice about how to get Donna Trumbull elected to the Fairport Town Council after what she'd told me. In fact, the more Neecy carried on about her dislike of Donna, the more I wondered why she'd agreed to host the rally in the first place.

What if Neecy was secretly planning to denounce Donna during the campaign kickoff? Could she be that devious, agreeing to host it and then sabotage it?

I shook my head. No way. Neecy was a Mount Saint Francis girl, and would never stoop that low. Would she?

"Don't worry about the rally, Carol," Neecy said, as if reading my thoughts. "I promise to behave myself and be a perfect hostess. Even Donna won't pick up on how much I dislike her. I've managed to hide it for years, even from Tony. I have no reason to humiliate her publicly. Tony would never forgive me. In fact, I'm sure he wishes he was the candidate himself, instead of Donna. He still hasn't gotten over the fact that he lost his own election. I think this is a way to get his name back into the public eye, in case he ever decides to run for office again."

I started to respond, but there was no chance of that. Neecy was on a roll. "I'll behave myself until Donna's check clears, at least."

"Check?"

"Donna made a very generous donation to Furry Friends, the new canine charity in town, in memory of Mary Pat. She's going to have the check enlarged into a poster and present it at the event. I'm the president of the board."

"That sounds like a bribe," I blurted out without thinking.

"That was my first reaction when Donna suggested it. But she convinced me that I was overreacting. She wanted to make an unselfish gesture to support a worthy cause in memory of someone whose death was what pushed her into running for office in the first place. You should think about getting involved with Furry Friends, Carol. I know how much you love your dogs."

Donna's donation still sounded like a bribe to me. I scribbled a note to myself to talk to Donna about nixing the public check presentation. I was sure the media and her opponents would have a field day with the so-called "donation" and it would torpedo her campaign before it even got started.

"Maybe once this election is over and I have more free time I can help out at Furry Friends," I said. "Now, about the rally..."

The rest of our conversation had to do with the nuts and bolts of putting the event together, and I'm not going to bore you with how we figured out how many people to plan for, how many chairs to set up, what to serve (if anything), and what to do in case it rained. Neecy insisted the rally be held outside, which was her right as the (reluctant) hostess, and we settled on renting a tent, in case of inclement weather.

I won a major argument when I convinced her that renting Porta-Potties was a tacky idea. "I just don't want a lot of strangers traipsing through my house," she said, and I didn't blame her. But fortunately, I had another of my brilliant ideas. "I know the perfect person to monitor anyone who comes in the house," I said. "Nancy Green has lots of experience with Realtor open houses. How about if we put her in charge of inside activities?"

"Great idea," Neecy said, mollified. I just hoped Nancy would agree with her. She hates to miss anything, and I was sure that convincing my BFF that monitoring indoor powder room usage during the event was critical would be a tough sell.

That's the least of your problems, Carol. You got involved in the campaign of someone you didn't bother to check out first. And, even worse, you roped your inner circle into coming along for the ride. What are you going to do now, besides pray for a hurricane so the rally will be cancelled?

Chapter 26

I know nothing. But I know that I know nothing. So I guess I do know something after all.

I wanted to put my head in my hands and weep. Or, better yet, bang my head on the kitchen table until I knocked some sense into my head. I hadn't ever felt this confused before, and for me, that was saying something.

For once in your life, stop and think before you overreact, Carol. Maria Lesco is as committed to Donna Trumbull's campaign as you are. You just have the official title of 'Campaign Manager,' and she doesn't. Maria's a smart businesswoman. She wouldn't be involved with Donna if she didn't trust her.

That made me feel a little better, but not much. Especially when I remembered the interaction I'd observed a few weeks ago between Donna and the owner of Fairport Garage. But the manager also told me this was an interaction they always had, that her bark was worse than her bite (with apologies to Lucy and Ethel for the reference), and that she always sent over a tray of tasty goodies from the bakery as an apology.

Even you have a temper, Carol. And if anyone overheard some of the things you've said, or could read your mind, you'd look pretty bad, too.

I remembered a classic movie starring Bette Davis, *All About*

Eve. In the film, Bette Davis is Margo Channing, a Broadway star who befriends a sweet young actress, Eve Harrington, played by Anne Baxter. Eve turns out to be a conniving witch who's only out for herself and will do anything she can to become a star, no matter what.

So, which one is Donna Trumbull, Carol? Margo Channing or Eve Harrington?

I made up my mind that I wouldn't put my Jane Hancock on any official contract Donna might send me until I did some serious checking on the bakery boss/town-council-member-wannabe. And I'd start with my nearest and dearest, Jim, who had mysteriously distanced himself from Donna's campaign after practically anointing himself as her campaigner-in-chief at the planning meeting. And had also, come to think of it, mysteriously distanced himself from his nearest and dearest—and main provider of all things food-related—for the entire day.

Putting aside my wifely thoughts, I resolved to start my research by finding out anything I could about Mel Trumbull's death. I hoped Google was in a cooperative mood today, and would quickly yield the information I wanted without forcing me to click on a bunch of useless sites before I found anything that was worthwhile.

Closely monitored by my two trusty research assistants, Lucy and Ethel, I woke my computer up from its sleep mode. Resisting the siren call of my email, I typed, "Mel Trumbull Death" into the search line. I ended up with a long list of death notices for people with a similar name from all over the country. Cursing my stupidity, I added "Fairport" to my request, which brought me to sites about other towns named Fairport. But no death notices. I added "Connecticut," which I should have done in the first place (I know, you're shaking your head at my amateur method), but for some reason I still couldn't narrow the search the way I wanted to.

Refusing to admit defeat, especially in front of the dogs (I like to impress them as often as possible), I decided to reach out to the one person I can always count on to help me out in these situations—my son Mike. I just hoped he had the time for an SOS from his dear old mom. Since I am a multi-tasker extraordinaire, I would also, subtly, inquire about what, or who, was new in his life.

Mike's nickname for me is Cosmo Girl, referring to my brief stint at *Cosmopolitan* magazine back in the last century. Knowing that he might ignore me if I texted when he was busy now with Cosmo's, his super successful South Beach, Florida bistro (yes, I am bragging again), I pondered how to best get his attention and, with apologies to my computer, grabbed my cell phone again.

Me: *Hello from your DESPERATE Cosmo Girl.*
Ping.
Mike: *What's wrong?*
Ping.
Me: *Need help.*
Ping.
Mike: *What's wrong????? R U sick? Dad?*
Ping.
Me: *No. Internet research help. IMPORTANT.*
Ping.
Mike: *Phew. Can it wait? Swamped right now.*
Ping.
Me: *NO!! Researching a death.*
Ping.
Mike: *Whose? R U in trouble again? Being 2 nosy?*
Ping.
Me: *NO!! Mel Trumbull. Died at least 10 years ago.*
Ping.
Mike: *I won't ask why you need to know. But okay.*
Ping.
Me: *Now?*
Ping.
Mike: *Okay, okay! Stay tuned. Over and out.*
Ping.

Waiting isn't my strong suit. I'm not as impatient as some other people (not mentioning anyone in particular, understand), but as I get older, and time is more precious, I hate to waste a single second sitting around doing nothing.

I decided to scribble a few notes on what Neecy had told me before they galloped out of my head. (I hope you don't need me to recap all that for you, and that you were as shocked as I was about what she had to say.) While I was in a scribbling mode, I also made a list for myself of what I still had left to do for Donna's launch party. Assuming I hadn't quit the campaign by then.

Mike did not disappoint his dear old mom. In less than ten minutes, he was able to find and text me Mel Trumbull's obituary. Why he was able to find it and I couldn't, I'll never know. And because he figured (correctly) that I'd have trouble reading the small print of the texted article, he told me to check my email for a duplicate. Bless him.

I resisted the urge to inquire about his life—love or otherwise—and responded with a "heart" emoji and quickly scanned the article.

TRAGEDY AT MR. T's TASTY TREATS

Mel Trumbull, 49, owner of well-known Fairport bakery Mr. T's Tasty Treats, died suddenly in a tragic accident late yesterday. Mr. Trumbull, well-loved in the community for his philanthropic work, was found dead at the bottom of the cellar stairs at the bakery by his wife of ten years, Donna. "The bakery had closed for the day, and I was out for about an hour having my car serviced," Mrs. Trumbull said. "Mel was doing prep work for the following day when I left. If only I'd stayed, he'd still be alive!" Fairport police are investigating, though there is no suspicion of foul play. Funeral arrangements are pending.

Hmm. I sat back and tried to process what I read. At first glance, Mel Trumbull's death seemed exactly what the newspaper had reported—a tragic accident. Falling down a flight of stairs could happen to anyone. All it would take was one wrong step and then....

Truth to tell, I've noticed that my own balance isn't as good as it used to be when I was younger. When I head downstairs after a rare foray to our second floor to do a little cleaning, I hold onto the bannister in a death grip, pardon the pun. And I'm paranoid about taking a shower if Jim isn't home. According to AARP, falling in the shower—or anywhere else in the bathroom—is a common occurrence for seniors and, if undiscovered, can be fatal. I always keep my cell phone with me, too. (Just not in the shower itself, of course.)

It certainly seemed that Mel Trumbull's death was a tragic accident. I thanked the Good Lord that, so far, something like that hadn't happened to us or any of our close friends.

"But there's one thing that's bothering me," I admitted to the dogs, still snoozing on the couch. For once, I actually got Lucy's attention. Usually, she hates it when I interrupt her beauty sleep, but she must have sensed that I needed the kind of feedback that only she can provide. She rose, stretched, and trotted over to sit at my feet. Ethel followed, of course. They are always a team.

Lucy yawned, clearly telegraphing that, although I had her attention at the moment, she had other plans for the rest of the day so I better get to the point. Ethel licked my hand, encouraging me to go on.

"We know Neecy Prentiss," I said. "Well, I do. And you know her dog, Porter. You've all played together outside several times." The dogs immediately reacted, which was probably to the magic word "outside" more than anything else, but I chose to interpret that as permission to proceed. "Neecy is one of the nicest women I've ever known, yet she said that Donna didn't seem upset by her husband's death. So, what exactly does that mean?"

Lucy gave me a skeptical look. *Are you implying that Donna Trumbull pushed her husband down the stairs? Don't be ridiculous.*

And, of course, Lucy was right. I was being ridiculous. Wasn't I?

I heard another ping, which scared me. Oh, please Lord, don't let this be Donna now.

It was Mike again.

Call me. More info.

I punched in Mike's number so fast that I dropped the blasted phone on the floor. And when I knelt down to retrieve it, I lost my balance and fell, pulling a muscle in my back. This was definitely not my day. Grimacing in pain, I heard Mike say, "I gotta make this quick, so just let me talk, okay? I started thinking more about the Trumbulls, and I remembered that a few of my buddies worked for them off and on during high school to earn extra cash. Emphasis on the word 'cash' because that's the way they were always paid. The guys thought it was great, but now that I'm running my own business, I wonder how legal that was. They also said the Trumbulls fought all the time. She was always telling him what to do, and he'd give it right back to her. They had some real loud fights in the back of the shop where the customers couldn't hear them. If my buddies happened to overhear one, Mrs. Trumbull would always give them a little extra cash for that day, and say she was sorry and that they shouldn't tell anyone. I thought you should know, even though I'm not sure what it means, and it all happened such a long time ago."

And in a millisecond, before I could respond, he was gone.

Chapter 27

If a husband speaks in the family room, and his wife is not there to hear him, is he still wrong?

The more I thought about what Neecy had said about Donna and Mel's relationship, added to the way he suddenly died and Mike's information about them fighting all the time, the more convinced I was that Donna could have been responsible for Mel's death. Okay, I wasn't really "convinced." But I had to find out more information, and fast.

On the other hand, my fertile imagination was fitting Donna Trumbull for an orange jumpsuit in state prison based purely on gossip and an old obituary notice. The police never suspected foul play, so why did I?

I needed to talk to the more logical person in this marriage; my husband. I wanted to share what I'd learned from Neecy, and what Mike had discovered about how Mel Trumbull died, and see what he thought. I knew I was risking being told I was over-the-top nuts to suspect Donna of causing her husband's death, but I was desperate for a mature sounding board.

My phone began to serenade me with "Unforgettable" by Nat and Natalie Cole, the kids' idea of the perfect ringtone for me. The way this day was going, it was probably Donna again, with even more jobs for me to accomplish in the next fifteen minutes. Or, even worse, telling me she'd emailed my contract and demanding I sign and return it ASAP.

I took the coward's way out and immediately changed my phone setting to the "mute" function without checking the caller ID first. Bad mistake. The call was from Jim, who sometimes prefers to contact me the old-fashioned way as opposed to texting. AARRGH.

I was dismayed to hear Jim's voicemail message inform me that he wouldn't be home for dinner tonight. In fact, he'd probably be very late, because he'd run into an old buddy from his NYC commuter days and they'd decided to have drinks and dinner and catch up. Double rats. One of the few times I really wanted my husband home and he had deserted me. I trust the irony of this situation isn't lost on you. If it is, you obviously haven't been married very long, or your husband has a job that requires him to leave the house for long stretches of time on a regular basis.

I needed to find another logical person to talk to right away. Someone who always tells me when I'm about to go off the rails, even when I don't want to hear it. That narrowed my list of choices to two people: Sister Rose and Claire. No contest there. Sister Rose still has the ability to make me squirm the way I did when I was in high school, so I eliminated her immediately and composed a text for Claire. Just as I was about to send it, I had a major case of second thoughts.

Are you crazy, Carol? Not Claire. No way. She'll just tell you that you're crazy, the way she always does. What you need is a creative thinker, not a sounding board, to help you find out if Donna Trumbull's a murderer.

I nodded my head. I love it when I agree with myself, especially when I know we're both right. I deleted the text to Claire and fired another off to the person who's been sharing adventures with me since we were kids. Nancy.

Me: *Hi. R u busy?*

Ping.

Nancy: *That depends. I am if u have envelopes to stuff or lawn signs to paint.*

Ping.
Me: *Very funny. No, I need advice. I'm desperate.*
Ping.
Nancy: *I'll be at your house in 10.*
Ping.
Me: *YAY!*

"I got here as fast as I could," Nancy said, arriving at my kitchen door in 8 minutes. "What's wrong? Jim? Jenny? Oh, God, not the baby."

"No, no. The family's fine," I said, pulling out a chair so Nancy could sit. "I called you about Donna Trumbull. I think she was responsible for her husband's death."

Nancy's reaction was a total surprise to me. She laughed. My very best and oldest and closest friend in the whole entire universe laughed at me! "You've got to be kidding, Carol. If you want my advice, here it is. Don't repeat your suspicions about Donna Trumbull to anyone. She's a powerful woman, and she could sue you for slander."

I was stung. And hurt. I couldn't believe I was hearing this from the same person who'd been my partner-in-crime (figuratively speaking) for years.

"I'm sorry I was so harsh, sweetie," Nancy said, looking contrite. "But there has to be some proof to back up this wild accusation, and I'm betting you don't have any. Usually I go along with your crazy hunches, but this one is too wild even for me. May I remind you," she held up her hand to forestall anything I could say in my own defense, "that earlier today we attended a meeting at the Trattoria where you proceeded to rope all of your best friends into supporting the same woman whom you now suspect murdered her husband? Do you understand how absolutely unbelievable that is?"

"This isn't just some random thought that popped into my

so-called feeble brain," I protested. "Just let me tell you what I found out today from Neecy Prentiss when I called her to thank her for hosting Donna's campaign kickoff rally." (I skipped the fact that I'd suggested Nancy guard the bathrooms in Neecy's house.) Then I added Mike's information, trying hard to make my narrative as short as possible.

I sat back and waited for Nancy to respond, hoping she wouldn't react like Claire and spend the next fifteen minutes or so poking holes in my narrative. Then she'd feel bad about how critical she'd been, apologize again, and we could finally get down to why she was here in the first place—to help me find out if Donna was responsible for her husband's death, or not. Because, as I summed up my "case," if Donna had any skeletons in her closet, we'd better find them now.

"What did Jim say when you told him all this?" Nancy finally asked.

I laughed. "I haven't seen Jim all day. He didn't come home for lunch, and called a while ago to say he wouldn't be home until late tonight because he was meeting a friend from his commuter days for dinner. I never knew he had any commuter friends. You don't think..."

Nancy dismissed my fear with a flip of her hand. "Sweetie, now you're *really* being ridiculous, and I can only handle one of your unsubstantiated conclusions at a time. So, let's get back to Donna. I admit you may have reason to be suspicious."

Phew. The Nancy Green I knew and loved was back! Thank goodness.

All of a sudden, a recent conversation with Donna bubbled up to my conscious mind from wherever it had been hiding. When added to all the other information I had gleaned, it was pretty damning. "There's something else I need to tell you, Nancy," I said. "Jim and I were at Donna's house for a preliminary campaign strategy session. Jim took over the whole meeting and didn't let me get a word in edgewise."

"Just like he usually does," Nancy said. "There's nothing new about that."

"I know. He just can't help it and he does know a lot about a lot of things."

"And is more than willing to share," Nancy added.

"You don't have to agree with me quite this much," I said, giving her a glare. It was perfectly okay for me to criticize my husband, but not okay for someone else to do the same thing. Which may or may not make sense. Take your pick.

"I didn't let him get away with it, and after a few dirty looks, he finally stopped pontificating and let me talk."

"Just like you usually do." Nancy nodded in approval.

"Donna later commented on our interaction, and said it reminded her of the way her late husband used to treat her, always taking over and bossing her around. She said that she hated it as much as I obviously did. And then her problem was solved. Conveniently and permanently. Those were her exact words. She suggested that mine could be solved the same way. What if she was hinting that she solved the problem herself by killing her husband?"

"My God, Carol, why didn't you say something before you roped all your friends into supporting the candidacy of a possible murderer? What's the matter with you?"

"I figured I'd misheard and I got caught up in all the campaign details and completely forgot about what Donna said. You can yell at me all you want, but that's what happened. When Donna and I had this conversation, it was before I talked to Neecy and heard what she had to say. And before Mike found the story about Mel Trumbull's death."

There was one other teensy fact that I had no intention of sharing with Nancy. I'm embarrassed to share it with any of you, but I will. You may remember that it was right after Donna told me about her husband's convenient death that she offered me a gigantic sum to manage her campaign. I'd concentrated on my soon-to-be-exorbitant salary and blocked out everything else. I'm not proud of myself, but that's what happened.

"I shouldn't have yelled at you," Nancy said. "I'm sorry. Forgive me?"

"Of course, silly," I said, squeezing her hand. "So, now that I've brought you up to date, what do we do now?"

Nancy had a determined expression on her face. "We have to see if we're right, and the sooner, the better. We have to set a trap for Donna and see how she reacts."

"What? Now you're the one who's talking crazy."

"I don't mean literally, Carol. But we need to get Donna into a private situation where she can let her guard down and talk." She grinned. "I know exactly where we should do it." She pushed my phone toward me.

"I get it. You want me to text Claire and Mary Alice. I'm not sure that's such a good idea. Do we want to involve them, too?"

Nancy laughed. "They'll be part of the trap, of course. You know how mad they'd be if they weren't. But they're not the key players. I'm surprised that you haven't figured out what my brilliant plan is already. In fact, I'm surprised you didn't think of it yourself."

"Okay, you're really starting to bug me. What the heck are you talking about?"

"Where is the one place a woman might go when she needs a little extra pampering, especially if she has an important event, like a kickoff campaign rally, coming up?"

"A hair salon!" I jumped up and gave Nancy a big hug. "You're a genius."

"I know," Nancy said, grinning. "Now text Deanna and see if she thinks I am, too."

"What do you want me to tell her?"

"You're the one who started this whole thing. I'm sure you'll figure it out. I'll go into the family room and text Claire and Mary Alice to come to Crimpers tonight around 7:00, and why. I'm sure Claire will call me when she gets the text, and I don't want our jabbering to disturb your concentration. With any luck, they'll both go along with another of your crazy schemes without batting an eye."

I was about to remind Nancy that setting a trap at the hair salon was her idea, but immediately had second thoughts. If the plan worked, she'd take credit for it, anyway. And if it didn't, I knew she'd blame me. So, why bother?

I thought for a minute and came up with what I hoped was the perfect strategy to enlist Deanna's help.

Me: *R u up for another adventure?*

Ping.

Deanna: *No way. I'm still recovering from our last one.*

Ping.

Me: *Not even to trap a murderer?*

Ping.

Deanna: *R u nuts? I am not going back to that crazy cat house again.*

Me: *No cats this time. Promise. Your salon tonight after regular hours.*

Deanna: *Why? Who r we trapping?*

Me: *Donna Trumbull. I think she killed her husband.*

Deanna: *What??? And if you're wrong??? I don't want to be sued or arrested!*

Me: *Relax. You'll just do her hair and spruce her up for the kickoff rally. I'll ask the questions.*

Deanna: *Just you, me, and a possible murderer? No way.*

Me: *No. Mary Alice, Claire and Nancy, too. Safety in numbers.*

Deanna: *Still not sure about this.*

Me: *Oh, come on. I'll be subtle. Maybe u'll get a new client.*

Deanna: *If u're wrong, I'll dye ur hair purple and orange for spite.*

Me: *It's a deal. R u in?*

Deanna: *I must be nuts, but, okay.*

Me: *C u at 7:30 sharp.*

I took a minute to congratulate myself on my powers of persuasion.

"Deanna said yes," I called into the family room. "Are we all set? What the heck's taking you so long?"

"Claire wanted to check first with Larry and tell him what we were up to," Nancy said, walking back into the kitchen and looking very pleased with herself.

"What? Why? He's a lawyer, for Pete's sake. He'll probably turn us in before we even—"

"Relax," Nancy said. "Claire knew Larry was swimming at

the Y and his phone was safely tucked away in his locker. But she wanted to go on record as saying she called him for some legal advice and, when she couldn't reach him, we just decided to go ahead with our plan. Claire called it 'covering your butt when you're married to a lawyer' and said it works every time. She and Mary Alice will be at Crimpers by 7:00. So all you have to do is get Donna there. I'll take care of everything else. See you later."

Chapter 28

Honesty is always the best policy, unless you're a politician.

I won't kid you. I was so nervous when I sent a text inviting Donna to a night of beauty at Crimpers that my hands were shaking. I hoped she was so surprised to receive such a generous offer that she'd accept, even though it was a last minute one. When my cell phone immediately rang with "Unforgettable," and her phone number popped up on my screen, I jumped.

Grow up, stupid. She wants to talk to you. You can do this.

"I always have my hair styled by Maurice at 5th Avenue Hair Salon in the city," Donna began, not bothering with basic niceties like saying hello. "He's been doing my hair for years."

"But he's not local," I pointed out. "I think you'd be smart to start using a local hair salon. It'd strengthen your ties in the community, and you'd probably pick up some votes there. My personal stylist, Deanna, is the best in town. She's generously offered to do a free consult and hair styling tonight after hours, so you'll look your absolute best for the kickoff campaign rally. You know there'll be lots of media there. She even said she'll come to the rally right before you give your speech to do final touchups. How can you refuse?"

"Well, when you put it that way." I could tell by Donna's

voice that she was weakening. "But I have an important business meeting later tonight that I can't be late for. She has to be finished by then."

"I promise, she will be," I said. And you may be, too, if I'm right. Of course, I didn't say that out loud.

"How about if I drive you? I can pick you up around 7:00."

"I need to drive myself so I can get to my other meeting," Donna said, sounding impatient with me for being so stupid. "I'll meet you there. I know where Crimpers is. And I'll bring your contract with me so you can sign it."

Oh, goody.

I sent a quick confirmation text to my co-conspirators, then scribbled a note to Jim and taped it to the refrigerator door, where I knew he'd see it. A quick change of clothes for me, a quick run in the yard for Lucy and Ethel, and I was ready to leave for Crimpers.

A sudden thought occurred to me like a bolt of lightning. What if Donna was really putting me off and had no intention of going to the hair salon after all? I already suspected she had a habit of bending the truth even more than other political candidates did.

You have to be sure she shows up at Crimpers.

I made a sudden decision. I had to follow her in my own car and hope she didn't recognize it. I nodded at my own brilliance and put the car in reverse. Good thing I double-checked my rearview mirror before I pressed the accelerator, because another car was coming into my driveway. Rats. I looked again and realized it was Jenny.

Now, you all know how much I love my darling daughter, but I didn't have any time to spare talking with her right now, especially if she and Mark were continuing to have marital problems. It was time for me to step back from that particular situation and let the kids figure things out on their own.

But I was a mother long before I became a "sleuth," so I

hopped out of my car, a welcoming smile on my face. "Sweetie, I'm surprised to see you," I said, giving her a big hug. "I was just on my way out and I'm on a tight schedule so I can't chat. Is CJ with you? Is everything okay?"

"Relax, Mom. Everything's fine and CJ's home with a babysitter because Mark's working tonight."

A babysitter who wasn't me? I felt a sharp stab at my heart and tried not to show it.

Reading my expression correctly, Jenny laughed. "Relax, Mom. You'll always be our favorite person in the world to watch over CJ. But I had a surprise for you, and it just couldn't wait. So I asked Cindy Page to do the honors. You remember her, right? The maternity nurse and Mike's possible new love interest? You really liked her."

Momentarily diverted, I had a brief fantasy of Cindy walking down the aisle in a white dress toward a beaming Mike, then shook myself back to reality. Time was ticking. No time for fantasies now.

"What's the surprise, sweetie? I don't mean to seem ungrateful, but I really have to go."

"Close your eyes and hold out your arms," Jenny ordered.

I bit my lip and did as directed. I didn't want to say something unkind to my only daughter. Then I was aware of a furry bundle in my arms and...something was licking my cheek.

I opened my eyes to see an adorable white dog wearing a pink collar. My heart melted as I hugged her close. But I knew how much care a dog required. In case you haven't already figured it out, Lucy and Ethel pretty much run our house. If the kids were thinking of adding a dog to their household right now, I knew I had to say something. (Even though I never interfere in the lives of my children.)

"You and Mark aren't getting a dog, are you? Don't you have enough to do with a new baby?"

"No, Mom. This isn't our dog. This is Harriet, Mary Pat's dog." She reached out and took the dog from me.

"I thought you'd be thrilled to meet her, but you're not. In fact, you look antsy, like you can't wait to leave. Which means you're up to something."

I started to protest, but Jenny knew me far too well.

"Forget it, Mom. What is it this time? I hope it's not dangerous." It's a humbling experience to be lectured by your own child.

I filled Jenny in as quickly as possible about Donna Trumbull, then waited for her to tell me I was way off base and should cancel the entire plan before it was too late.

"You never stop surprising me," Jenny said. "Some mothers are content to bake cookies and babysit their grandchildren. But not you. Don't think I'm criticizing you. In fact, I've learned the past few years that no matter how wild some of your schemes may seem, they're not. You have good instincts about people, and if you say there's something fishy about Mel Trumbull's death, you may be right. There's only one way to find out for sure."

She opened the rear door of her car and placed Harriet on a blanket on the seat. I bit my lip before I blurted out that the dog should be in a secure carrier for safety. Instead, relieved that I had made my case so efficiently, I decided I'd better leave before Jenny changed her mind and called Mark to tell him his mother-in-law had finally gone over the edge.

"Not so fast," Jenny said, grabbing my arm. "I'm coming with you." She yanked open the passenger door. "You're not going to let me miss this and Donna won't recognize my car. Besides, there should be a credible witness to document what we find out, and who better than the wife of a police detective?"

"I don't want you to get in trouble with Mark," I protested. *And blame me again.*

"Don't worry about that, Mom. We've talked things over and he knows I'll never put myself in danger. But he realizes that being your daughter comes with a unique set of traits and opportunities, some of which are even helpful to him. This situation is a prime example." She waved her phone. "Besides, I can keep in constant touch with him on his private number. Now, fasten your seatbelt and let's get to Donna's so we can follow her to Crimpers."

"What if she doesn't go there?" I asked. "Or she figures out we're following her? What'll we do then?"

"We'll figure something out. What's Donna's address?"

"She lives a few blocks away. Turn left out of our driveway, drive two blocks and take another left. I don't remember her house number, but it's on the right hand side of the street. Trust me, you'll have no difficulty spotting it."

Jenny gave me a quizzical look, checked to be sure Harriet was safe, and we were off.

"Drive to the end of the block, then turn around and park," I suggested as we sped by Donna's house. "And why are you driving so fast?"

"I don't want to let her think we're checking out her house, of course," Jenny said. "Although, with that patriotic paint job, I'm sure she's used to people gawking. I see a pickup truck in the driveway and a white convertible behind it. Is the convertible hers?"

"I assume so," I said, craning my neck to look around.

We parked on the opposite side of the street so we could get a better view. I was nervous, and Jenny could tell. "This is my first stakeout," she said, trying to break the tension. "It's nice to have such special bonding times with you, Mom. I know other mothers and daughters go on shopping trips together. This is much more fun."

I started to laugh, then grabbed Jenny's hand. "There she is now on the front porch. There's a man with her. If you put the windows down, maybe we can hear what they're saying."

Jenny looked doubtful, but did as I suggested. I leaned forward in my seat, but we were too far away for proper eavesdropping. My line of sight was perfect, however. "That's Doug from Fairport Garage," I said. "He takes care of servicing all the bakery trucks."

"I guess he does a lot more than take care of the trucks," Jenny said. OMG. Donna and Doug were now locked in a passionate embrace, right there on her front porch.

"That's what I call personal service," I said. "Wait, they're talking louder now."

"The shipment is due to arrive at the beach at ten," Doug said as he walked Donna down the driveway to her car. "Give me a little time to load everything into my truck. Can you meet me at the bakery at eleven?"

"No problem," Donna said, giving Doug another intimate embrace. "But I hope this is the last time. I'm getting nervous."

"You worry too much, babe. You don't have to do everything yourself. That's why we hired more people, remember?"

Donna nodded. "I love you. See you there."

"Love you too. Now get going so I leave, too."

"What are they talking about, Mom?" Jenny asked. "This doesn't make any sense."

"I guess Doug picks up some of the ingredients Donna uses for the baked goods," I said. "He's a very helpful guy."

"Obviously."

Donna didn't waste any time backing out of her driveway. Her headlights flashed onto Jenny's car for a brief moment, and Jenny pushed me down on the seat so Donna wouldn't see me.

"Give her a few seconds, then pull out slowly," I whispered. "But don't get too close. We don't want her to figure out she's being followed."

I sent Nancy a quick text to tell her Donna was on the way and I was following her, adding: *R U all set?*

But Nancy didn't respond.

Chapter 29

Underestimate me. It'll be fun.

My clever daughter improvised a route that would get us to the hair salon at the same time as Donna, but from a different direction. I was very impressed and told her so.

"Years of practice watching you, Mom. You're the most creative person I know. In a good way."

"Thank you. I think."

"You look nervous," Jenny said. "Better put a smile on your face, because we're here. Remember, this was your idea, and as far as Donna knows, it's supposed to be fun."

"I am nervous. I have no idea how this is going to play out. It could be a complete disaster. Nancy said she'd take care of everything, but I have no idea what she's planned." I had a sudden vision of Hercule Poirot gathering suspects together in the drawing room of a country house for the big reveal of whodunnit. Except in this case, we had one suspect, no witnesses to the murder, and we were in a hair salon. Plus, we didn't even know if a murder had been committed. I doubted Hercule would approve.

Jenny double-checked to be sure Harriet was comfy in the back seat. "We won't be too long," she assured the dog, giving her a treat. Big mistake, because the dog, who'd been snoozing away, now started to yip, wanting another treat. And she wasn't taking no for an answer.

"I hope Harriet settles down soon," I said, waving to Donna to let her know I was here. "Maybe you should stay outside with the dog until she stops barking. I don't want any neighbors complaining about the noise. When she calms down, you can come inside."

"I assumed you'd already be here with everything all set up for me, Carol," Donna said, joining Jenny and me. "I'm on a tight schedule tonight. And who's this?"

"My daughter," I said, as Jenny reached out and grasped Donna's hand.

"I'm Jenny Anderson, and I'm so glad to meet you," Jenny said. "I've heard such wonderful things about you from my mother, and I begged her to let me tag along tonight. It's about time the women of Fairport had a voice in how this town is run."

My brilliant daughter had said exactly the right thing, because Donna immediately turned on the charm. "I'm so glad you feel that way," she said. "Perhaps you'd like to become active in my campaign. It's so important to encourage younger women to get involved."

"That's why I'm here," Jenny said. "I'm sure I can recruit some of my friends to volunteer, too."

I nudged Jenny and pointed to the car, where Harriet now had her face plastered against the window and was continuing to yip. "Please take Harriet for a quick walk so she'll calm down."

"A dog!" Donna exclaimed. "How wonderful, Carol! We can take some pictures of me with the dog and use them in the campaign. What a brilliant idea you had, surprising me this way. Your mom is amazing, Jenny."

"You have no idea," Jenny said, shooting me a look. "If you both go into Crimpers, I'll calm the dog down and walk her."

"I'll check with Deanna first to be sure it's okay to bring Harriet inside," I said, hoping the sudden addition of a dog wouldn't complicate the plan.

Jenny nodded, waving her phone. "Text me."

Praying everything was really set inside (with Nancy, you never know), I linked my arm with Donna's to hurry her into the salon. But nothing prepared me for the sight that greeted us.

My bestie had truly gone over-the-top this time. The first thing I saw was a huge banner that proclaimed: "The best man for the job is a woman. Donna Trumbull for Town Council." Plus, Claire, Nancy, Mary Alice and Maria Lesco were all wearing white t-shirts with the same slogan in green and blue. Of course, the Dream Homes logo was prominent on the t-shirts too.

Honestly, that Nancy!

"I've never been so surprised in my life," Donna said, giving me a huge hug. "Nobody ever gave me a party before. Who are these wonderful women?"

"We're some of your volunteers," Nancy said, pushing in front of me to shake Donna's hand. "We're so excited to be part of your campaign. I'm Nancy Green, from Dream Homes Realty."

"This is Claire McGee and Mary Alice Costello," I said, finally finding my voice. "And I'm sure you recognize Maria Lesco from Maria's Trattoria."

"I wanted to do something special, just for us girls, so we could all get to know each other a little better before the official campaign kickoff," Nancy said. "I hope you don't mind, Carol."

Mind? I was in awe. How the heck did Nancy pull this together so fast?

"This is Deanna," I said. "The best hair stylist in Fairport."

"If you'll just sit here, and put this smock on over your clothes, Mrs. Trumbull," Deanna said, patting a chair that had been strategically moved into the center of the salon.

"Oh, no, not Mrs. Trumbull," Donna said. "Call me Donna, please. We're all going to be such good friends."

"Let's get this party started!" Nancy said, handing a glass of what looked like champagne to Donna as she settled herself in the styling chair.

"Oh, I shouldn't have any wine," Donna said, pushing Nancy's hand away. "I don't drink and drive. Confidentially, the last time I did, I got into a little bit of trouble. But she stumbled, so it wasn't really my fault. Some people just aren't steady on their feet."

My ears perked up. Was Donna referring to her husband's death? And who was "she"?

"Oh, come on, you can have just a few sips," Nancy said. "After all, we're celebrating you tonight, and we have to have a toast. What's a toast without a little champagne? I don't ever drink and drive, either. But we're having coffee in a little while, so I guarantee you'll be fine to drive."

"I better be," Donna said, taking the glass from Nancy's hand. "I have a very important meeting later tonight." She took a small sip, then said, "Um. Delicious. I can't remember the last time I had champagne."

"Carol, don't you want some, too?" Nancy said, pressing a glass into my hand.

"I need to stay sharp tonight," I said, pushing her hand away. "No champagne for me."

"Don't be such a party pooper," Claire said. "Try a little bit."

"You really should," Mary Alice echoed. "I think you'll be pleasantly surprised at the taste."

I took a tentative taste, and smiled. It was ginger ale. "I knew you'd like this particular vintage, Carol," Maria said. "I chose it from my personal wine cellar just for you. Donna's is a different vintage." She looked at me to be sure I understood that Donna's was really champagne, and I nodded.

By this time, Deanna and Donna were chatting away. Well, that's not totally accurate. Donna was chatting and Deanna was listening, along with everyone else. There's nothing like being able to let your hair down (sorry, couldn't resist) while being primped and pampered. "I think a few highlights around your face would take years off and make you even more appealing to the voters," Deanna said. "And I want to change your root color, make it softer. How does that sound?"

"Great!" Donna said, taking another sip of champagne. She swiveled around in the chair to look at me. "I'm really enjoying myself, Carol. This is going to be a night to remember for me."

"I can't wait to see what happens next," I said with a straight face.

Deanna returned with a bowl of noxious glop which she proceeded to slather all over Donna's head. "Sit here and be comfortable for about twenty minutes," she said. "Then I'll add the highlights and you'll sit for another twenty minutes." She mouthed to Nancy, "What next? She can't go anywhere for a while. Start asking your questions."

I tried to jump in before Nancy. I was dying to have Donna clarify her earlier comment about the "little bit of trouble" she got into the last time she'd had a drink and then driven.

But Nancy was quicker. She shot me a look that told me to play along with her. "So, Donna," she said with all the subtlety of a brick, "Carol's asked me to get some background information from you for the bio we'll be handing out at the kickoff event."

"I'll take notes," Claire said, pulling her chair close so she wouldn't miss a word. "I know we all admire what a success you made of the bakery business after your husband died." She waved her pen. "What can you tell us about that?"

Mary Alice, who so far had been her usual quiet self, spoke up. "I'm a widow, too, Donna. It occurred to me that you worked so hard to build the business up as a memorial to your late husband." This was a point of view I'd never expected. I was impressed to see that Mary Alice had whipped up a few tears to add credence to her comment. "I can tell that, like me, you must have had a very happy marriage."

"You're very fortunate that you and Brian had such a great relationship, Mary Alice," Nancy said. "I can't say the same for my own, and neither can Carol. In fact, I was glad to be able to get out of the house tonight and away from Bob for a change. Maybe by the time I get home he'll already be in bed and we'll avoid another argument."

"That sounds a lot like how my marriage was, Nancy," Donna said.

Yay! Now we were getting somewhere.

My phone pinged with a text. Not now!

Jenny: *Can we come inside? Harriet's being a good girl now.*

Rats. I'd completely forgotten.

"Deanna," I said, "Jenny's outside with a small dog. She'd like to bring her inside for a little while. Is that okay with you?"

"Of course, Carol," Deanna said, rolling her eyes. "The more, the merrier. Any other surprises?"

"I don't think so, but you never know."

Deanna grinned.

Me: *All clear.*

My memories of what happened next are a little blurry, but bear with me, okay? Jenny brought Harriet into the hair salon, where they were immediately surrounded by adoring fans. The biggest fan was Maria Lesco, who was understandably thrilled when she saw Harriet after all this time. Jenny passed Harriet over to Maria to cuddle. By this time, Maria was crying. "Oh, Harriet, I thought I'd never see you again." Harriet responded by covering Maria's face with doggie kisses.

"I guess they know each other," Jenny whispered.

I nodded. "Maria wanted to adopt Harriet after Mary Pat's accident. Maybe that'll happen now."

Maria turned to her right, giving Harriet a clear view of Donna, who was sitting in the styling chair. The next thing we knew, Harriet had wiggled out of Maria's arms, jumped onto Donna, and began biting her so hard that she was drawing blood.

"Get this damned dog off me!" Donna screamed. "She should be put down for attacking me."

"Over my dead body," Maria said, grabbing Harriet and holding her tight.

Something clicked in my brain. Call it an "aha moment" or a stroke of brilliance. Your choice.

"You're the driver who hit Mary Pat Ryan and left her there to die," I said. "Harriet recognized you. That's why she attacked you."

Donna bolted out of the styling chair and ran toward the door, but Maria stopped her cold. Brandishing the snarling Harriet in front of Donna, she said, "Stop right where you are or I'll let Harriet have another chance at you. Somebody, please call the police."

And that, as they say, was that.

Chapter 30

The road to true crime never runs smooth.

I've always considered myself an excellent judge of people, but when the list of Donna's dirty deeds finally came out, I was shocked. I couldn't believe how she had deceived me, and through me, all of my closest friends. The fact that she was the hit-and-run driver who killed Mary Pat Ryan, then used her crime to launch her campaign into local politics, made me sick to my stomach. I never knew anyone who was so evil.

Thank goodness the real Donna was unmasked long before the election. I shudder to think of what she and her paramour, Doug (whom I also thought was a nice person) had planned for Fairport once Donna was on the town council.

I'll try to explain the facts to you as I know them. Please pay attention. It's complicated, and I tend to get confused. But every time I add extra details that I think are important, "Some People" (not mentioning any names, but you can figure out who I mean) accuse me of taking too long to get to the point of my story.

First of all (and this should come as no surprise), I was in big trouble with Sister Rose. Nancy had included her in the group text for the Crimpers caper, but she was interviewing a potential volunteer for the thrift shop at the time and didn't see it. By the time she finally read the text and showed up at the hair salon,

Donna had already been arrested and carted off to the Fairport Police Station in handcuffs. The fun nun was angry she'd missed out on all the action and said that, if I had been more organized, I would have figured out the whole mess much earlier so that everybody (meaning her) could have been notified about the plan in enough time to be present for the arrest. This was so ridiculous that, instead of dissolving into tears at the criticism, I didn't bother responding. She'll get over it. And maybe she'll leave me alone for a while.

Moving on.

I found out much later that the big case Mark and Paul were working on was to find the source of the drug epidemic in Fairport and shut it down for good. Every time they'd get a tip from one of their regular informants, it led nowhere, and there was concern (which turned out to be unfounded) that there could be a leak in the police department itself. Hence, the secrecy about their schedule. Then they got lucky.

Remember the guy who confessed to being the hit-and-run driver? And Jim's sense that there was something fishy about his confession? It turns out that my husband was absolutely right. The more the police questioned the guy, the more he kept changing his story. He finally admitted that he'd been bribed to confess to the accident, but refused to say who'd paid him without a plea deal. When he told the police that he could expose the masterminds behind all the drug trafficking in town, he got his deal. It was quite a story. He named Donna and Doug as the two behind the whole operation. The drugs would arrive by boat, then be delivered all over the area using the bakery trucks. It was a brilliant plan and had been going on ever since Donna took over the business.

Donna and Doug each accused the other of being the boss behind the operation in an effort to lighten their sentences, and it's going to be impossible to prove which one of them is lying. Doug did add one crucial piece of information that convinced the police to take another look at Mel Trumbull's death, though. Donna had told Doug that when she found her husband at the bottom of the bakery stairs, he was still alive. But instead of calling for help, she left Mel there to bleed to death. It wasn't until after Donna was sure he was dead that she called 911. What a sweetheart. I added to Doug's story by sharing that Donna had hinted the same thing to me—without the gory details. But Donna hadn't actually admitted committing the crime to me, so it was doubtful that conversation would be used at her trial.

Mark was impressed that I was the one who figured out Donna was the hit-and-run driver. (I gave credit to Harriet, too.) I didn't tell him what a lucky coincidence that was. As for her (and her paramour) being behind all the drugs pouring into Fairport, it boggled my mind. I made a solemn promise to myself that, if I ever decided to get involved in a political campaign again (heaven forbid!), I'd research the candidate all the way back to before they were born. Maybe if more of the electorate did their homework before they cast their ballot, we'd have better people running the country.

Speaking of elections, Carla Grimaldi, The Campaign School at Yale graduate, easily beat Frank Bologna and was elected to town council. Both Jim and I voted for her, as did all my friends. I had generously offered Carla my help in her campaign, but she said, "Thanks, but no thanks." I think I get points for voting for her anyway.

I took Nancy on a best friends' jaunt to New York to thank her for organizing the trap that unmasked Donna Trumbull. She's no longer having nightmares, and I think being Watson to my Holmes has restored her self-confidence. My two cents, for whatever it's worth.

Oh, there's one more piece of important news I almost forgot to share. Harriet has a new home. You may recall Maria Lesco wanted to adopt the dog, but since she works such long hours at the Trattoria, and couldn't bring Harriet to work with her because of Board of Health regulations, that wasn't possible.

Harriet's new owner is none other than Elaine Lambert, the soon-to-be ex-wife of Mary Pat's nutty neighbor, Marty. She accused Marty of loving his precious cat more than her, and when he didn't deny it, she walked out and rented a pet-friendly apartment in town. Turns out that Elaine was (secretly) a volunteer dog walker for Furry Friends, and through them, was able to adopt Harriet. I know she'll give her a loving home. They've both been through a lot.

I just love happy endings, don't you?

Addendum

According to historical sources, Election Day was a big deal back in the eighteenth century. It usually took place in May, though it could happen anywhere from mid-January to June.

Connecticut, unlike most other colonies, elected its own governor. The ballot counting at the end of the day featured a banquet and a special cake for dessert, followed by a ball.

The original cake recipe came from England with the early colonists, who called them 'great cakes' and served them at large gatherings. Similar to fruit cakes, they could weigh as much as 12 pounds. The first recipe for American election cake appears in 1796 in the first U.S. cookbook, *Amelia Simmons' American Cookery*.

Simmons notably substituted ingredients like maize for English oats. Her recipe called for 30 quarts of flour, 10 pounds of butter, 14 pounds of sugar, 12 pounds of raisins, three dozen eggs, a pint of wine and a quart of brandy — plus spices.

The cakes got linked with Hartford, Conn., and are sometimes called Hartford election cakes or Hartford cakes. One reason for that could be that prominent Hartford native Catherine Beecher, sister of Harriet Beecher Stowe, also published a cookbook that included a much-copied recipe for the cake.

The Connecticut Colony paid roughly £3 for the first documented election cake in Hartford in 1771.

Here's a recipe for Election Cake from the *Boston Cooking-School Cook Book* by Fannie Merritt Farmer, 1911 edition.

1/2 cup butter
1 cup bread dough
8 finely chopped figs
1 1/4 cups flour
1 egg
1/2 teaspoon soda
1 cup brown sugar
1/2 cup sour milk
2/3 cup raisins seeded, cut into pieces
1 teaspoon cinnamon
1/4 teaspoon each of clove, mace and nutmeg
1 teaspoon salt

Work butter into dough, using the hand. Add egg well beaten, sugar, milk, fruit dredged with two tablespoons flour, and flour mixed and sifted with remaining ingredients. Put into a well-buttered bread pan, cover, and let rise one and one-fourth hours. Bake one hour in a slow oven (350 degrees).

Some helpful websites:

The League of Women Voters has an excellent guide to being an informed voter on its website: www.lwv.com.

For information on the Coton de Tuléar dog breed, the American Coton Club is the place to go: www.americancotonclub.com.

And finally, if you're a woman thinking of running for political office, or know someone who is, The Campaign School at Yale University is a great resource. Their mission is to increase the number and influence of women in elected and appointed office in the United States and around the globe. The web address is www.tcsyale.org. The glass ceiling is yours to break. Go for it!

Retirement
Can Be Murder
A Baby Boomer Mystery (#1)

Every wife has a story. **Retirement Can Be Murder** is the story of Carol Andrews and her Beloved Husband, Jim, members of the fastest growing demographic in history, the Baby Boomer generation. Carol dreads her husband Jim's upcoming retirement more than a root canal without Novocain. She can't imagine anything worse than having an at-home husband with time on his hands and nothing to fill it—except interfering in the day-to-day activities of their household and driving her crazy. Until her plans to stall Jim's retirement result in her husband being suspected of murdering his retirement coach.

https://amzn.to/2SEpB3K

Moving
Can Be Murder
A Baby Boomer Mystery (#2)

A *Baby Boomer Mystery* by the author of **Retirement Can Be Murder**. Empty nester Carol Andrews would prefer leaving her beautiful antique home in Fairport, Connecticut, "feet first" to selling it and moving on. But her Beloved Husband Jim convinces her that a nearby active adult community is the best fit for them at this time of life. Their house sells, and Carol returns alone the night before the closing for a "pity party" farewell tour. And discovers the dead body of the buyer in her living room. Wow. Talk about seller's remorse!

https://amzn.to/3fpzBaX

Marriage
Can Be Murder
A Baby Boomer Mystery (#3)

Empty-nester Carol Andrews is thrilled when daughter Jenny announces her engagement. She's dreamed of planning her daughter's wedding since the day Jenny was born. But with only two months to pull together a destination wedding on Nantucket, Jenny insists on hiring Cinderella Weddings to organize the event. Father-of-the-bride Jim objects to the cost, and Carol objects to having her opinion ignored. When Carol finds the wedding planner dead at the bottom of a creepy staircase at a Nantucket inn, and the cheating husband of Carol's BFF Nancy is accused of her death, Carol has more to worry about than getting to the church on time!

Named a 2012's Best Mystery by *Suspense Magazine*

https://amzn.to/2RMWLMY

Class Reunions
Can Be Murder
A Baby Boomer Mystery (#4)

Baby Boomer Carol Andrews has no interest in her upcoming fortieth high school reunion. Her memories of days at Mount Saint Francis Academy are mixed, to put it mildly. But BFF Nancy convinces her to join the reunion planning committee, so she'll have some say in how the event is organized. All is going smoothly until the dead body of one of their classmates is found the night before the reunion—in Carol and Nancy's room.

https://amzn.to/2RLcR9I

Funerals
Can Be Murder
A Baby Boomer Mystery (#5)

Baby Boomer Carol Andrews is shocked to hear that her hunky landscaper, Will Finnegan, has died, and feels obligated to pay her respects to his family. But this Finnegan's wake is shut down before it even starts, when Carol discovers someone has added a pair of scissors to the guest of honor's chest. Once again, her husband Jim and the Fairport police forbid Carol to get involved. But the always curious Carol can't help herself when one of the most important people in her life jumps to the top of the suspect list.

https://amzn.to/2NqiCvf

Second Honeymoons
Can Be Murder
A Baby Boomer Mystery (#6)

Carol Andrews can't believe her luck when her husband, Jim, surprises her with a second honeymoon trip to Florida. But there's a catch—it's really a business trip, not the romantic getaway Carol expects. Jim's been called out of retirement to create a marketing plan for a new television game show aimed at Baby Boomers, *The Second Honeymoon Game*, and the pilot episode will be shot in the Sunshine State. The honeymoon is really over when the show's executive producer, none other than Carol's grammar school boyfriend, winds up dead on Carol and Jim's first night in Florida. And their son, Mike, is the police's number one suspect.

https://amzn.to/2No53fC

Dieting
Can Be Murder
A Baby Boomer Mystery (#7)

There's a little too much to love about Carol Andrews these days, thanks to the extra calories she consumed during her second honeymoon in Florida with her husband, Jim. Determined to shed the extra pounds before the birth of her first grandchild, Carol joins Tummy Trimmers, a new, holistic approach to fighting—and winning—the battle of the bulge. But her weight loss regimen is interrupted by another group member, who collapses on Carol right after completing a meditation exercise to help lose weight, and dies. When the evidence points to murder, the always curious Carol can't resist adding sleuthing to her personal weight loss routine.

https://amzn.to/2YqC3VE

In-Laws
Can Be Murder
A Baby Boomer Mystery (#8)

Carol Andrews doesn't share well. Especially when it comes
to her precious, long-awaited first grandchild, CJ. So when her
son-in-law's pushy mother, Margo, arrives in town and horns in on
Carol's happiness, it's hate at first sight. But when Margo thinks
she's committed a murder and reaches out to Carol for help, then
vanishes without a trace, it's up to Carol to put aside her petty
jealousy and crack the case before the police get involved.

https://amzn.to/2Xm1rPG

About the Author

Susan Santangelo is the author of the best-selling *Baby Boomer* mystery series. She is a member of Sisters in Crime, International Thriller Writers, and the Cape Cod Writers Center, and also reviews mysteries for *Suspense Magazine*. She divides her time between Clearwater, Florida and Cape Cod, Massachusetts, and shares her life with her husband Joe and two very spoiled English cocker spaniels, Boomer and Lilly. Boomer also serves as the model for the books' front covers, and Lilly is featured on the back. She is also a proud, lucky two-time breast cancer survivor, and credits early detection by regular mammograms with saving her life twice.

www.ingramcontent.com/pod-product-compliance
Lightning Source LLC
Chambersburg PA
CBHW070014120726
47909CB00003B/926